Carly whimpered when Pat's tongue moved past her lips and danced with her own for the first time. She needed no encouragement from Pat as her lower body molded itself to the other woman. And God, it felt so good to be held and kissed this way. She crushed Pat to her, her arms holding Pat tightly against her body.

They drew apart, their breathing ragged. Carly opened her eyes, looking into Pat's. So blue. She wanted to drown there. She pulled Pat's mouth to hers again, softer, gentler now. The fury of their first kiss was absent as they explored each other with gentle tongues.

Finally, Carly pulled away, separating herself from Pat.

"You drive me absolutely crazy, you know that, don't you?" Carly asked.

"You could pretend you're smashed and I'm a stranger and you won't know my name in the morning," Pat suggested quietly.

"You know I can't do that. You're not a stranger and I'm not going to use you to satisfy my . . . hunger."

"Please, use me," Pat whispered.

Carly reached out a hand and touched Pat's face. "I would never."

Visit

Bell Books

at

BellaBooks.com

or

call our toll-free number
1-800-729-4992

Gulf Breeze

GERRI HILL

Bella
BOOKS

2004

Bella Books, Inc.
P.O. Box 10543
Tallahassee, FL 32302

First Edition

Cover designer: Sandy Knowles

ISBN-10: 1-931513-97-X
ISBN-13: 978-1-931513-97-5

Dedicated to
my brother, Danny.

Acknowledgments

Thanks to Angelique Rader for your tireless editing. To Sandy Knowles, thanks for everything you've done to make this a reality. Sincere thanks to Julie Black, Sherry Morton and Stephanie Solomon. And a very special thank you to Diane, for your constant support and encouragement.

CHAPTER ONE

"God, already?"

One blue eye peeked out from beneath the mass of tangled dark hair an instant before a fist unceremoniously silenced the alarm clock for the third and final time. She groaned and made herself get up. It was either that or throw the alarm across the room again.

Long legs swung over the side of the bed and Pat Ryan immediately grabbed her head, wincing at the aftermath of tequila shots the night before. Straightening her tall frame, she rubbed her still-closed eyes and walked into the bathroom without turning on any lights. She stumbled into the shower, letting the cold water bring her around.

"Jesus!"

She quickly turned the knobs before sticking her face into the warmer spray.

One of these days, she would learn. She was getting

too damn old for this, she thought wryly. The local guys down at The Brown Pelican always thought they could out-drink her and she was never one to pass up a challenge. Especially when it involved money.

She usually started her day with a jog along the beach, but not this morning. And it had nothing to do with tequila shots. She had to be in Rockport before dawn. *Texas Wildlife Magazine* had commissioned her to photograph nesting shorebirds and she had found a nest of newly hatched curlews the day before. She was familiar with the Long-billed Curlews, once she learned their name, but the local birders in Rockport assured her it was rare for them to nest this far south. Old Mrs. Davenport had offered her a hundred dollars to show her where the nest was located.

She shook her head. Birdwatching! What a total waste of time! She didn't doubt that the news was already on the birding hotline and she pictured a thousand Mrs. Davenports combing the area, looking for *her* nest.

She found her favorite baseball cap and pulled her hair through the back before grabbing two camera bags and trudging as quickly as her headache would allow to her Jeep. The gulf breeze felt good on her face and she breathed deeply, the damp salt air bringing a smile to her face. She loved the mornings, especially before dawn, when the tourists were still tucked safely in their condos and hotels, out of her way and out of her sight. Pat Ryan hated tourists. In the summer months, the normally peaceful Mustang Island was transformed into total chaos. Bumper-to-bumper traffic on every street, hour-long waits for the ferry, the beaches crowded and littered, not to mention the restaurants. It drove her crazy. Even the old dives that only served baskets of fried fish had long lines on the weekends. The Shrimp Shack was about the only place the locals could still go without worrying about tourists. The old building, tucked away off of the main drag, was in desperate need of a paint job. If the building didn't turn people away, the blaring country music from the jukebox would. That, and the colorful assortment of patrons who frequented the place deterred even the most eager tourists from venturing inside.

Pat knew though, without the tourists, the island would die. She depended on their dollars as much as anyone. She had photographs for sale in nearly every gallery in Port Aransas, as well as Rockport. It hadn't always been that way. When she first moved here, she'd had to beg and plead just to get a few to carry her small prints, relying mainly on her magazine credits to pay the bills. But, having finally made a name for herself as a wildlife photographer, most of the gallery owners came to her now. That was why she'd been toying with the idea of opening up her own gallery, selling only her own work.

It was ironic, really. Pat couldn't tell the difference between a Sandpiper and a Plover if her life depended on it, but she had a knack for capturing them on film. She had little patience for tourists, but, if need be, she could sit for hours waiting for that perfect shot. She remembered the "Great Blue Heron," her most famous photograph. She had found him splashing in the marshes around Copano Bay, seemingly playing in the water without a care in the world. Upon further inspection, she discovered that what the bird was actually toying with was a snake. Pat wasn't sure which one was hoping the other would be dinner, but she got a perfect shot as the heron, with feathers ruffled and eyes wide, bent low to the water just as the snake jumped vertically out and over the heron's head. The expression on the bird's face was priceless and she had made a small fortune on the reproduction of that photo alone.

But that was five years ago, she reflected, as she

3

waited for the ferry. Nothing had really changed, except she could pay her bills without worrying now. She still lived in the same old beach house. It was pale blue, battered and in need of a fresh coat of paint, but what it lacked in beauty, it made up for in the view. She still drank the guys under the table at The Brown Pelican, still got up before dawn in search of the perfect shot, and still lived her life alone. She had thought that, at thirty-six, she might have found someone to share her life with by now, but she hadn't met anyone she could stand being around long enough to develop a relationship. Patience to wait for that perfect shot, she had plenty. Patience with people, women particularly, she had none.

CHAPTER TWO

She stood at the edge of the grass and watched the sun rise out of the water, flooding the sky with brilliant pinks and reds. The cool breeze lifted her short blonde hair slightly and she absently brushed it away from her face, her eyes never leaving the sunrise. Two pelicans flew into her sight, crossing the sun, the colors bouncing off their white feathers and she watched them for a second, then slid her eyes back to the pinks and reds. Carly had missed this. It had been too many years since she'd been here.

"It's beautiful, isn't it?"

Carly jumped as the voice startled her.

"I'm sorry, Dr. Cambridge. I didn't mean to sneak up on you."

"It's okay, Martin. I just didn't expect anyone else to be out here this early."

"I was at the site when I saw your lights."

Carly nodded. She couldn't believe the progress they had made on the Visitor's Center in just a few short months. It wasn't going to be large, not like the Visitor's Center of neighboring Aransas Wildlife Refuge, but every square foot was accounted for as usable space. Martin had pushed the contractors hard, trying to get it finished before fall, when the migration would be in full swing.

"Got some news last night," Carly said. "The federal grant passed. We'll have enough money to begin restoring the marshes now instead of next spring."

When Habitats For Nature had purchased the ranch last year, they found that most of the marshland had been drained and filled in, then replanted with non-native grass for cattle. It would be a huge undertaking to try to restore it all to its natural state, but if they were going to make this preserve work, Carly had insisted that be their first priority. The migrating shore birds, ducks and especially the endangered whooping cranes relied on marshes for survival. Without healthy marshes, they would be hard-pressed to attract any wildlife to the preserve.

"I know that's what you've been most worried about, Dr. Cambridge. I've got contractors already lined up. We can start digging this week."

"Good. But please, stress to them again the importance of disturbing the land as little as possible. I don't want it to look like a construction site out there."

They began walking back to their vehicles and Carly turned to look back at the sunrise, the soft colors having faded already, the sun sparkling bright now, only hinting at the heat it would bring on this spring day.

Martin showed Carly the progress they had made on the Visitor's Center in the past week. She had been in Washington, lobbying for their grant and kissing up to politicians, something she absolutely detested. One reason she had quit her job with the state was to get away from the politics of it all. When she started with the Parks and Wildlife Department, she had naïve aspirations, thinking she could come in and change it all, clean up the rivers, preserve land for native species. But she quickly found that all things revolved around politics and money. That was why she had jumped at the chance to work for Habitats For Nature, a non-profit organization whose only goal was preservation. It afforded her the opportunity to come back to the Gulf Coast, where her family still lived.

"They should be through with the wiring this week, then we're ready to go full force on the interior. If the weather stays dry, another month and a half, two at the most," he assured her.

It wasn't that she was anxious to get the Visitor's Center ready for the public. It would be another year before they would open their gates for tours, but she wanted the staff in place and the field technicians out there when the fall migration started. Their bird count would determine how much of a state grant they got next year.

She knew it would be several years before the habitat was back to its native state, several years before the wildlife would return for good. Oh, they already had deer, raccoons, skunks and most of the other small mammals native to the area. Mammals didn't rely on the marshes for survival. What she really wanted was to attract the endangered whooping crane. The Aransas Wildlife Preserve, which was federally managed, was only a mile down the coast from them. She saw no reason why the cranes wouldn't find the new marshes eventually. But she knew the ducks would find it first, then shorebirds and wading birds. And unlike the Aransas Preserve, they would not allow hunters to come in during the fall. She understood the need to cull the deer herd, but she also believed it put an enormous stress on the other wildlife with hunters tromping through the woods firing guns. The previous ranch owner had run day leases and the first thing Carly had done was take down the tree stands that had been put up in the big oak trees that the ranch was famous for.

The second thing she had started, even before they broke ground on the Visitor's Center, was to begin renovations on the old ranch house, making it into offices for the staff and remodeling the upper floor into an apartment for her. Eventually they would hire a manager to live full-time on the property, but for now, she would stay here while they got things underway.

"My assistant, Elsa Sanchez, is going to be moving down this weekend, Martin, to set up our computer system. I'll bring her around on Monday. I want you to show her the blueprints so she can get an idea of what we'll need. They supposedly have it all mapped out but I want her to take a look. I want the servers in the ranch house where the offices will be, but I want to network the Visitor's Center, too."

"She's the computer whiz you were telling me about?"

Carly smiled and nodded. She knew Elsa from college, but they'd lost touch soon after. Then she met Elsa again in Austin years later when they'd both worked for the Parks and Wildlife Department. Elsa was a field technician and she had been assigned to work with Carly on a project involving the Edward's Aquifer. The development boom in the Hill Country was quickly draining the aquifer and they were studying the effects on the natural springs in the area. Actually, they were watching them dry up before their very eyes. Carly's face hardened as she remembered the political pressure of that study. Development brought tax dollars and her findings were swept under the rug for nearly two years until environmental groups protested loudly enough. The development had been curbed, but it was too little too late.

Elsa had been as disenchanted by the whole process as Carly had been. That's when she decided to change careers. She went back to school, getting another degree in computer science and adding a M.C.S.E. certificate to it as well. They had remained friends and Elsa had been more than willing to give up her job as a network administrator in the city for a chance to work on the preserve, combining her computer and networking skills with her love of protecting the environment.

"She's wonderful, Martin. You'll love her. And it'll give you a chance to brush up on your Spanish. She gets on a tirade sometimes and loses me when she launches into Spanish," Carly explained.

Martin chuckled. "I'll try to keep up but the only practice I get these days in when I visit my grandmother."

Carly shook her finger playfully at him. "It's sad, Martin, when an Anglo such as myself knows more Spanish than you do."

CHAPTER THREE

"Good God, you'd think they'd never seen a goddamned bird before," Pat muttered under her breath. She stood with hands on her hips, surveying the crowd that lined the pond. Her pond. Her curlews. She shook her head, cursing Mrs. Davenport. The old woman had no doubt been following her.

She tossed one of her cameras on the front seat in disgust then childishly kicked at her back tire. Of all the luck, she thought. Yesterday, she had accidentally stumbled upon a nest of long-billed curlews and had no idea what she had found. Pat had been searching her field guide frantically for a bird that fit their description when Mrs. Davenport had ambled over, voluntarily pointing out she wasn't even in the correct category. *"You've got a bird book. Why don't you learn to use it?"*

Everyone told her Mrs. Davenport was *the* local authority on native birds. Of course, Pat had run into

10

her numerous times while working, but she avoided her as best she could because the old biddy made her nervous, always decked out in some outrageous birding outfit and sporting not one, but two pairs of binoculars around her neck. Once she broke the ice, though, the old woman was as hard to shake off as a flea. She seemed determined to call attention to all of Pat's mistakes.

"Oh, Ms. Ryan! There you are! Come have a look! We haven't spotted the nest yet."

Pat turned, a biting retort on her lips as Mrs. Davenport walked over, dressed in all her birdwatching garb. Pat couldn't decide what part of the ensemble was the most outrageous — the scarf imprinted with every species of bird that was knotted loosely around her neck, the army surplus wading boots, or the wide-billed camouflage hat sporting yards and yards of mosquito-netting that flowed down the old woman's back like a strange bridal veil. Pat pulled the bill of her cap lower and pierced Mrs. Davenport with an icy blue stare.

"Nice crowd. Must have hit the . . . hotline, huh?" she got out through clinched teeth.

"Oh, yes. This is big news," the old woman stated importantly as she adjusted her hat over her thinning gray hair. "I'm trying to get the local paper out for a picture."

"Great. Thanks a lot."

"Well, Ms. Ryan, I assure you, in my circle, this is very good news. The Audubon Society is positively beside itself. Why, the long-billed curlew hasn't nested in these parts in years. My dear departed Elbert, God rest his soul, was still in his prime the last time we saw them, and that was before Carla hit."

"Carla?"

"The hurricane, dear. Surely, you remember Carla?"

Pat Ryan drew her eyebrows together and tried another scowl on old Mrs. Davenport.

"Look, do you really think it's wise to have all these people . . . gaping at this nest? I mean, wouldn't it be tragic if the birds abandoned their nest and the poor babies were left to starve and die? All because *you* put it out on your hotline?"

Old Mrs. Davenport brought one hand to her chest, eyes wide.

"Do you think they're too close? I mean, we haven't even seen the nest yet and the parents haven't flown."

"Oh, sure. They're just sticking around, trying to protect the young, but tonight, maybe they'll think, hey, what are we going to do when twice this many people show up? How are we going to look for food and protect them at the same time? Maybe we should just abandon the nest and head up north, like we usually do and start over. What then?"

"Oh, well I would feel horrible, of course. But these are birders. They wouldn't approach the nest."

Pat rolled her eyes. *Birders.*

"Look, I think you should just ask everyone to leave. I mean, is it worth it?"

But Mrs. Davenport held her ground.

"I see you have *your* cameras, just like us. What's the difference?"

"I'm a professional. I know how to do this," Pat said.

"Just like you knew that they were curlews, right?"

Pat rolled her eyes again, just in time to see a brand new Cadillac skid to a halt next to her Jeep.

"Oh, I see your Aunt Rachel heard the news, too."

Pat watched her elderly aunt jump from her car, binoculars swinging from around her neck.

"Where are they?" she called to Mrs. Davenport.

"Wait," Pat put up a warning hand. "Not you, too. This is a protected area," she said lamely.

"This is public land," Mrs. Davenport corrected.

"Why, Pat, I didn't expect to see you here. Did you hear the news on the hotline?"

"No. I found the goddamn nest. I should be the only damn person out here," she said, her voice rising with each word.

"Oh, pooh, you hate birds," her aunt said. "Come along, darling, show me the nest."

Aunt Rachel linked arms with Pat and drew her after Mrs. Davenport as they headed toward the pond.

Pat took a deep breath, clutching her camera to her chest as she hurried along beside her aunt, nearly choking on the perfume that hovered around the older woman.

"You know, I'm shooting for a magazine. Maybe you could use your influence and get everyone out of here," Pat whispered to her aunt. "What do you say?"

"They're curlews, Pat. Nesting . . . with young. We all want to see."

"And since when have you gotten into this?"

"Isn't it exciting, Pat?"

Pat rolled her eyes again. Her own aunt was decked out, head to toe, in her version of birdwatching gear, completely impractical white linen Bermuda shorts and matching boots.

"Nice hat," she murmured, sparing a wry glance for the lace and straw confection perched on her aunt's head.

"I got it at that cute little Birds and More shop on Austin Street."

"Looks great on you."

Aunt Rachel was really her only family. The rest had deserted her years ago. If truth be told, they had deserted Aunt Rachel as well. The eccentric old woman was a bit too much for her stuffy, Catholic family. Oh, the occasional Christmas card was exchanged and sometimes a phone call, but that was about it. Pat assumed they did that so they wouldn't be left out of the will.

"Come by the house for lunch, Pat," her aunt said. "I've some things I want to discuss with you. We haven't visited in ages."

Pat stood at the edge of the crowd, watching as the birders spied across the small pond with their binoculars, looking for the elusive nest. Then she grinned. Of course. They all knew there was a nest here — somewhere. But only she knew exactly where it was. She could either wait them out or sneak around the back side of the pond. She doubted anyone in this crowd would be inclined to follow her through the mud and tall grass.

Oh, let them fumble around a bit. The sun was already too high anyway for a decent shot. She walked back to her Jeep, mentally planning another trip tomorrow morning, well before dawn. That way, maybe she could still get a few good shots before the crowd showed up.

"Pat? Wait," her aunt called. "We don't see them. Did you?"

"No. They probably hate crowds."

"Where are you going?"

"To your place."

Her aunt nodded. "I'll be along shortly."

CHAPTER FOUR

Carly walked through the dust of the downstairs and eagerly mounted the steps that would take her to her new quarters. A plastic dust cover was nailed at the top of the stairs and she moved it aside, stepping onto the newly carpeted hallway. She took a deep breath, the smells of fresh paint and new carpet a welcome change from the dust and debris on the lower level. It would still be at least another three weeks before the first floor was finished and they could start outfitting the offices, but the apartment was complete.

"What do you think?" he called.

"Nice. Clean," she called back, walking to the top of the stairs. "But Martin, I'm not sure about moving in here yet. Not with the construction workers going in and out all day. I won't get any work done."

He shrugged. "Well, then wait. I know it looks a mess down here, but they assure me only another three, four weeks tops."

Her current apartment, although small, was already set up with her computer and fax and other office equipment. She knew she would work much better undisturbed by construction workers, who were already beginning to gather. Before long, loud male voices called to each other and she rolled her eyes.

"I'll wait, Martin."

He chuckled but nodded.

CHAPTER FIVE

Pat stretched her long legs out in the hammock and closed her eyes. It was cool in the shade and the breeze off of the bay kept most of the mosquitoes away.

A quick nap, lunch with Aunt Rachel, a trip to Corpus to drop off the film she'd shot yesterday, then an early dinner, maybe the Shrimp Shack tonight. Angel would be bartending. At least she'd have a female to talk to instead of the usual guys.

She sighed, willing sleep to come. Moving one leg to the ground, she set the hammock in motion again. It was a warm day for April. She should really take advantage of it and be out looking for nests, not trying to sleep in a damn hammock. But she was still pissed off at Mrs. Davenport. Oh well, she could always just go to the wildlife refuge and bug the staff there to show her some nesting sites. She needed at least ten. So far, she had four.

She opened one eye when she heard the car approach. Her aunt. Guess the curlews were safe again.

"Pat?"

"Out here," she called back. She rolled her head and watched her aunt, still decked out in her birdwatching getup, walk across the lawn towards her.

"Oh my, it's warm today, isn't it?"

"It's hot."

"I thought we could have lunch on the veranda, but I think we should choose the shaded deck in the back. I had Alice fix us up something nice."

Pat finally sat up and swung both legs over the side of the hammock. She pulled her cap off and shook out her hair, then tilted her head at her aunt.

"You haven't invited me to lunch in two years."

"Nonsense. You eat here all the time."

"I eat here if I happen to drop by during mealtime. Now, what's going on? You've got something up your sleeve," Pat accused.

Her aunt had the grace to blush, but lifted her chin in defiance. "Can't I simply invite my favorite niece over for lunch?" she asked as she turned and headed back to the house.

"Uh-huh," Pat murmured, but dutifully followed after her.

She went into the house just long enough to wash up and steal a beer from the fridge. Her aunt was already waiting on the back deck.

"A beer? We have tea," her aunt offered.

"No, thanks," Pat said as she tipped up the bottle.

"Oh, hell. Alice," she called. "Bring me a Tom Collins." She turned to Pat and grinned. "You are a terrible influence on me."

"Yeah, well, we'll blame it on our upbringing," she said.

"You can hardly blame the Catholic Church for your drinking habits. God knows you blame it for everything else."

"Speaking of that, have you heard from them lately?"

"Your father called me at Easter. I'm sure it eased his conscience somewhat, being a religious holiday and all." She hesitated before continuing. "He did inquire about you."

"That's nice," Pat said dryly.

"Well, the conversation was short, anyway. I'm sure he was just making sure I was still alive."

"Checking on his inheritance, no doubt."

Her aunt snorted. "As if he'll be mentioned in the will. And it's not like he needs any more money." Aunt Rachel reached out and grasped Pat's hand. "Speaking of money, why haven't you cashed the last few checks I've given you?"

Pat shrugged. "I don't need any money, Aunt Rachel. I've told you that."

"That's not the point and you know it. It won't hurt you to pad your accounts, in case you have an emergency of some sort."

"If I have an emergency, then I'll ask you for money."

"You are so stubborn. I sometimes wonder if you're from this family at all. Money is and always will be the most important factor in the Ryan family. Your great-grandparents are probably rolling over in their graves this very moment."

Pat laughed. "I'm sure they've been rolling for awhile and it's not because of money."

Aunt Rachel laughed too. "Yes, you're probably right. I'm sure they've turned several times over my eight marriages alone. Your being gay, however, was the last straw."

Pat managed only a ghost of a smile.

Aunt Rachel reached out and grabbed her arm.

"I'm sorry, Pat. Fuck them. We've got all we need right here."

At that, Pat laughed. It was a rare occasion that Aunt Rachel used the F-word. And usually, it was during a discussion about the family.

Alice interrupted them with a Tom Collins and a fresh beer for Pat. They smiled at each other and touched glasses before drinking.

"God, I love days like this," her aunt said. "Beautiful spring weather, sitting out here enjoying the day with you." She leaned closed and whispered, "You are my very favorite person in the world, you know that."

"You keep telling me that, although I don't know why," Pat said.

"Your parents are total fools. They have no idea the wonderful person you are. Or how talented you are. Or that you've grown into such a beautiful woman. I pity them. They chose to see only one thing about you and they couldn't live with that one thing. Well, too bad for them. I never desired children, Pat, I've told you that before. But if I had ever had one, I would have wanted a daughter, just like you."

Pat moved her hand across the table and grasped her aunt's wrinkled fingers in hers. She gave a slight squeeze then pulled away.

"Enough of that," Aunt Rachel said as she cleared her throat. "I'm too damn old for tears in the middle of the day. Now, I'm wondering if I should get you drunk first."

"Before what?" Pat asked warily.

"I have a rather large favor to ask you."

"Ask," she said. "We'll decide about drinking later."

Her aunt drew up her arms and rested her elbows on the table before speaking.

"Well, since you're a local, I'm sure you know about the Habitats For Nature project."

"What?"

"Habitats For Nature," her aunt repeated slowly.

At Pat's blank stare, Aunt Rachel slammed a hand on the table.

"Good God, woman, you make a living taking pictures of wildlife! Don't you keep up?"

"No. I go out, shoot, then I leave." Her aunt's disapproving stare deepened as she pursed her lips. Pat raised her eyebrows. "What?"

"You go out. What if there was no place to go out *to*? What if there weren't these wonderful projects that are trying to preserve nature? Then where would you take your pictures?"

Pat rubbed the cold beer bottle against her forehead, desperately trying to figure out where this was heading.

"Habitats For Nature," her aunt repeated slowly. "They bought the old Thompson Ranch."

"Oh, yeah," Pat said, finally remembering. "Up the coast from Aransas Wildlife Refuge?"

"Yes. Only the government won't have a hand in this. They have wonderful ideas, Pat. They are going to bring the marshes and wetlands back to their natural state. Can you imagine the wildlife?"

Pat stared at her, wondering when her aunt had turned into an environmentalist. For that matter, when had she started birdwatching?

"And your favor is?" Pat asked hesitantly.

"Well, I have become a contributor. A major contributor," she added as Pat stared at her. "In fact, I've even offered some input."

"Uh-huh?"

"Well, I was hoping you would volunteer your talents to them."

"What?" Pat demanded.

"They need some promotional material and they'll need photos for the Visitor's Center. Naturally, I thought of you. I told them I was certain you'd be thrilled to donate some time to this wonderful project."

"Are you out of your mind?" Pat demanded. "People pay money for my photos. That's how I make a living. That's why I don't have to ask you for money. Because I charge people for my photographs." Her voice rose slightly. "And, I don't have time. I've got six goddamned more nests to find and today was wasted because old Mrs. Davenport put it on the hotline, for Christ's sake!"

"Will you calm down?"

"You volunteered me already, didn't you? They think I've already agreed to this, don't they?"

"I may have said you'd be thrilled to do this. I mean, you do make your living out there in nature."

"Aunt Rachel, I just take pictures. I'm not really active in these things, you know? All those environmental rights people kinda make me nervous. They're strange."

"Oh, pooh," she said. "Dr. Cambridge is one of the nicest people I've ever met. She's devoted her life to preserving nature. She's got such a passion for it, I just couldn't resist. And, because funds are very limited, they don't really have the budget to hire a photographer. So, naturally, I thought of you."

"Naturally," Pat murmured. She leaned back in her chair and lifted her hair off of the back of her neck, letting the breeze cool her skin. Dr. Cambridge was probably as flighty as old Mrs. Davenport.

"I've arranged for you to meet Dr. Cambridge first thing Monday morning, on site. She'll show you around and give you some ideas on what they're looking for. Just a few nice shots for promotional material, posters, brochures, things like that. Something to send out to potential donors. Then, of course, they'll need some really nice shots to display in the Visitor's Center."

Pat stared at her aunt, her eyes narrowing. "So, you've got it all arranged, do you? Just a few shots? Sure. It's not like I've got a goddamned deadline for this magazine! It's not like I've got six more nests to find!" she finished, her voice rising with each word.

But her aunt simply smiled and patted her hand.

"I knew I could count on you. And, Mrs. Davenport has agreed to show you some nests if you'll agree to show her the curlews."

"What?" Pat demanded.

"Yes. In fact, she said there are plovers nesting in her own yard."

Pat scowled. What the hell did plovers look like again? Were they considered shorebirds? Damnation!

CHAPTER SIX

"Will you keep quiet?" Pat said for the fourth time. "They're over there."

"I see the damn nest," Pat growled. Not only did she have to show Mrs. Davenport the curlews, she had to suffer her presence at each and every nest the old woman had shown her. She tried to ignore her, moving closer for another shot of a ruddy turnstone. A drab brown bird until they flew, then their beautiful wing patterns unfolded and even Pat had to admit they were pretty. But she was really only taking shots now to appease Mrs. Davenport. She would come out before dawn and photograph the nests early, just at feeding time. And she would come out alone.

"I think that's enough," Pat said.

"You didn't get very close."

Pat tapped her 500mm lens. "Close enough."

"Do you want to see another?"

Mrs. Davenport had shown her seven nests, two on her own property. The thought of spending any more time with the old woman hovering over her shoulder did not appeal to Pat. Not that she wasn't already in her debt, but the entire Sunday was nearly gone.

"I really appreciate you showing me the nests, but I've got enough for now. I think I'll just head back to the island and start developing these."

They crept quietly back along the marsh until they reached the road. Pat tossed her camera bag in the back of the Jeep. She laughed softly as Mrs. Davenport tied a scarf around her hat. It had blown off earlier in the open Jeep and they had to turn around to retrieve it after she'd insisted to Pat that it was her lucky birding hat.

She dropped Mrs. Davenport off at her bayside house, just across from Fulton Beach. She thanked her again, a bit grudgingly, and headed back to the island. If there was one person in the birding community that she hated being indebted to, it was Mrs. Davenport. She would never live it down.

Going home, going back to bed might have improved her sour mood, but she didn't make it to her house. She stopped at The Brown Pelican instead. Beer and pool. Sounded like just the thing she needed to unwind after spending the entire day with a bird fanatic.

"Pat."

"Hey, Shorty," she called. "Where's your partner?"

"Oh, his wife made him go to some birthday party," he said as she pulled up a barstool next to his.

"And you? Your wife run you out again?" She nodded at Sam as he placed a draft beer in front of her.

"No, she's in Corpus shopping. I'm a free man today."

"Hell, Shorty, you spend more time here than at home anyway."

"And where were you last night? We had a tournament. Me and Davey came in second."

"Yeah? I drove by but it was packed. I went to the Shack instead."

"You should have come in. Had some biker chicks in here. Looked kinda dangerous. Right up your alley."

Pat snorted. She wanted no part of the biker chicks. She'd tried that last year and had woke in a hotel room with three naked women in bed with her, not recalling what had transpired. She did, however, remember the empty tequila bottle.

"No, no, Shorty. Did that last year. Had a hangover for three days."

Shorty laughed. "I remember. Four of them, right?"

"Three."

"Damn, woman, you have all the fun."

Pat let a ghost of a smile cross her face. Fun? Well, maybe at the time. She couldn't recall. It was after that episode that she started to realize how empty her life really was. Three women in bed with her and she didn't even know their names.

"Fun. Right. That's me," she said dryly.

"You want to set up a game?" he asked, motioning to the pool table.

"One game," she nodded. "I've got to go to Corpus, then an early date over in Rockport tomorrow." An early date with old Dr. Cambridge. She could hardly wait.

CHAPTER SEVEN

Carly laughed when she bit down on the lime wedge, the tartness nearly bringing tears to her eyes.

"God, I can't remember the last time I've done tequila shots." She placed the lime wedge inside the empty shot glass and reached for her beer mug instead.

"Me, either. College?"

They were sitting on the floor of Carly's crowded apartment, catching up. Elsa Sanchez had arrived early that morning and Carly had helped move her things to the apartment next door. Elsa was nowhere near settled in, but they had called it a day and ordered pizza instead. Now, empty beer bottles and a half-eaten pizza lay scattered on the floor around them.

Maybe it was the tequila or maybe it was just being around Elsa after all this time, but the mention of college brought back a flood of unpleasant memories.

"Jesus, Carly, that still get to you?"

Carly nodded.

"I'm sorry, chica. But it's been nearly ten years."

"It could be a hundred years and it would still get to me."

"But the last time we talked about it, in Austin, you said you didn't even think about it anymore."

"I don't think about it, Elsa, but that doesn't mean it's not still there. It'll always be there."

Elsa shook her head sadly, not believing that, after all these years, her friend still couldn't let go of the pain and betrayal.

"She's taken so much of your life, Carly. Why can't you just let it go?"

"I have let it go, I just haven't forgotten."

"And that's why there's been no one else?"

"There'll never be anyone else." Carly sighed. Yes, Carol had taken so much of her life, nearly all of it, she remembered. She looked up and met Elsa's eyes. "Did you know I almost killed myself?" she asked in a whisper.

"Over her?"

Carly nodded. "A few months after she left, I had a bottle. . . I hadn't been sleeping. . . I had a prescription. . . and I had all the pills in my hand, a bottle of whiskey and I just wanted it to be over," she said quietly.

"*Dios mio*," Elsa whispered. The petite woman clapped her hands over her mouth, large brown eyes growing even larger.

"She had already taken everything else. My money, my love, my dignity, not to mention a car, furniture and jewelry, why not my life?"

"Are you serious?"

"I know, it sounds silly now. I can't even believe the thoughts I was having then. But I was . . . devastated. I was alone and I had no one to turn to. It wasn't like I was out, Elsa."

"What happened?"

A hint of a smile flitted across Carly's face. "My mother called."

Elsa squeezed her hand.

"Mom could always make me feel better, no matter what. That time was no different." Carly leaned back against the sofa and brushed her hair away from her face. "I told her everything that had happened. She was shocked, to say the least. But supportive. I decided that night I would never, ever give myself to someone again. I will never be *used* like that again. She took every last shred of dignity I had, Elsa, and she *laughed* about it. God, I remember how she laughed. I was so stupid. So naïve. No, I'll never do that again."

"You'll meet someone," Elsa insisted.

"No. I won't. I don't want to. My life is full. Especially now. I've got this wonderful project here, I'm close to my family again. They've included me in everything. I don't need anyone else in my life. I know that, I've accepted that. Any love I have to give, I give to my nieces and nephews. I'm happy with that."

"Carly, everyone needs someone."

"You're single," Carly stated.

"Yes, but only because I haven't found Mr. Right. It's not because I've decided there is no Mr. Right and I've quit looking. He's out there somewhere. I just know it."

"Well, I hope you find him. But for me, no. I just can't take that chance again. I lost too much the first time."

Elsa nodded and patted Carly's hand lightly.

"Enough of that. Let's have one more, then I'll flip you for the last piece of pizza," Elsa suggested.

"Oh, no. No more. I'll feel like hell the way it is. I'm meeting a photographer in the morning. Remember I was telling you about Rachel Yearwood, she's one of our major donors. Well, she said her niece has volunteered to shoot the promotional material we need, as well as some photos for the Visitor's Center."

"Is she a real photographer or just your weekend variety?"

"I think she's real. Rachel said she does it for a living," Carly said as she began cleaning up their mess.

"That's wonderful, then. I think it's great that so many people are volunteering for this project."

"Yes. It is coming together, isn't it?"

"Do you need me to come with you?"

"No, no. You have plenty to do here. Tomorrow afternoon, I'll take you on the grand tour. Martin will have all the blueprints. They've run cables and all, but you'll need to take a look and see if there's anything we missed."

"Okay," Elsa said as she reached for the last piece of pizza. "You weren't going to eat this, were you?"

"My God, we ate a large pizza," Carly stated. Then she looked at the tequila bottle, nearly half gone. "You're a very bad influence, Elsa Sanchez."

"Be quiet," she said and shoved the rest of the pizza in Carly's mouth.

CHAPTER EIGHT

Pat stopped her Jeep at the gate, wondering if she was at the right place. There were no signs. She stepped out, pulling her cap more firmly on her head and walked to inspect the gate. The chain hung loosely, but it was unlocked.

She shrugged, then opened it. If she were at the wrong place, she would find out soon enough.

The dirt road wound through oak mottes and open fields before leading her to an obvious construction site. Most of the activity was centered around a new building, but several vehicles surrounded an old ranch house. After a moment's hesitation, she drove to the ranch house, parking well out of the way.

She slipped one camera around her neck, then slung the camera bag over a shoulder. Her sunglasses shielded her from the bright sunshine and she looked around, looking for anyone who might be looking for her.

She finally found someone who looked out of place, a small blonde woman wearing tan shorts and a white blouse tucked inside. She was talking to one of the construction workers. Perhaps she knew where Dr. Cambridge might be.

Carly stopped talking as she watched the tall woman approach. Dark hair was pulled back in a ponytail and covered with a ball cap. White shorts accented tan muscular thighs. Carly found she couldn't tear her eyes away from them. When she finally raised her eyes, she watched in fascination as the woman pulled off sunglasses and folded them, hooking them neatly into the collar of her T-shirt. Her eyes were bluer than a winter sky.

"Excuse me. I'm looking for a Dr. Cambridge."

Oh dear Lord. Those eyes. Carly could only stare.

"Uh, this is the Habitats For Nature place, right?" Pat asked, looking around. *Shit, I'm probably at the wrong damn place.*

Carly finally came to her senses and cleared her throat.

"Yes, it is."

Pat flashed her a relieved smile. "Good. Is Dr. Cambridge around? I'm Pat Ryan. I'm supposed to meet her this morning."

Carly nodded, finally finding her voice.

"I'm Carly Cambridge," she said.

It was Pat's turn to stare. *This* was old Dr. Cambridge? Surely not.

"Are you sure?"

Carly chuckled. "Quite sure."

"I mean, I was expecting someone older. Not that this isn't a pleasant surprise," Pat said, recovering. She stuck out her hand. "Nice to meet you."

Carly took her hand briefly and smiled in return. "Someone older?"

"Aunt Rachel didn't elaborate. I just assumed," she said.

Carly smiled at the mention of Rachel's name. They had become friends over the months that they had corresponded.

"Rachel is a wonderful woman. We have quite a few donors already, but none as sincere as she is. She really cares about this project. I'm so glad you do, too. It's difficult finding a quality photographer, especially one that gladly volunteers their time."

"That's me," Pat said lightly.

"Great. Well, let's head out and I'll show you around. Of course, we'll want shots of the Visitor's Center, but I don't think it's necessary to get the ranch house. We're redoing it for office space, mostly. We'll be starting on the reconstruction of the marshes and that'll take much more money than we have. We're hoping you'll get some great shots of that. The bay area is relatively undisturbed, thank goodness, and I'm sure you'll find plenty there that suits you."

Pat followed behind Dr. Cambridge, trying to follow her ramblings, but her eyes were locked on the woman's nicely rounded backside as she walked. *This might not turn out to be such a bad assignment after all.*

Carly stopped at the edge of the Visitor's Center, very conscious of the silent woman walking behind her.

"Do you want to go inside today or would you rather wait until off hours when the workers are gone?"

Pat looked through the windows at the workers milling about and shook her head.

"No. Not today."

"Very well. Let's take my Jeep and I'll give you the tour. After that, I'll let you wander around alone. You can come out here anytime, the gate's unlocked during the day."

"I like to work early mornings or late afternoon," Pat said. "The colors are much better then. Not so bright."

"Well, I guess I could give you a key to the gate. You're free to come and go as you like."

"Thanks."

Dr. Cambridge's Jeep was much newer than her own. Pat immediately rolled the window down and stuck one arm outside, moving her eyes away from the woman and focusing on the sights around her.

Carly watched as Pat Ryan shoved sunglasses on, covering those beautiful eyes. *Beautiful? Where did that come from?* She pulled away, moving down the dirt road to the bay.

"We'll extend this road into the woods. It's so grown up in places, the oak mottes have nearly disappeared with all the brush. We'll make a loop around the marshes and have places for people to stop and watch the wildlife, but most of the marshes will be off limits to the public."

"If it's off limits to the public, what's to draw them here?" Pat asked.

"We're not a resort or state park," Carly said sharply. "This preserve is for the wildlife, not people."

Pat turned and looked at Dr. Cambridge, raising one eyebrow above her sunglasses. "But, if I'm not allowed to *see* the wildlife, why should I donate money?"

"Perhaps you should try the zoo, then," she said curtly.

Pat laughed and it caught Carly by surprise.

"Is that what you'll tell your donors?"

"Most of our donors understand the purpose of this preserve. And they'll still see plenty of wildlife. Ducks and shorebirds are not usually disturbed by a few cars and people milling about. And the deer will become accustomed to cars, too. Once they get past the fear of being hunted, that is."

"If that's the case, then why limit access?"

Carly sighed, exasperated. Was she a photographer or a politician?

"We're not a publicly funded preserve," she said slowly. "It's technically private land. We're making it accessible to the public for their enjoyment, but we don't have to."

"You're making it publicly accessible so you'll get donations. If it were to be strictly private, no one would give you money."

"Look, Ms. Ryan, obviously you don't understand the concept behind Habitats For Nature. Native land is scarce. And this," she said, waving her hands around her, "is hardly native anymore. The marshes have been drained. Cattle have grazed here on imported grass. The natural landscape has been changed to suit man's needs. The ducks and shorebirds have disappeared. Our main concern is returning this land to its natural state. With the help of donors, yes. People who love this land and want it restored. For that, we're willing to open it up, minimally, to the public."

An environmental nutcase, Pat mused. Why couldn't she have been an *old* Dr. Cambridge? Pat flicked her eyes over the small woman sitting beside her. Her blonde hair looked like it was in need of a cut and she had it tucked behind her ears. Her arms and legs were tanned and she noticed the fingers that drummed against the steering wheel impatiently. She was too damn cute to be an environmental wacko.

"I apologize, Dr. Cambridge. What do I know about it? I'm just a photographer."

"Can I ask you something, Ms. Ryan?"

"Of course."

"Why did you volunteer for this?"

Pat cleared her throat and grinned.

"Well, I didn't exactly volunteer. It seems my aunt volunteered my services without asking."

Carly stared, her mouth opening slightly. Rachel Yearwood had come to her, saying her niece had graciously offered her services, free of charge, all for the benefit of the preserve.

"I see."

"I'm not really into all this nature stuff," Pat admitted.

Great. Just great. Could she even take pictures?

"You *are* a photographer, right?"

"Yes, of course."

Carly nodded. "Well, if you were coerced into this, I'll understand if you bail out now. In fact, we probably would do better paying someone. At least then, they might actually care about what they shoot."

"Hey, look. I make my living shooting wildlife. Forgive me if I'm not political about it."

Carly let out her breath, her impatience with this woman growing thin.

"Ms. Ryan, we all have different agendas in life. Ours, apparently, don't seem to cross paths. However, we are in need of a photographer and our budget doesn't exactly allow us to hire one. If you're not able to do this, perhaps you know someone in your profession who might be willing to lend a helping hand. Time is what we don't have. Our resources will run out by the end of summer without new donations. We're planning on starting on our mailing lists by mid-May, at the latest and we would like to have a brochure put together by then."

"I didn't say I wouldn't work for you, Dr. Cambridge. I promised Aunt Rachel," Pat said. "Just don't expect me to go door-to-door with you, looking for donations."

"Fair enough. We do appreciate your sacrifice," she said.

Pat laughed again, surprising Carly for the second time. She had intended her comment to be an insult. Apparently, this woman was too thick-skinned to even realize it.

CHAPTER NINE

Carly was still trying to recover from her encounter with the insufferable Pat Ryan when Elsa knocked on her door.

"I thought I heard you," Elsa said. "You've been banging."

"The photographer is a jerk," she blurted out.

"A jerk?"

"Yes. She probably voted for Bush. She cares nothing about this."

"I thought she volunteered."

"So did I."

Carly couldn't understand why she let the woman upset her so. It's not like she hadn't met hundreds of others just like her. But the fact that she made her living taking pictures of wildlife without having an inkling as to the destruction around her was just something Carly could not comprehend.

"So, we're still looking for a photographer then?"

"No. She's going to do it. We don't have the time nor money to find someone else."

"Okay. But do you even know what kinds of pictures she takes? I mean, she might suck," Elsa said.

"She's a wildlife photographer. Surely she can manage this."

"But still, we should check her out," Elsa said, moving to Carly's computer.

"What are you doing?"

"Maybe she's got a Web site," Elsa said and she was already doing a search when Carly looked over her shoulder.

"Pat Ryan Photography. Port Aransas."

Elsa clicked on the link and Pat Ryan's blue eyes appeared on the screen, staring right at Carly.

"*Mamacita!*" Elsa murmured. "She's a goddess."

Carly had to admit that she was quite attractive. It was only when she opened her mouth that she became insufferable.

"Check out the pictures, Elsa," Carly said lightly, pointing to a link.

Then they both laughed as a startled Great Blue Heron appeared before them, snake and all.

"She took that?" Elsa asked. "I've seen that photo several times. In fact, I think I have a coffee mug with it on it."

Other photos lined the page and Carly's eyes were drawn to a doe and fawn, hiding in the trees in the early morning. The doe's head was turned, across the fawn's back, looking right at the camera. The big, brown eyes were full of trust as if knowing the photographer would not harm her baby.

"Great shot of the whooping crane," Elsa said, pointing to one where the sunrise engulfed the beautiful white bird.

Carly stood up and nodded. Pat Ryan certainly had talent, that much was evident. She should be happy to have her working on this project. She looked again at the photos, all so carefully constructed, as if she'd set a stage for the wildlife she'd shot. If she didn't know better, she'd say that all the photos were made with love of the animals and the nature surrounding them. Not by some woman who barely gave notice to the destruction of the very things she took photos of.

"Well, I suppose I'll have to tolerate her views. You're right. She's good. We can't very well turn down talent like this. Maybe just having her name on this project will help with donations. She's obviously successful." She didn't add that she, too, had a coffee mug with the heron's face embellished on the side.

"Come on. Let's go out to the site and I'll show you around. Time to get to work."

CHAPTER TEN

"Hey, Pat."

"Angel," Pat drawled, pulling out a barstool and leaning her elbows on the counter.

"What brings you here in the middle of the day?"

"I need a beer."

"Ah. Coming right up. Want lunch, too?" she asked as she filled a frosty mug with draft beer.

Pat thought for a moment. Knowing there was nothing at her place to eat, she nodded.

"Shrimp po'boy, extra tartar," Angel called to the kitchen. "So, what's up?"

"Just trying to recover from a meeting," she said. "I met the most obnoxious woman today. An environmental wacko, the type that you just want to muzzle to get them to shut up."

"A Mrs. Davenport clone?"

"If only," Pat said with a smile. Angel had never met Mrs. Davenport, but she'd heard all the stories from Pat. "Aunt Rachel volunteered me to shoot photos at that new wildlife thing outside of Rockport."

"What's that?" Angel began filling salt shakers, tilting her curly blonde head in Pat's direction while she concentrated on her task.

"The old Thompson Ranch. Habitats For Nature bought him out and they're turning it into a preserve."

"Well, that'll give you another place to work, won't it?"

Pat narrowed her eyes at Angel and gave her best scowl, only causing Angel to burst out laughing.

"Your tough-guy act doesn't work on me, remember?"

Pat grinned and sipped from her beer.

"Yes, it'll give me another place to work," Pat agreed stiffly. "Only I'm working for free, it seems."

"So, what about this woman? You usually don't let anyone get to you."

"Oh, she's just so gung-ho. Got all upset with me just because I'm not active in the environmental movement. Hell, I like wildlife as much as the next one, probably more. But I'm just not all *out there*, you know? She just rubbed me the wrong way."

"I see that." The other woman smirked, wrinkles deepening at the corner of her eyes and mouth.

"And to top it off, she's damn attractive," Pat said, finally uttering the thing most bothering her. If the woman had just kept her mouth shut, Pat might have considered asking her out.

"Oh. So not Mrs. Davenport."

"No. She's probably younger than I am. Dr. Carly Cambridge."

"Doctor?"

Pat grunted. "Some environmental degree, no doubt. And I'll be spending the next several weeks if not months, out there working for her."

"Oh, well. Can't be that bad," Angel said and moved away to another customer.

Not that bad? Please . . . the woman will drive me insane.

CHAPTER ELEVEN

Using the gate key Dr. Cambridge had given her, Pat drove down the dirt road just as the sun was rising over the bay. She stopped and stood on the back of her Jeep, camera pointing to the sunrise. She captured the dunes as they glowed pink, then hurried on past the Visitor's Center and stopped where the trail snaked down to the water. She jogged the last few yards, then fell to her knees, taking several shots of the water as it shimmered with the red and pink reflection of the sun, seemingly still dripping with water as it hovered above the bay. When the colors changed, she put her camera down and watched, unconscious of the smile that appeared on her face as pelicans flew across the bay.

She had seen more sunrises than she could count and the quiet beauty of it never failed to thrill her. Finally she stood, dusted the sand off her knees and walked slowly back to her Jeep, eyes scanning her surroundings for any sign of movement. She spotted a few seagulls as they started their hunt for food and then the ever-present vultures that left their roosts in the oaks. In the winter, there would be ospreys, too, wings spread beautifully as they soared over the bay. She grudgingly admitted that the preserve was a wonderful idea. The Thompson Ranch had been around forever, but the public was never allowed on the property. Now, this part would be opened for others to enjoy, just as she had enjoyed the sunrise.

She went back to her Jeep and followed the rest of the road until it stopped where the marshes were going to be reconstructed. Earth-moving equipment was already present, but no work had yet begun. She took several shots of the flat grassland, trying to envision what it would look like with water instead of grass. Carly had told her they would restore this area first, so that visitors could see their progress and eventually move inland to restore the fifty-something acres which had been filled in by the Thompsons over the years.

She walked on into the woods, trying to get her bearings. She assumed she would spend many mornings out here, hiking. She swatted at a mosquito that was trying to have her for breakfast and knew the number would increase dramatically when the marshes were back. It was one of the curses of living near the bay, but, she knew, also food for the birds.

She walked on until the oak mottes became too dense, the underbrush growing so thick she could not penetrate. It made her wonder how the deer managed to get around in there but she knew they did. She also knew Dr. Cambridge planned on thinning the underbrush in places to allow the oak trees to grow unimpeded by the thick cover.

Much to her surprise, she found a newly hatched nest of cardinals in the low brush. The male was not at all happy with her appearance so she stayed back and sat for nearly a half-hour until the parents grew accustomed to her and continued to visit the nest. She shot nearly a roll of film on the nest alone.

Finally she stood, her aching muscles complaining at having been inert too long. She made her way back to her Jeep and drove to the ranch house. Carly's Jeep was parked out front. Pat debated whether to drive right past or stop. She decided to stop.

****

Carly and Elsa were both on the floor, flat on their stomachs as they pulled cables behind the built-in desks. Elsa insisted that they move them and Carly, knowing little about the workings of computers, agreed. A loud voice from behind startled them.

"Am I interrupting?"

Carly banged her head on the desk and cursed. Elsa poked her head out without hitting anything, her eyes widening.

"*Dios mio*," she murmured.

Carly looked up, right at long, tanned legs. Her eyes followed their length, finally stopping at the amused face of Pat Ryan. *Shit.*

"Dr. Cambridge, hello again," Pat said, squatting down beside the prone woman. "Busy doing environmental stuff, I see."

I hate her. Carly sat up to face Pat Ryan's smiling eyes only inches away.

"You're a little late, aren't you?" She reached behind her and rubbed her head where she'd smacked it.

Pat laughed and leaned back on her heels, away from Carly.

"I was here at sunrise, thank you. Where were you?

46

Still in bed? There's land to preserve, you know. Wildlife to save."

Carly gritted her teeth and ignored the soft chuckle from Elsa as she stood. Pat stood, too, and pulled the cap off her head, letting her dark hair cascade around her face.

"I wanted to shoot the Visitor's Center before the men showed up, but I ended up playing with some cardinals instead. I'll try to get it tomorrow," she said.

Carly stared, dazzled by the woman before her, high cheekbones now framed in dark hair, blue eyes shining back at her. But only for an instant. Pay Ryan secured her hair again and slipped the cap back on.

"Cardinals?"

"Yeah. Found a nest in the brush. Thought it might look good on one of your little brochures," she said.

"Good. Glad you're working."

"I don't believe we've met," Elsa finally said, standing as well. "I'm Elsa Sanchez. Computer nerd."

"Nice to meet you, Elsa. Pat Ryan. I *volunteered* to photograph this — work in progress."

"Yes. I hear your aunt is very persuasive," Elsa said with a smile.

Pat laughed again. "I see you've heard. But, I'm sure it will be enjoyable. Entertaining, at least," she said and smiled at Carly.

"Don't you have to get going and — develop something?" Carly asked, suddenly feeling uncomfortable in the woman's presence.

"Well, I can help you down on the floor there, if you need?"

This time Elsa laughed and Carly neatly ignored both her and Pat Ryan. *I hate them both.*

"We don't need any help, thank you. In fact, we were nearly done."

"Well, then I guess I'll go — develop something."

47

Pat grinned at Elsa. "Nice meeting you. I'm sure I'll see you about."

"Same here."

Pat tipped the bill of her cap then turned and walked purposefully from the room, leaving both women staring after her.

"*Dios*," Elsa said again.

"I really wish you would quit saying that."

"She's . . . outstanding," Elsa murmured. "Do you think she's . . .?"

"Do I think she's what?"

"You know, gay?"

"How the hell should I know?" Carly exploded. "And why the hell should I care?"

"Sorry."

"Don't start, Elsa," Carly warned.

"Don't worry. I wouldn't dream of it."

"Because for one thing, I don't even like the woman. She's arrogant. I can hardly stand to be around her."

"Yes, I can tell."

"And another thing, she's . . . insufferable," Carly said for lack of finding another suitable word to describe the obnoxious Pat Ryan.

"Yes, insufferable."

"Obnoxious."

"Yes, obnoxious."

Carly turned on Elsa, hands on hips as she glared at her. "Are you mimicking me?"

"Me? Why in the world would you think that?"

Carly pointed at her, shaking her finger in Elsa's face. "Because I know you and I can see the wheels turning. Don't even think about it."

"I wouldn't dream of it."

"Are you two fighting?" a male voice asked and they both turned to see Martin watching them from the doorway.

Carly recovered first. She moved away from Elsa and towards Martin.

"Of course not, Martin. We don't fight. She just delights in irritating me," Carly said and tossed a glance back at Elsa who stuck her tongue out at her, causing Carly to laugh.

"I'm glad you're here, Martin. You can help me with these cables. Dr. Cambridge has . . . environmental stuff to do," Elsa said.

"I hate you," Carly whispered, but Elsa only grinned as she pulled Martin down with her. The smile that Martin gave Elsa caused Carly to raise her eyebrows. It appeared Martin was smitten with her assistant. Good, Carly thought grumpily. That'll keep Elsa busy.

CHAPTER TWELVE

"I'll have it tomorrow, I promise."

For all of Pat's skill as a photographer, she lacked the patience to develop her own color prints. For that, she used a lab in Corpus. Her darkroom was used only for the occasional black and whites. She dropped off the three rolls of film she'd shot that morning, stopping just long enough to give Randy, the manager, a hard time.

"Don't wash out my cardinals, okay?"

Randy grinned. "You're never going to let me live that one down, huh?"

"No. It keeps you on your toes."

"Sure it does. Maybe it makes me nervous," he said.

"Hardly. You're the best."

"Thanks, Pat. Coming from you, that means a lot. I've seen your color prints."

"Yeah. Now you know why I come here. I'll see you tomorrow."

Pat and Randy had a similar conversation nearly every time she dropped off film. At first, he thought it scandalous that a photographer with her reputation would allow someone else to develop her film. But she trusted him completely.

She drove across the bridge back to the island, her thoughts on the ranch and what she would shoot tomorrow. The Visitor's Center, for sure. She wanted to get some shots before it was completely done and Carly said only a few more weeks before they started on the interior. The ranch house, too, looked like it was nearing completion and she was doubtful that they'd taken any photos of it before they started the renovations.

She wondered if Carly would still be out and about in the morning. Probably. She suspected the woman practically lived out there. She grinned, remembering the sight of the doctor sprawled on the floor, her tanned legs spread out behind her.

Pat chuckled. The satisfaction she felt at flustering the doctor amused her. She wanted to dislike Carly Cambridge, for all her pompous views, but she'd enjoyed their banter that morning. She assumed the woman wanted to dislike her just as much and maybe she did.

CHAPTER THIRTEEN

"Shit." Carly let her hands fall from the steering wheel to her lap in dismay.

Pat Ryan's Jeep was already at the site.

"Well, so much for an early start."

Her own Jeep was loaded with some things from her apartment. She spent so much time driving back and forth, she couldn't argue with Elsa and Martin when they suggested she start moving into the apartment upstairs. It made sense. And Martin was certain the workers would be out of her hair in two weeks.

Grabbing a box from the back, she hoisted it to her hip and walked to the house, trying unsuccessfully to stop herself from searching the area for Pat.

After unlocking the door to the ranch house, she flipped on the lights, surprised to find that Martin had started painting. She'd left early yesterday, shortly after the photographer had tried to drive her insane, and spent the afternoon in her apartment answering email and putting together the mailing lists. A secretary would be nice. Hopefully, Elsa would be able to assist her as soon as the network was up and running. They could only afford to hire possibly one other full-time staffer this year. The rest of the help would be made up of volunteers. Rachel Yearwood had assured her there were plenty of willing bodies right here in Rockport. Her main concern was the fall migration bird count. She had lined up a few professionals, contacts she'd made while working for the state, that were going to lend a hand, free of charge. She was hoping the local birding club, headed by Mrs. Davenport, would supply the warm bodies. Or so Rachel had promised.

It made Carly a little nervous to think she was trusting people she'd never met, especially when the outcome would determine the amount of next year's state grant.

"Good morning," a soft voice said next to her ear.

Carly jumped, a hand going to her chest automatically.

"Jesus! Must you do that?"

"Do what?" Pat asked innocently.

"Sneak up on me all the time? Do I need to put bells on you?"

Pat arched one eyebrow and grinned. "That would be interesting, depending where you decided to attach them. But, kinda hard to sneak up on birds, don't you think?"

"Ever heard of knocking?"

"Knocking? I work here. I didn't think I'd have to knock everywhere I went."

"Are you always so difficult, Ms. Ryan?"

Pat paused, tilting her head and meeting Carly's sea-green eyes. "Yes."

"Wonderful," she said dryly. "It'll make the next few months so enjoyable then."

Pat laughed. "You really don't like me, do you?"

Carly's eyes widened in mock surprise. "Whatever gave you that idea?"

Pat shrugged. "I guess my glowing personality is not rubbing off on you, huh?"

"Yes, it's rubbing off on me, alright," Carly murmured.

Pat laughed again. "So, are you always this uptight?"

Carly turned, her green eyes flashing. "What exactly does that mean?"

"Uptight? I thought you were a doctor. You don't know what that means?"

Carly closed her eyes, imaging with delicious clarity, her hands clinched around the photographer's neck. She wondered if a quick punch to the face would ensue jail time.

Instead, she silently counted to ten, then twenty, and opened her eyes. She caught herself looking right into the baby blues of the woman standing next to her. Amused baby blues, she noted. In fact, they nearly danced and a ghost of a smile appeared on her own face. The woman was insufferable, but damn, those eyes . . .

"So, you need help unpacking? I noticed your Jeep was loaded down."

Carly was about to decline the offer, then realized it would take her several trips up and down the stairs alone.

"I'm not interrupting your work?" she asked, pointing to the camera hung around Pat's neck.

"No. I took some in the Visitor's Center already. I want to take some outside, once the workers show up. Oh, Dr. Cambridge, I noticed a road going back into the brush, behind the ranch house. Where does that go?"

"To an old barn and whatnot. There are actually several roads back there, snaking across the property. Behind the first line of oak mottes, they've cleared sports for grazing. In the fall, they used to lease it out to day hunters. There were tree stands all over the place," she said. And then, "You can call me Carly. Dr. Cambridge is so . . ."

"Stuffy?" Pat supplied.

"I was going to say formal."

"Oh. I was going to say uptight."

Carly walked out towards her Jeep. "Why is it every time I'm around you, I just want to throttle you?"

"Throttle me? Well, you know, I haven't been throttled in quite a while now. Could be fun," Pat teased.

Carly bit back a grin and shoved a box into Pat's arms. "Upstairs."

"Yes, ma'am."

Carly watched her walk off, not immune to the long tanned legs, silky dark hair and blue, blue eyes. She sighed. It would be so much easier to dislike her if she wasn't so damn attractive. And, Carly had to admit, her sense of humor, though somewhat demented, was engaging.

"Hey, there's like . . . an apartment up here," Pat called.

"Good. Then they didn't lie to me," Carly called back. With arms loaded, she climbed the stairs, finding Pat in the bedroom.

"Great view," she said, pointing out the windows that opened to the bay.

Carly followed her gaze and nodded. Actually, this was the first time she'd been in here. She'd only checked out her office, which to her was the most important room. She could sleep anywhere.

"No bed?"

Carly turned around, seeing only the new dresser she'd found at an antique shop in Rockport. Other than that, the room was mostly bare.

"I have an apartment in town," she said. "I'll probably move the furniture in over the weekend."

"Well, need some help?" Pat offered.

"Oh, no," Carly shook her head. "That's okay. Martin and Elsa will help. We should be able to manage."

"Really, I don't mind helping." Then, she flexed her right arm, showing off her well-defined biceps. She pointed at it and grinned. "Strong as an ox."

Carly couldn't help but laugh. "Stubborn as one, too," she murmured as she walked back downstairs.

"I heard that, Doctor."

Together, it only took them three trips to unload the Jeep. Actually, it wouldn't take Carly long to move. She's only been in the apartment since January and had not bothered to unpack everything, knowing she would be moving to the ranch eventually. Hopefully, in a year or so, they would be able to hire a full-time manager and Carly could get her life somewhat back to normal. Then, she could concentrate on *environmental stuff*, as Pat would say.

"Thank you for helping," Carly said.

"No problem. I'm just hanging around until the activity starts up."

Pat leaned against the doorframe and fidgeted with her camera. Carly stood on the porch, hands shoved into the pockets of her shorts, surveying the ranch. Her eyes moved from the bay to the Visitor's Center, then finally to Pat. Without thinking, Pat raised the camera and captured Carly just as she turned questioning eyes to her.

"I'm not part of the wildlife," Carly murmured.

"No?" Pat lowered the camera and grinned. "Sorry.

The light was perfect. Couldn't resist. Besides, surely we'll want one of you in the brochures?"

"Absolutely not."

"Why not? Don't you think donors will want to know who is going to spend their money?"

"I think they would rather see on *what* it will be spent rather than by *whom*," Carly stated.

Pat shrugged. "You're the boss."

"And speaking of the brochure, when do you think you'll have enough pictures to start? I'd like to begin the initial mailing as soon as possible."

"Why don't you explain to me the different mailing cycles that you're going to do," Pat suggested.

"Sure. Why don't we walk down to the bay while we talk."

Pat fell in line next to Carly as they made their way down the dirt road. The sun was already creeping higher in the sky and out of habit, Pat scanned the horizon, looking for movement.

"We've secured mailing lists from most of the environmental and conservation groups. That's where we'll start. We'll send the smaller brochures to them." Carly felt herself growing more animated as she described the campaign. "These potential donors will be the ones that'll send in ten or twenty bucks here and there. The large, multi-page brochure we're going to do will be sent to known donors across the nation who are more likely to send in hundreds of dollars. That'll be our second wave. By the end of the year, I hope to have a booklet put together that we can send to local business owners and some of the larger corporations in the area. And I want posters. We'll put those in shop windows around Rockport and Port Aransas. I want to get those up before tourist season, which gives us about a month."

"Wow. That sounds like a lot."

"Yes. Time consuming and definitely a big expense.

But as the old saying goes, you have to spend money to make money."

"So tell me, what kinds of photos do you want in this first brochure? The construction? Birds?"

"Both. I want them to see what we've accomplished so far, mainly the Visitor's Center. Right now, there aren't a lot of birds, wetland birds anyway, making this their home. That's unfortunate, because it would be nice to have a pond with ducks on it, something to show what we're trying to protect."

"I've got lots of prints laying around of birds. Do they have to be taken here?"

"Isn't that the idea?"

"Well, we could put some shots in of pelicans, egrets, herons, etc. Something to show what will make this their home once the wetlands are back."

Pat paused, thinking. She had hundreds of discarded photos which weren't marketable that would be suitable for this project.

"Right now, I've only got cardinals," Pat said. "I mean, I can hang out here on the bay and get gulls, terns, pelicans and maybe some shorebirds. But that's not really going to be the focus of this preserve, right? The wetlands are the focus. And you don't have wetlands."

"Okay." Carly shrugged. "Sad, but okay. Listen, I'm really out of my league with this, anyway. I wrote the verbiage. That was the easy part. In fact, I've got the first two brochures ready to go, other than the pictures. The booklet, I'm really doing that as we go. That's where I'll want the sequence of breaking ground to the completed Visitor's Center and the building of the marshes."

"But I don't have any shots of you breaking ground," Pat reminded her.

"Well, I managed to take a few. I haven't even developed them yet so I have no idea if the quality will even be good enough, but hiring a photographer was not top on my list at the time."

"Did you say hiring?"

Carly laughed. "I'm sorry. How about finding a willing volunteer?"

"Better," Pat nodded. "Okay, how about I bring over what I shot yesterday and I'll get today's developed so we can go through them. I'll also get together some others I've taken."

"I know this is asking a lot, but do you think you could find the time to go with me to the printer? I've met with them before and they know what I want, but I'd feel more comfortable if you were there to present the pictures and help pick out which ones are best. We've got the layout, as I've said, and left blanks where we want photos to go."

"Do you have a copy?"

"On my computer."

"Why don't you let me read it. That'll help. But yes, I'll go with you," Pat agreed. So why was she volunteering more of her time? She was going to be busting her ass as it was to meet her deadline on the nesting shorebirds.

"Can you come in the morning?"

"Actually, I have another assignment I'm working on. A *paying* one," Pat said with a smile. "Nesting shorebirds," she said at Carly's silent question. "Ten nests. I have initial shots on all ten, but I'm not nearly finished."

"Okay. Well, we'll be moving over the weekend so my computer will be here on Monday. I'll print out the brochure for you then."

"I'll get it over the weekend. I'm helping, remember?"

"Listen, you really don't have to do that."

"I don't mind. I'll probably be out here anyway," Pat said.

"Okay," Carly finally agreed. She didn't know why, but she didn't want to spend any more time than was necessary with this woman. She didn't want to like her.

As they walked back towards the ranch house, Carly suddenly felt she owed Pat some sort of apology. After all, today was the only day she'd even been half-way civil to the woman and Pat was going out of her way to help with the project.

"Pat, I want to thank you," Carly started. "I know you were roped into this project by your aunt, but I sincerely appreciate it. We got off on the wrong foot. I'm sorry."

Pat glanced at her, conscious of the fact that this was the first time Carly had called her by her first name.

"Oh, hell, Doctor, was that an apology? Don't be doing that," Pat drawled. "Then I'll have to start being nice to you."

Carly smiled. "You'd rather we argue? I doubt an apology will stop us. I still find your views to be incomprehensible."

"Good. Because I still find you to be opinionated and damn near an environmental wacko."

Carly laughed. "Well, that's original."

CHAPTER FOURTEEN

The Brown Pelican was crowded for a Thursday evening and Pat felt a pang of guilt as she drove past. She hardly ever missed a Thursday. She and Davey usually paired up in pool. It was a good escape, but mostly, it gave them all a chance to act like idiots after tequila shots. But not tonight. She was tired. After she'd left Rockport, she'd driven to Corpus to pick up yesterday's film and drop off what she'd shot that morning. Then, on her way back to the island, she'd caught the sunset over Corpus Christi Bay and she couldn't resist. Like a good sunrise, the sunset called to her and she'd grabbed her camera. Using her Jeep as a tripod, she snapped off several shots before it dipped out of sight, leaving a beautiful rosy glow to the sky.

It had left her feeling melancholy. At the first beach access road, she turned off the highway and drove along the gulf as the color washed from the sky.

She passed The Brown Pelican with only a glance. But she was hungry. Instead of going straight home, she drove to The Shrimp Shack. The tables in the cramped restaurant were packed, as were the picnic tables on the deck out back. She was happy to see Angel still working.

"Hi Angel," she said as she pulled out a barstool, moving it slightly away from the guy next to her, who appeared to be chain-smoking.

"Hey Pat. Get you a beer?"

"Yep. And dinner," she said. "To go."

"Usual?"

"Yeah. No crab this time," she said. "Extra shrimp." She hated the stuffed crab they insisted on including with the seafood platter. Glancing once again at the chain-smoker, she tapped him on the shoulder. "Hey, man, move your cigarette, would you?"

The man glared at her. "The non-smoking section's over there," he pointed, the cigarette nearly brushing her hair.

"Hey, Johnny, lay off," Angel said. "Jesus, you're like a chimney over here. I can hardly breathe."

"This is still a smoking bar, ain't it?"

"Oh, move down to the other end. You can second-hand smoke down there without lighting up."

"Damn women," he muttered but he moved down four stools.

"Thanks," Pat said. "I was afraid I was going to have to deck him. Who is he, anyway?"

"I don't know. He's been here about a month. Doesn't talk much."

Pat nodded. She dismissed the man and sipped from the draft beer Angel slid in front of her.

"What are you doing here, anyway? It's Thursday."

"Had a busy day. Didn't feel up to The Pelican tonight," Pat explained. "How's Lannie?" she asked, referred to Angel's lover. Lannie was one of only two women cops in Port Aransas.

"Still as bitchy as ever," Angel said. "Complains I'm not home enough."

"You're not. Every time I come in here, you're working. Do you ever take off?"

"She's working the night shift now, so I don't mind pulling doubles," Angel said.

She moved away to refill beer mugs at the end of the bar and Pat watched her. Angel was the first friend she'd made when she moved here and she realized that was still a very short list. Oh, the guys at The Pelican, she'd call them friends. Sort of. Just drinking buddies, really. It wasn't like they shared in each other's lives. She really didn't have that much to share, actually. She lived a rather boring life, all things considered.

****

Saturday morning found her running silently along the surf, long legs pounding in the soft sand as the first light of dawn cut into the darkness. Her thoughts drifted, moving easily to the shots she'd taken yesterday. She'd returned to five of the nests and shot a full roll at each. She'd even managed to shoot the curlews without interruption. Maybe she would try to hit the other five during the week. Hopefully, she'd have enough to submit to the magazine. Then she would meet with Steve Anderson, the guy assigned to the story, and they would write short articles on each nest. She hoped her field notes would be enough.

When the sun started creeping above the waves, she turned and retraced her steps, her eyes locked on the sun as it rose miraculously out of the surf. Her steps faltered with the beauty of it, yet again. Pinks graduated to red, then orange, as the giant orb climbed higher on the horizon. She finally stopped and stared, letting the beauty surround her. When the colors faded, she picked up her pace, racing the last several yards to her front steps.

She stopped on the bottom step and looked up at her old beach house. It sorely needed a paint job, but she didn't want the commotion of painters hanging around for days as they painted the relic. At least her neighbors would be happy when she finally got around to it, she suspected. Hers was the shabbiest of all the houses on this stretch.

"Later in the summer," she said to no one.

She brought her coffee and juice outside and sat, watching the endless procession of waves as they crashed on the surf. The beach was coming alive as other joggers followed her path of earlier. She picked up the stack of prints and shuffled through them, picking out several she thought would look nice in the brochure. The shots she'd taken of the cardinals had turned out great and she hoped Carly would want to use at least one. Actually, there was one she was quite pleased with. It would make a great centerpiece for the Visitor's Center. The male cardinal had been guarding the nest, glaring at Pat, but behind him, four hungry mouths stood wide open, begging for food.

She should really get going. She had no idea what time the big move was taking place and she should have suggested meeting them at Carly's apartment to help load furniture. Well, she assumed they would be making more than one trip anyway.

CHAPTER FIFTEEN

"Dr. Cambridge, you've got to lift your side up a little," Martin hissed as the entire weight of the bookcase fell against him.

"Martin, I've told you a hundred times, my name is Carly," she grunted as she tried to lift the bottom of the bookcase. It wasn't moving. "I can't," she said. "Shit."

The bookcase was her favorite piece of furniture. Her desk was a close second. But this piece was so beautiful. Hand-carved over a hundred years ago, her grandfather had given it to her when he retired.

"Do you need help?" Elsa asked as she stood behind Martin, her hands perched importantly on her hips.

"Elsa, you're smaller than I am," Carly said. "Why don't we leave it for later?" she suggested. "Pat Ryan said she would be out today and offered to help. Maybe we can get her to make a trip over here later."

"Well, she looks strong," Martin said.

"As an ox," Carly said without thinking.

"Excuse me?" Elsa said.

"Nothing," Carly murmured. "We're going to have to make two trips anyway."

"I told you to get a bigger trailer," Elsa said for the second time.

"Do you want me to slap you?"

"Girls," Martin warned. "You know, we could have hired someone to do this."

"What would be the fun in that?" Elsa asked.

"Come on. I'm getting cranky," Carly said. "Let's take this load. We'll get the rest later."

"*Getting* cranky? You were there at eight this morning," Elsa teased.

"Elsa, watch your mouth or I'll send you back to Austin," Carly threatened.

"As if, chica. You need me."

Carly relaxed. Yes, she needed Elsa. As a friend and a co-worker. Elsa knew all her secrets. She was the best kind of friend.

Carly drove her Jeep and Martin and Elsa followed in Martin's truck, pulling the trailer. She could have asked her brothers to come over from Corpus to help. She knew they would have. But she didn't want to burden them on a Saturday. She knew they both worked much more than forty hours each week and Saturday was their time to spend with the kids. She didn't want to cut into that.

She was pleased to find Pat's Jeep at the ranch when they pulled up, although the woman was nowhere to be found. The three of them were tussling with Carly's desk about half-way up the stairs when Pat appeared in the doorway.

"I see that the desk is winning," Pat said with a grin. "Are you going up or down?"

"*Dios mio*," Elsa murmured. "She should wear more clothes. She's not safe . . . bella."

Carly glanced over Martin's head and met Pat's laughing eyes. Then her eyes took in the woman's perfect shoulders exposed by the tiny tank top she wore. *Perfect?*

"A little help?" Carly managed.

Pat nodded and moved behind Martin.

"If I get up there, can you handle this end?" she asked him.

"I think so."

Pat squeezed between the desk and Elsa, their bodies brushing as Elsa was pressed against the wall.

"*Dios mio*," she said again as Pat moved away from her.

She fanned her face dramatically and Carly rolled her eyes. Elsa was such a pushover. But when Pat joined her at the end of the desk, their bare thighs touching as they both lifted the end, Carly felt her own blush creeping onto her face. The woman was so . . . powerful. The desk lifted with ease and she couldn't pull her eyes away from the woman's arms as muscles strained with the weight of the desk. *Dios mio was right!*

"Where to, Doc?"

"Office," Carly said. "Second door down."

Once the desk was situated, they alternated taking boxes up the stairs and moving furniture. The move was going smoother than Carly had anticipated and she knew it was because Pat had joined them. She was much stronger than she looked and Pat and Martin moved the sofa up the stairs as she and Elsa looked on from below. Carly found she couldn't look away from the long length of legs exposed by Pat's shorts. She had runner's legs. Carly could picture her jogging along the beach in skimpy shorts and sports bra. Then she shook her head, wondering where in the world that image had come from.

"I like her, Carly," Elsa said quietly. "*Diosa* . . . a goddess." Then she grinned. "She almost makes me wish I was gay."

Carly playfully hit her arm, then pulled her outside, shoving another box into her arms.

"Why do you assume she's gay?"

"Oh, come on. For one thing, no man could handle her. But, you know, she just has that look about her. That one, she would be a handful. A heartbreaker. I don't know if even a woman could handle her. She's just so . . ."

"Powerful," Carly murmured, speaking her thoughts aloud. "And overbearing and obnoxious," she added.

"Where the hell do you want this?" a voice called out the opened window above their heads. They both looked up and found Pat staring down at them.

"Coming," Carly said. Jesus, if she just wasn't so damn attractive.

That same thought echoed again as they found Pat draped across the sofa. Her legs were parted and Carly found her eyes creeping along their length to where her shorts were bunched between her legs. *Jesus!*

She turned away with a slight blush and pretended to survey the room, anything to avoid looking at the woman sprawled on her sofa. Should it face the windows and the open view of the bay? Or face the back wall where her TV would go once they had the entertainment center moved in? She seldom watched TV. She would move her recliner in the corner. She could see the TV from there.

"Here," she pointed. "Facing the windows."

"Excellent choice," Pat said. "You're going to see

some great sunrises."

"That would mean, of course, that you'd have to get up in time," Elsa teased. "Or have your sleeping habits changed?"

"We don't really need to discuss my sleeping habits," Carly said. "And yes, they have changed, thank you very much."

Elsa laughed. "She used to be cranky as hell when she had an early morning class."

"No wonder you're usually in a foul mood when I see you in the mornings," Pat said with just a hint of a smile.

"No. That has absolutely nothing to do with the time of day," Carly shot back and they all laughed.

"Come on, Martin. Let's get the rest of the boxes," Elsa said and grabbed Martin's hand and led him from the room. Carly didn't miss the flirtatious glance that Elsa gave him.

"Thank you, by the way. We couldn't have done this without you," Carly said and lightly touched Pat's arm as she walked past. "But, I think the hard part's done."

"Carly?"

Carly turned. It was the first time she'd heard Pat call her by name. She liked the sound of it.

"You shouldn't lie to the help, you know."

"What do you mean?"

Pat walked over to her and playfully pinched her cheek. "Martin told me about the bookcase. He said I would hate you after we moved it."

Carly laughed. "But, you said yourself, you're as strong as an ox."

"Yes. But I think you'll probably owe me dinner for this."

Carly watched her walk away, not liking the

accelerated beat of her heart. She reached up and touched her cheek where Pat had gently squeezed. Oh, don't go there, she told herself. It would be nothing but trouble.

But even with Pat's help, the bookcase was still a bitch to move. It took all four of them to haul it up the stairs and even then, they stopped twice to rest.

"Tell me again why we didn't hire a moving company?" Elsa asked.

"I only have a few heavy pieces," Carly said. "It's not like I have a house full of furniture."

"Let's see. Bed, sofa, entertainment center, that bitch of a desk," Elsa checked off on her fingers. "Table," she added.

"The table is small."

"This monster."

"This and the desk belonged to my grandfather. He had them in his office."

"They're beautiful," Pat said. "Heavy as hell, but beautiful."

When they finally managed to get it into her office, it was Martin who spoke first.

"Dr. Cambridge . . . Carly, please be sure of where you want it. I think I speak for all of us when I say, once it's down, it's down."

"You mean, I can't try all four walls to see where I like it best?"

"Here," Elsa pointed. It was the wall closest to where they stood.

"Wimp. I want it over there, closer to the desk."

"Are you sure?" Pat asked.

Carly turned around and surveyed the room. Martin tapped his fingers impatiently on the wood. Elsa rolled her eyes. Pat watched Carly's every move.

"Yes. This wall," she said.

"Okay. On three," Pat said and they all pushed and shoved the giant bookcase against the wall.

"Next time, we're hiring men," Elsa stated as she leaned against Martin. "Big, burly men."

"What are you saying?" Martin asked.

"Oh, chico, nothing against you," Elsa said. "You're very strong. But, I mean, like . . . *burly*, you know?"

"Elsa, you better stop while you're ahead," Pat suggested.

"How about pizza and beer? My treat, of course," Carly said.

"Of course it's your treat," Elsa said. "But I don't really feel like going out. Why don't we go back to my apartment, since I still have chairs, and order in?"

"Okay. I'll stop and get some beer on the way," Carly agreed. "Pat? Martin? That okay with you?"

They all agreed. Martin and Elsa left first, with Martin pulling the now empty trailer behind him. Pat waited at the entrance while Carly locked the gate.

"I'm going to stop at the liquor store for beer," Carly said as she walked up to Pat's Jeep. "Is beer okay or would you rather have something else?"

"No, no, that's fine," Pat said. "Do you want me to go with you or just meet you at Elsa's?"

"You go ahead. I won't be long."

Carly followed Pat's Jeep down the winding road until they reached the highway. Then, she let Pat pull away from her as she took her time. She was really tired and she suspected they all must be. It had been a full day, but fun nonetheless. She enjoyed Pat being there today. Of course, without her help, they never would have managed. And, she had to admit, she liked the woman. She would never admit this to anyone else, but in oh so many years, she felt a tingle of attraction to another woman. She would allow it to go no further, she knew, but still, it was there.

When she arrived at Elsa's apartment, lugging in a case of Corona and a bag of limes, they were all sprawled on the floor, already drinking.

"I ordered two large pizzas," Elsa told her.

"Good."

Pat got up to help her with the beer and they crammed twelve into the fridge.

"That'll do for now," Pat said, snagging another one. She pulled out a lime and sliced it into several wedges, passing it around to the others.

"I feel like I've been beaten," Elsa stated. "Just in case you wanted to know," she told Carly.

"And just in case I haven't said thank you enough. . ."

"Don't worry. I'll bring this up on numerous occasions during the summer. Whenever I need a day off because my back *still* hurts."

"I'm sure you will."

"How long have you two known each other?" Pat asked.

"College," Elsa said. "We lost touch for awhile, then ended up working together in Austin."

"Yeah, until you escaped and went *back* to college." She turned to Pat. "We worked for the state. But our ideals were shattered by politics. Elsa was smarter than me and left. I hung on, still hoping I could make a difference."

"I don't doubt that you managed that somehow. I can't see you taking no for an answer," Pat said.

"You've heard of the Edwards Aquifer?"

"Yeah. San Antonio gets its water from there, right?"

"Yes, among others. But it spreads all the way to Austin. It was my project. I did research for years and they were killing it, draining it dry. Too much development, too much runoff. The streams were drying up, thus the springs were, too. But, it was all politics. The developers had money and politicians love money."

"Now you've done it," Elsa warned Pat. "She'll go on for hours now if we don't stop her."

Carly laughed. "I'm over it, Elsa."

"Sure you are. That's why you still send hate mail to a former governor who is now in the White House."

"I do not send hate mail." Then she grinned. "At least, not any more."

The pizzas arrived and they all dug in, devouring both of them until only one piece remained. Pat and Martin both eyed it, but politely offered it to the other. Elsa finally tore it in half and watched as they fought for the largest piece.

Carly offered them all another beer, but Pat declined.

"I live on the island. I should really get going," she said. She'd had a wonderful time. She didn't really know these people, but they had included her in their conversations and she'd enjoyed herself. She'd made new friends and Carly had warmed up to her, too. In fact, they hadn't had a single argument all day. Not really. The herons, well, Pat had just been teasing Carly.

"I can't thank you enough," Carly said as she walked her to the door.

"No, you can't," Pat teased. Then she lowered her voice. "Don't think this counted for the dinner you owe me."

"I never thought it did," Carly said easily.

"See you two later," Pat called to Elsa and Martin. Then she paused at the door. "We still need to get together and go over the brochure. I've got some photos I want you to look at."

"Okay. I should have printed it out for you today, but I didn't think of it," Carly said. "If you're out and about tomorrow, come by the ranch. I'll be there. If not, Monday?"

"I'm doing some work out this way in the morning. After I'm done, maybe I'll swing by."

"Good."

Carly watched her as Pat went to the back of her Jeep, then pulled on a sweatshirt. Yes, she imagined the ride back to the island would be cold in the open Jeep. Pat looked up and saw her watching, then lifted one hand in a wave as she drove away.

"You going to stand there all night?" Elsa asked.

"No, sorry," Carly said and closed the door.

"I guess I should be going, too," Martin said. "I promised my mother I would take her to church in the morning."

"Is all of your family here?" Elsa asked him.

"Just my mother and one sister. I'm from the Valley, most everyone still lives down there."

"Martin, thanks again," Carly said. "I know it wasn't exactly in your job description."

"No problem, Dr. Cambridge."

"Carly, please. I'd like to think we've become friendly enough to use first names."

"I'm sorry. Habit."

"Martin, I enjoyed spending time with you," Elsa told him as she walked him to the door, much like Carly had done Pat.

"Me, too. Goodnight, ladies."

"Buenas noches," Elsa replied.

Elsa closed the door and leaned against it and closed her eyes.

"I don't know what it is, but he does something to me," she finally said.

"Martin?"

"Yes, Martin. Who else?"

"Well, I had hoped you weren't just flirting with him all day for the fun of it," Carly teased.

"I was not flirting." She began clearing away the empty pizza boxes, then looked up. "Has he been married?"

"Yes."

"Oh, good Lord, he's not *still* married?"

Carly laughed. "No. Actually, I think he's been single for quite awhile. I got the impression he was married and divorced down in the Valley. He's been living in Corpus for about five years."

Elsa digested this news with a frown. "Must be a reason he's still single, then."

"Elsa, *you're* still single," Carly pointed out.

"Well, he just seems like a normal man, you know. They're kinda hard to find these days."

"Yes, Martin is wonderful. Very dependable, trustworthy. He came highly recommended when I was looking for help with this project."

"And I'm certainly glad you hired him. Now, what about Pat?" Elsa asked, changing the subject.

"What about her?"

"You seemed to get along with her today. I didn't notice any quibbling, other than the argument over the herons," Elsa said.

"They were egrets. Who can't tell the difference between a heron and an egret?"

"Obviously your photographer."

"I think she just likes to argue with me. She seems to get great joy out of irritating me."

"So I noticed. But it was really nice of her to help out today."

"Yes, it was. I mean, we're all practically strangers to her, but she fit right in."

Elsa smiled at her, then patted her cheek. "Good."

"Good? Good, what?"

"Just good."

"Elsa . . ." Carly warned.

"Elsa what?"

"I know what you're thinking."

"You couldn't possibly. Your thoughts don't go in that direction, remember?"

"I can still beat the crap out of you," Carly warned.

"In your dreams, chica."

CHAPTER SIXTEEN

Pat found her aunt sitting on the deck, sipping a Bloody Mary while she read the Sunday paper.

"Pat? My, my, back from church already?"

Pat grinned. It was a running joke with them.

"Yes. I see you took in the early Mass."

"And I sang in the choir. Needed a little something to soothe my throat," Aunt Rachel said, pointing at her drink. "Want one?"

"Sure. Breakfast?"

"No. It is past the breakfast hour, you know that. Brunch. Alice is making omelets. Let her know you're here. Oh, and freshen this up, will you?" she asked, handing Pat her nearly empty glass.

Aunt Rachel put the paper aside when Pat rejoined her at the table.

"Perfect," she said after sipping the fresh Bloody Mary. "I taught you well."

"You know perfectly well this is Angel's recipe," Pat said.

"Oh, pooh. I was making these before Angel was even born. Now, tell me what you've been doing all week. Mrs. Davenport says you sneaked onto her property one day."

Pat laughed. "Where was she hiding? I wanted to get some close-ups, which is impossible to do with her running her mouth the whole time."

"What about Dr. Cambridge? She hasn't called to complain, so I assume you kept your appointment."

"Yes, Aunt Rachel, I kept *your* appointment. And as I suspected, she was a little on the nutty side," Pat said.

"What do you mean? She's perfectly normal."

"Normal? I meant her views. I called her an environmental wacko and it didn't even phase her."

"You *what?* Patricia, Dr. Cambridge is so . . . wonderful. She is so passionate about her cause."

"*Patricia?*"

"She genuinely cares about this land and the wildlife. She has no hidden agendas. She's not out to make money by scheming donations from poor, old widowed women like me. And believe me, you would be surprised at how many people try to take advantage of that."

"Poor? Aren't you exaggerating?"

"I didn't mean poor, as in no money."

"Yes, I know what you meant. And aren't you exaggerating? You're the least helpless woman I know."

"Why, thank you. I think that was a compliment. Now, tell me what you're doing to help Dr. Cambridge."

Pat shrugged. "I helped her move."

"I meant with your camera. Move where?"

"To the top floor of the ranch house. The bottom floor will be offices, but she's going to live upstairs."

"Why did you help her move?"

Pat shrugged again. "I was out there anyway. She wants to put the first brochure together this week."

"So you've already been taking pictures?"

"Yes. I've been out there quite a bit this week. In fact, I'm supposed to go out today and we're going to go over the prints that I have and decide which ones she wants to use."

Aunt Rachel smiled and grabbed her hand.

"Thank you, Pat. I knew once you met her, you would warm up to this idea. It's hard to say no to her."

"Yes. I found that out."

"So, I know you said you had some deadline," Aunt Rachel said. "Can you do both? I would really feel terrible if this is going to take up too much of your time, you know."

"I'll manage. Thanks to Mrs. Davenport," she added. "I've got my ten nests. The clouds this morning aren't helping, though. And it's supposed to rain this week, so that'll cut into my time."

"Oh, well, we can't control the weather. I should warn you though, Mrs. Davenport has listed all the nests on the birding hotline."

"Son of a bitch! What in the hell is she thinking?"

"She's thinking you don't own them."

"Goddamnit! That woman is going to drive me completely insane!"

"Oh, calm down. She helped you, didn't she?"

"The woman's a fruitcake," Pat said. "I think she just likes the attention."

"Yes. You may be right. Although, you should really be nicer to her. I think I've got her talked into donating money to Dr. Cambridge."

"And what does that have to do with me?"

"Well, I may have mentioned that you would be happy to show her around the new place, maybe take her . . ."

"*What?* Have you lost your mind? Aunt Rachel, the woman is damn near crazy. I'm not going to show her around the ranch."

"Pat, she's worth millions, surely you know that."

"I don't give a shit! That has nothing to do with me."

"Think of Dr. Cambridge, then."

"Oh, Jesus . . . Aunt Rachel, why do you do this to me?"

"Because I don't have any children of my own to torment."

CHAPTER SEVENTEEN

Carly was unpacking yet another box. She hated moving. But it wasn't like she'd gotten used to the apartment. In fact, she hated the apartment. Especially her upstairs neighbors, who were apparently night people, and came and went at all hours. That, she would not miss.

She stood in her living room and looked around. It was coming together. She had spent the entire morning putting her kitchen in order, then moved to her office. She'd actually hooked up her computer last night and unpacked several boxes of books. Once she had everything set up, she did remember to print out the brochure, just in case Pat stopped by today.

Now, after stopping long enough to eat canned soup for lunch, she was tackling the living room. The first thing she did was hook up her stereo. She sorted through her box of CDs and pulled out a Sarah Mclachlan, setting the volume high while she stacked her CDs, all in alphabetical order. Then, she added the few DVDs she owned.

The framed prints she loved were leaning against various walls. She would hang them later. She stared at one in particular, that of a whooping crane at sunrise, and it reminded her of the one on Pat Ryan's website. Maybe later . . . someday, she would inquire about buying one of Pat's.

"Hey."

"Jesus!" Carly jumped, hand going to her racing heart.

"Sorry. I need bells, I know," Pat said with a grin.

"How do you do that?"

Pat shrugged. "Lots of practice. But I did knock."

"Where?" Carly asked.

"On the front door."

Carly hit the remote, turning the music down and faced Pat. Today, she wore jeans and Carly thought she looked even more attractive than she did in shorts, if that were possible. She suddenly felt terribly underdressed. Her old sweat pants were baggy and worn and the T-shirt she'd grabbed that morning had seen better days.

"I guess I need a doorbell," Carly said.

"Am I interrupting?"

"No, of course not. I'm just unpacking. I printed out the brochure for you earlier," Carly said and she moved past Pat and into her office. When she turned, Pat was standing in the doorway.

"Looks good," Pat said. "The desk and bookcase. . . beautiful pieces."

"Thanks. My grandfather had them forever in his office. When he retired, he gave them to me."

"Retired? From?"

"He was an attorney. As are my father and both brothers," Carly said.

"Why didn't you follow?"

"I just didn't have the calling, I guess. I always wanted to be a vet. My grandfather was the only one who supported my decision."

"But you're not a vet. Or are you?"

"I was two semesters away and switched to wildlife biology. I thought I could make more of a difference that way. But I was young. I didn't realize all the obstacles."

"Politics?"

"Politics and indifference."

"Well, we do tend to take things for granted," Pat said.

"Yes, most people do." Carly stopped before she launched into one of her sermons. "Let's go to the table. Do you have photos?" she asked.

Pat held up the large, manila envelope she'd had tucked under her arm. Following Carly, she smiled at the baggy sweats she wore. She looked comfortable. Adorable, she added, surprised at her thoughts.

Pat handed the envelope to Carly and took the printed brochure. She pulled out a chair and began reading, hearing Carly's voice in the words. Concise and to the point, no sugarcoating. She frowned. It needed sugarcoating, she realized.

Carly spread the prints out, her eyes widening. They were great. God, the sunrise over the bay was beautiful. She smiled. Pat's cardinals. She ran her finger over the nest, as if to touch the young. Then she laughed. The male was definitely defending his nest.

"This one's great," she said.

"Yes. I thought that would make a great print. For

the Visitor's Center," Pat said. "Aunt Rachel said you wanted some to display there."

"Yes, we do. But this is very good. I mean, this is your profession. You could sell this."

"I shot it on your time," Pat said.

"It's not like I'm paying you. And this doesn't really reflect the preserve. We're all about shorebirds and ducks and marshes," she said.

"Well, obviously, cardinals live here, too."

"You're very good."

"Why, thank you, Dr. Cambridge. I know you had your doubts."

"Not really. I checked out your Web site."

"Ah, so you did have your doubts."

Carly laughed. "Okay, well, yes. After our first meeting, I may have had doubts. I thought maybe Rachel sent you here just to irritate the hell out of me."

"And I thought she was doing it just to irritate me."

"What do you think of the brochure?"

Pat raised her eyes and met green ones for just an instant. "It's . . . harsh," she said. "It doesn't paint a very pretty picture."

"It's not supposed to. The marshes have been destroyed. The land has been changed to meet man's needs — and cows' needs. Of course it's harsh."

Pat shook her head. "If I got this in the mail, I would think all was lost and I would not want to give a dime."

With hands on her hips, Carly glared at Pat. "What the hell are you talking about?"

"This. It's all doom and gloom. I'm depressed reading it. It doesn't give me the warm fuzzies."

"You're supposed to be depressed reading it. That's what makes people give money."

"You're joking? No, I disagree."

"*You* disagree?"

"Yes. People want to feel like they're giving to a good cause. Something with a bright future. You paint this dismal picture, as if all hope is lost. What good is money going to do to help this place? You've already doomed it."

"As if you know anything about preserving land!"

"I'm just saying, we're contradicting ourselves here. You paint this dismal picture of this place, yet we put pretty pictures of birds in the brochure. What is it we are really trying to tell people?"

"We're telling people this is what it *could* be."

"Why not tell them the land's been fucked over, but you're restoring it and look, beautiful cardinals are already nesting here."

They stared at each other, green eyes locking on blue for an instant, then Carly smiled and Pat did the same.

"Okay. It's fucked. Let's tell them that," Carly said and laughed.

"Carly, the statistics are great, the outlook is great but in between, it sucks."

"Jesus, I hate you, you know that?"

"Yes, I figured."

"Okay. It's just everything's always been black and white with me. I have a hard time glossing over things."

"I think you should focus on what's being done to improve and restore this place instead of what's been done to destroy it. Talk about restoring the marshes, talk about wanting the whooping crane to locate here, talk about the hundreds of ducks and shorebirds that can make this their home. That's what people want to give money to."

Carly stared at her, wondering where the indifferent photographer had gone. The woman speaking these words was sounding like an activist.

"You're not quite as uncaring and indifferent as you make yourself out to be, huh?"

Pat smiled. "I guess I never really thought much about it before."

Carly sighed. "Okay. You're probably right. I was on my soapbox when I was writing this." She pulled the brochure from Pat's hands, scanning the words she'd written, seeing them with different eyes. Yes, it was harsh. Yes, it was dismal. God, she hated her.

"Got any beer in this place?" Pat finally asked.

Carly looked up, embarrassed. She was a terrible host. "I'm sorry, yes." She moved to get up but Pat stopped her.

"I'll get it. Want one?"

"Please."

Carly continued reading the brochure, mentally making changes. She noticed the beer Pat put in front of her and she reached for it silently, her eyes still scanning the document.

"You don't mention the Visitor's Center in much detail," Pat said. "That'll be the first thing people see when they come here, the first place they go. Why don't you talk about what you want the Visitor's Center to be," Pat suggested.

"Perhaps I should let you write this. You seem to be the only one with ideas."

"No. I have a hard enough time writing captions for my photos." Then she shuffled through the stack on the table, finding the ones of herons and egrets she'd shot previously. "What about these? Don't you think we could use something like this to show what will be here eventually?"

Carly studied them, each bird captured uniquely in its setting. Yes, they could use them.

"Shorebirds?" she asked.

Pat found some others. Unidentified shorebirds, she liked to call them. They all looked alike to her.

"Greater yellowlegs. Willet. Marbled godwit, that's a great shot," Carly said as she named them.

Pat stared, stunned.

"Hopefully, these will all be here. Yes, we can use them. I'll rewrite this. We can include these, along with your cardinals, of course. I'm supposed to meet with the printer Wednesday afternoon. Do you think you can go with me?"

Pat still stared at the prints. "How do you know what these are? They're not in the goddamn field guide," she said.

"Of course they are," Carly said.

"They're not in *my* field guide."

"They're in *all* field guides, Pat. Can you go with me, please?" Carly asked again.

"Yes. I'll go with you."

"Good. It's in Corpus. There's no point in you coming all the way out here just to go back again. I'll pick you up."

"Okay. When you get off the ferry, stay on the main road and go to the third light. Go right on Sandpiper. Take the second left, Gulf View . . ."

"I should probably write this down," Carly said. She found pad and pen. "Okay, right on Sandpiper. Second left, Gulf View."

"Right on Perry's Landing. Fourth house down."

"About two?"

"That's fine. And I'm sorry if I offended you with all this," Pat said, pointing at the brochure that lay between them.

"No. In fact, I should thank you. No one's read it other than you. To me, it made perfect sense. I guess I wasn't looking at it objectively."

"Well, I better head back. Supposed to rain later. My Jeep is still topless."

"Yes, mine too. I guess I'll pull it into the old barn out back."

"Well, if the weather holds, I may be out this way. If not, I'll see you on Wednesday."

"Thanks, Pat. I really appreciate everything you're doing."

"No problem. I'm actually beginning to like it myself. All this environmental stuff is brainwashing me, I think."

Carly walked down the stairs with Pat, just now noticing the dark clouds gathering over the bay. Rain for sure tonight.

"Be careful," she said as Pat slammed the door to her Jeep. She doubted Pat would make it home before the rain hit. She had half a mind to ask her to stay but thought better of it.

Later, as she sat at her computer rewriting the verbiage for the brochure, she thought of Pat. She really had no intention of liking her as much as she did. In fact, after their first meeting, she was certain she could not stand to be in the same room with the woman. But, as Elsa had said, she was a goddess. One of the most attractive women Carly had ever met. Her thoughts went to Carol, the woman who had used her so thoroughly all those years ago. She, too, had been attractive. Too attractive. And Carly had been too blind to see anything but that. Carol had wined and dined her and before Carly knew what happened, she had fallen in love. She had sold her soul. And almost lost her life.

She had vowed she would never again give herself to another person. The pain was too great. She poured herself into her work and was never even tempted by another woman.

Why, then, did Pat Ryan fill her thoughts?

CHAPTER EIGHTEEN

She found the sweatshirt she kept crammed between the seats and pulled it on, cursing herself for not pulling the top up on the Jeep before she left Carly. Little good it would have done. She didn't have the windows with her. By the time she pulled into her driveway and parked under her stilted beach house, she was soaked. Her wet hair was plastered to her back and she went straight to her utility room and stripped off her wet clothes.

After a hot shower, she poured a glass of wine and sat in the dark, watching the lightning as it danced over the gulf.

Her thoughts drifted to Carly and she smiled slightly. Without really trying, she seemed to irritate the woman to no end. Oh, but she was damn cute. Especially when she got riled and her green eyes flashed. Which was often. Pat's normal impatience with people, women, didn't seem to apply to Carly. She found she enjoyed the other woman's company. Actually, what Pat found refreshing was Carly's indifference to her. Pat wasn't naïve about her looks. She had used to it her advantage on numerous occasions, in fact. But Carly seemed oblivious, even though she was obviously gay. Maybe Carly was involved with someone in Austin. Maybe that was the reason for her indifference.

But still, Pat noticed the attraction she felt for the other woman. She'd hardly recognized it at first, they had been too busy arguing. But the blonde woman who was so devoted to her cause still managed to stir Pat's libido.

CHAPTER NINETEEN

The rain that had started on Sunday afternoon lingered until Tuesday. Pat paced back and forth in front of her windows, watching the waves churn angrily against the wet sand. A mist, even a light rain, Pat could handle. She could still get out and run, if nothing else. But this, this continuous downpour had her stuck inside for the second day.

"Fuck it." She had to get out.

She had put the top on the Jeep yesterday morning, but the seats were still damp. She put a dry towel down and turned the heater on high. Pat hated April. Some days, so warm you would swear summer was making an early appearance. Then, like today, cold and damp, making you wonder if the brief winter they enjoyed was still hanging on.

She drove through the downpour, her wipers barely keeping up with the rain. There was only one car at The

Shrimp Shack. It was Angel's. She pulled the hood of her raincoat over her cap and ran inside, stopping to wipe her muddy boots on the mat.

"I figured I'd see you today," Angel said.

"I hate this shit. I have cabin fever," she stated.

"Beer?"

"Sure. I've got nothing else to do." Pat looked around the empty bar. "I guess I'm the only one that braved the weather?"

"Oh, we had a handful at lunch, that was it. You eating?"

"No. Had a delicious frozen dinner earlier." Pat took a swallow from her beer, then put it down on the coaster Angel had provided.

"Hey, Lannie has the weekend off. She said to invite you over for dinner Saturday night."

"Please tell me she's not trying to set me up again," Pat said.

"No. She knows you're hopeless."

"So you're actually taking a Saturday off?"

"I'm taking the whole weekend off. We haven't spent an entire weekend together in months."

Pat's cell phone interrupted them and she searched her coat, finally finding it in one of the pockets. She checked the ID before answering.

"Aunt Rachel? What's up?" Pat asked.

"Where are you?"

"Are you checking up on me again?"

"I'm simply trying to find you. Dr. Cambridge called, looking for you. Apparently, you didn't leave her any phone numbers. She said she needed you."

Pat raised her eyebrows and grinned. "She *needs* me?"

"She found a nest. Egrets. She was very excited."

"It's been raining for two days. When did she get out to find a nest?"

"She didn't go into details. But she was very excited. I told her I would hunt you down."

Pat looked out the window at the steady rain. She didn't relish driving to Rockport and the ranch in this. She certainly didn't want to go outside in it, looking for a damn egret. But, the idea of seeing Carly, a possibly wet and soaked Carly, appealed to her. Oh well, she didn't have anything better to do.

"Okay. You can call her back and tell her I'm on the way to her rescue. I'm just going to finish my beer."

"Tell Angel hello for me."

"And what makes you think I'm here?"

"Where else would you be in this mess?"

CHAPTER TWENTY

The rain had eased up somewhat by the time she turned onto the dirt road of the ranch, but Pat was still thankful Carly had left the gate open for her. She pulled up to Carly's now covered Jeep and ran to the porch. She raised her hand to knock just as the door opened.

"Didn't want me sneaking up on you today?" Pat asked.

"I've been waiting," Carly said. "Come inside." She stood back and let Pat enter, then closed the door behind her. Pat took off her raincoat and pulled off her cap, shaking her long dark hair. Carly could only stare. No woman had the right to look that good in jeans.

"So, an egret," Pat said. "Are you sure it wasn't a heron?" she teased.

"Funny. Don't think I won't drown you if I get the chance."

Pat laughed, a loud, rich laugh that Carly found delightful.

"Here," Pat said. She handed Carly her business card. "My cell number is on the back."

"Thanks."

"It's been raining nonstop. What possessed you to wander outside?"

"I pulled my Jeep into the old barn Sunday after you left. I walked there today to put the top on, then decided to drive the back roads. There's a pond in the back. A rather large pond. That's where I found them. Snowy egrets," she said.

"Oh. I know that one. Dark legs with yellow feet."

"My, my. We'll make a birdwatcher out of you yet."

"Don't threaten me, Carly. That label will never apply to me. I refuse to end up like old Mrs. Davenport."

"I can't wait to meet this woman. Between you and Rachel, she's practically a birding legend around here."

"So, you really want to brave the rain? We could wait for a sunny day," Pat suggested.

"I would really like to use them in the brochure. That is, if you think you can get a shot in this mess."

"It'll be dark, but I can try. Shooting a white bird in weather like this will make the color look washed out. But maybe they can touch it up." Pat pulled on her raincoat again. "I'm ready if you are."

They took Pat's Jeep. The rain had let up even more, but dark clouds hovered to the north, a threat of more rain to come.

"There's the barn," Carly said, pointing to the structure that had seen better days. "Looks bad on the outside, but I didn't find any leaks."

Pat drove down the bumpy road, pausing when it forked. She looked at Carly with raised eyebrows.

"To the left."

Just a short way down the road, Pat saw the water. The pond, obviously dug to supply the cattle with fresh water, was larger than she imagined. The oaks and brush had grown right up to the edge on the far side and she suspected that this was where Carly had found her nest.

"I saw the bird over there, in the shallow part. I was so thrilled to find him here, I never suspected they had a nest."

"Did you see both parents?"

"Yes. The nest is about five feet high. I didn't get very close. I didn't want to disturb them." She pulled out her binoculars and scanned the brush, looking for white in all the green. She finally found the head of the egret. She handed Pat the binoculars. "They are to the right, about three o'clock," she said.

Pat searched the trees, finally spotting one egret on the ground. She looked higher and found the other, she assumed on the nest. Or nearby. Did egrets sit on nests?

"I'm certainly not an expert or anything, but don't they normally nest in colonies?"

"Normally, yes. Maybe they're starting a new colony."

Pat lowered the glasses and studied the area, planning the best route to take. From the left, she decided. There would be less cover but she would more likely get a clean shot from there. She reached into the back and pulled out her camera bag, taking the smaller lens off the camera and replacing it with the 500mm. The lighting wasn't good for the larger lens, but she doubted she would get close enough to use the smaller one. She shoved it into her coat pocket just in case. "Okay, wish me luck."

"Wait, you won't disturb them, will you? I mean, I want the shot, but I don't want to run them off."

"I promise I won't get too close."

She got out and closed the door silently, taking slow, quiet steps away from the Jeep. Carly watched as she disappeared into the brush, wondering why she was going away from the nest. But a short time later, Pat reappeared, now much closer to the nest, but still in the cover of the brush. Carly picked up the binoculars and watched the egrets. They didn't seem to notice Pat.

The steady dripping of the rain on the canvas top increased and Carly wondered if Pat would be able to get a shot before the next downpour hit. She raised the glasses and focused on Pat. The woman's clear complexion and tanned face appeared, intense eyes glued on the nest. She barely moved.

"Jesus, but she's attractive," Carly whispered. "Why does she have to be so attractive?"

Pat inched along, her boots silent on the wet leaves. She barely noticed the rain. When the egret on the ground, presumably the male, flicked its head in her direction, she froze. After a few seconds, it looked away and Pat moved again, slowly, silently.

"So that's how she sneaks up on me," Carly murmured. If the birds knew of her presence, they didn't show it. Finally, with hardly any movement at all, Pat raised the camera.

Both birds looked her way at the sound of the shutter and Pat kept still, camera still held to her eyes. With her thumb, she advanced the film, waiting until they looked away. The light wasn't as bad as she'd feared, but they would still be washed out. She snapped several more, finding that the egret was indeed sitting on the nest. She wanted to change the lens. She needed to get closer, but she was totally exposed. She suspected the birds were getting nervous and she'd promised Carly she wouldn't disturb them.

Carly held her breath as the male fidgeted on the ground. "No closer," she whispered.

When she looked again at Pat, she noticed that the woman had moved back several feet. The male settled back down. But they all jumped at the crack of thunder overhead. The downpour had begun.

Pat finally became aware of the rain as it ran down her back. She hadn't put the hood up, fearing it would spook the birds. With as little movement as possible, she slipped the camera under her coat, protecting it from the rain. She continued backing up, away from the nest. However, a lightning strike and a loud clap of thunder caused her to jump.

"Shit," she whispered. "What the hell am I doing out here?"

"Jesus Christ! Will you get back here?" Carly bit her lip, watching as Pat disappeared into the brush again, knowing she would reappear near the Jeep. She reached over and opened Pat's door, not caring if she startled the egrets. Pat was going to be drenched, that is, if the lightning didn't get her first. Another flash across the sky followed by a boom of thunder made her jump. Then Pat was there, sliding into the Jeep, dripping wet.

"Are you insane?" Carly demanded. "Do you have any idea how close that was?"

"Yes. I damn near shit on myself."

She flashed Carly a grin. Carly returned it reluctantly.

"I'm sorry. I never should have made you do that."

"Dr. Cambridge, I've never been one to pass up a shot. I'm all in one piece."

"You're soaking wet. I'm sure I'll never live it down if you end up with pneumonia."

"Thank goodness you're a doctor," Pat quipped as she started the Jeep and backed away. The egrets never moved.

Carly couldn't resist. She pulled out a tissue from her coat pocket and dabbed at the rain dripping down Pat's nose. Pat brushed her hand away.

"Jesus, I'm going to run into a goddamn tree," she said. She grabbed the tissue from Carly's hand and wiped at the windshield, now fogged. They managed to make it back without hitting anything and they both ran for the porch.

Pat stood dripping by the door as Carly went to find towels.

"Leave your coat down there," Carly called from the top of the stairs.

"I guess that means I'm to come up," Pat murmured. She tossed her raincoat on the floor and pulled off her muddy boots. Even her socks were wet.

"You look like a drowned rat," Carly observed as Pat leaned against the bathroom door. She walked over and pulled Pat's cap off her head, then lifted up her hair.

"You are so wet," she said, her hand squeezing water from Pat's hair.

The statement, made so innocently, nonetheless caused Pat's mouth to lift in a grin. She couldn't resist.

"You just seem to do that to me, Dr. Cambridge."

Carly refused to let Pat see the blush that covered her face. Instead, she covered Pat's head with the towel and escaped into the kitchen, but not before she heard the rather loud chuckle coming from beneath the towel.

"Damn the woman," she murmured.

But when Pat reappeared, she still looked like a drowned rat. It was Carly's turn to laugh.

"Have you looked in the mirror?"

"No. In my mind, I still look perfectly groomed."

"Trust me, those words do not fit that . . . look," Carly said with yet another smile.

"I believe you. Now, if you're done having your fun

with me, can we turn on the heat? I'm actually freezing to death."

Carly noticed the flushed appearance and saw that Pat was shivering. She frowned. The woman would be lucky if she didn't come down with the flu.

"You need to get out of those clothes." As soon as the words left Carly's mouth, she saw the grin Pat flashed her.

"If you insist. I thought you would never ask."

Carly decided to ignore the comment. It was safer that way.

"I have nothing that will fit you, though. And unfortunately, the washer and dryer won't be installed until the utility room is finished downstairs."

"How about those cute baggy sweats you had on the other day?" Pat asked.

Cute? They were her oldest pair.

"And a pair of socks," Pat added.

Carly looked down at Pat's feet. "You wear what? Size twelve?"

"Nine."

Carly pointed at her own feet. "Seven."

"That'll do."

Carly shrugged. She hadn't washed the sweats, but she doubted Pat would care. They were at least dry. She found a thick pair of socks, knowing they would still be small.

Pat disappeared into the bathroom. Carly poured them each a glass of wine, then found two cans of soup and heated that. When Pat returned, she couldn't help but laugh. The sweats reached just below her calf and the socks were stretched tight over her feet.

"May I borrow your camera?" Carly asked.

"No, you may not. And you're not to tell anyone about this."

"You actually look adorable," she said before she could stop herself.

Pat's reply died on her lips and she saw embarrassment, followed by confusion in the other woman's eyes.

"Well, I thought they looked adorable on you, too," Pat said quietly.

Carly didn't try to hide the blush this time. She simply handed Pat a glass of wine and went to stir the soup.

"I thought a bowl of hot soup might warm you up some."

"That'll be great."

"Do you think any of the shots will turn out?" Carly asked, trying to find a safe subject to talk about. She cursed her traitorous body. She wanted to ignore the attraction she felt for this woman, but inappropriate thoughts seemed to form words and leave her mouth without her even being conscious of it. *Adorable? What are you thinking?*

"Maybe. The light was better than I thought. But I never saw the eggs or even if they'd hatched. The mother was completely on the nest."

"Well, I'm sorry I made you do that. Especially if we don't end up using them."

"Maybe later, after they've hatched, we can take more. You can always use them in your next brochure," Pat suggested.

They sat across from each other at the small table, eating the soup silently. Carly refilled their glasses for the third time. She felt she was giving Pat the wrong signals. She had been practically flirting with her. Well, as much as Carly knew how to flirt. Actually, she wasn't flirting. She was just reacting. But she had to stop things right now. When Pat got up to put her empty bowl in the sink, Carly took a swallow of wine before speaking.

"I think we should talk," she said.

"Talk?"

"I just wanted you to know that I'm not . . . well, I'm not interested in you," she said.

Pat leaned against the counter and crossed her arms, waiting for Carly to continue.

"I think we can be friends," she said. "Despite the outcome of our first couple of meetings," she added with a small smile. "But, I'm not interested in anything else. Just in case you were."

"In case I was interested in you?"

"Yes. I just wanted to make sure you were clear about that. I'm not . . . I'm not attracted to you. At all," she added. "So, in case you were thinking that I was . . ."

"Well, it's not really up to you, is it?"

"What is that supposed to mean?"

"I am attracted to you. You don't really have a say in that."

"Of course I do! There will never be anything between us. Trust me."

"Okay, I trust you," Pat said. But she walked purposefully to Carly and bent down, kissing her full on the mouth before the other woman knew what was happening. "I've got to go. Thanks for the dry clothes. And the soup."

Carly sat there, stunned. Absolutely stunned. She heard Pat leave the bathroom, presumably with her wet jeans, heard her walk quietly down the stairs, heard the front door open and close, heard the Jeep start up and leave.

Only then did she dare raise her fingers to her mouth and touch it where Pat's lips had rested. The kiss had been too brief, too hard to be passionate. It was a kiss of possession, of ownership.

"Shit. I can't believe she did that."

But yes, of course she could believe it. She had no doubt Pat Ryan would go after whatever, whomever she wanted.

"I'm in big trouble," she murmured.

CHAPTER TWENTY-ONE

It took Pat forever to get warm. Even a hot shower did little to chase the chill. She poured a small glass of brandy and huddled in her own sweats, covered with a blanket.

"You actually kissed her. What in the hell were you thinking?"

She was actually thinking that Carly Cambridge was the first woman she'd been attracted to on more than a sexual level. There was certainly that, she noted with a smile. But, there was an energy between them. Carly excited her. She doubted she would ever be bored in her company. And that had always been the problem. When she was younger, she tried to have relationships. But beyond the sex, there was nothing there. And she soon lost patience. She grew restless. She needed conversation that was as passionate as their nighttime activities but it never was.

Pat knew she attracted her fair share of women just on her looks alone. And years ago, when she had the energy, she took advantage of that. But she always craved more. She wanted what Angel and Lannie had. A home. Someone to share her life with. Someone she could relate to on all levels.

Now, what really scared her was that for the first time, she'd met someone who actually stirred her soul. What if Carly had been telling the truth? What if she wasn't attracted to her?

"That would hardly be fair," she said out loud.

CHAPTER TWENTY-TWO

Carly was dreading the trip to Corpus. She'd made up excuses in her mind to call Pat and cancel. But, she had to meet the printers. And Pat had the prints.

Now, as she sat on the ferry and crossed Aransas Bay, nervousness set in. She wanted to be angry with Pat. In fact, when she'd gotten up that morning, she was angry. But as the hours passed, so did her anger. It wasn't fair to blame Pat. She knew nothing of her past. She didn't know that Carly had vowed to never give herself to another soul ever again.

Oh, but that kiss. The more she thought about it, the longer it lasted. And it was never long enough.

"Shit."

She drove off the ferry, grabbing her scribbled directions. She found the streets with ease, finally pulling up behind Pat's Jeep. Before she could get out, Pat bounded down the stairs. Shorts today. Great. Just what

I need. Those long legs tempting me. Carly noted that Pat had her sweatpants in her hands, neatly folded.

"Hi," Pat greeted. She slammed the door and Carly backed out without saying a word. "Beautiful day, isn't it? I never thought we'd see the sun again."

Carly kept her mouth closed. She could at least pretend to be angry.

"Flu symptoms haven't set in, in case you were worried," Pat offered.

Carly only nodded.

"Oh, please. You can't possibly still be mad about last night."

"I most certainly can."

"That was *hours* ago. You have to actually work at being mad for that long."

Carly suppressed a smile. Just barely.

"It wasn't really a kiss, anyway," Pat continued. "When I really kiss you, you'll know."

"That was your one and only chance."

"Now you don't really believe that, do you?"

Carly paused at the light. "Which way?"

"Next light. Go left."

They were driving the length of the island, the gulf on one side, the bay on the other. In the distance, they could see the high-rises of Corpus Christi.

"Are you going to tell me?" Pat asked.

"Tell you what?"

"Tell me what happened to you."

"What are you talking about?"

"Someone's hurt you. Tell me about it."

"You have got some balls, you know that."

Pat laughed and glanced down between her legs. "No, I don't. Trust me. No balls. Now tell me."

"I will not. It's . . . painful."

"That's why you need to tell me."

"Are you always like this?"

"Yes."

Carly gripped the steering wheel hard. Shit. Maybe she should tell Pat. Maybe then Pat would know why Carly was off-limits.

"I met her in college. I was in my last year and we had a biology class together. She had always dreamed of being a veterinarian, however biology and chemistry were not her strong points. They were mine. I began tutoring her."

"And ended up in bed?"

Carly glanced at Pat quickly, then back at the road. "If it were only that simple," she said. "She was my first. She was beautiful, really. Athletic. A people magnet. I fell head over heels. We spent every spare minute together. Finally bought a house. I was paying for school out of a trust my grandfather had given me. Carol didn't have time to work, she struggled with her classes as it were. So, I pretty much took care of all the expenses. About a year and a half later, I got a job in Austin. I moved into this tiny apartment and drove back on weekends. We decided that we should share the driving, so I bought her a new car, since she would be making the trip to Austin every other weekend.

That worked out fine for awhile, but then her driving was cutting into her studying, so I ended up making the trip most often. But still, it was working out. I helped her with her classes when I could, I cooked on the weekends so she would have as little to do as possible. She was barely hanging on as it was. But she made it. When she graduated, I was so proud of her. I took off work on that Friday and drove up early. I was going to surprise her. I found a U-Haul truck in the driveway and most of my furniture inside it. I found her in the kitchen. She was laughing with this other woman when I walked in. She then introduced me to her girlfriend."

Pat was quiet. She didn't have any witty comment to make to ease the tension in the Jeep.

"I was . . . floored. I mean, I had absolutely no idea. They had been seeing each other for almost two years. She had a job waiting in Dallas. She was packing to move."

"So, the furniture, it was hers?"

"No. I paid for it all. Like I said, she didn't work. I was just too stunned to argue. I think I was actually in a state of shock. The worst part was how she laughed at me. She said, 'Did you really think that someone like me could be with someone like you?'" Carly glanced again at Pat. "The only thing I took that to mean was that she was this beautiful woman and I was a homely looking bookworm."

"Bookworm, maybe. But homely? No, you'd have to wear dark-rimmed glasses and grow a beard for that look," Pat teased. In fact, she found Carly to be beautiful. Her short blonde hair, although always unruly, framed a smooth, clear face. And those wide sea-green eyes, Pat loved looking into them.

"She said, 'Face it, Carly, I needed you to get through college. I'm sorry you thought there was more to it.'"

"Talk about balls," Pat said.

"So, Carol left that day with her girlfriend driving the U-Haul and she waved at me through the window of the car I bought for her," Carly said. "And I wanted to die." This time, when she looked at Pat, compassionate blue eyes stared back at her. "I felt lifeless. I wanted to make that a reality. It seemed the only way to make the hurt go away."

Pat reached over and took her hand, folding it warmly between her two larger ones.

"I had sleeping pills. And a bottle of whiskey."

Pat trembled at the words, spoken so softly, but clearly.

"But my mother called to check on me. She told me what a wonderful daughter I was and how proud she was. They never knew about Carol until that night. I stayed on the phone several hours, pouring it all out. My mother was wonderful. I took a leave from work and spent a week in Corpus with them. I got past the hardest part while in the company of my family. Even my brothers were so supportive."

"I'm glad your mother called you that night. What would this day be if you weren't here?"

Carly smiled and squeezed Pat's hand before reclaiming her own.

"Thank you. So, there's my horrid little story. The devastation of a broken heart. And why I will never, ever do that again."

"You said she was your first?"

"Yes."

"So, all these years, there's been no one?"

"No."

"But, I mean, surely you get lonely. Surely your body needs attention occasionally," Pat said.

"Yes. There have been a couple of occasions where I've gotten smashed and went home with strangers. It's not something I'm proud of. I didn't even know their names."

"And Carol? I assume you never saw her again?"

"No."

Pat nodded. "Thank you for telling me. But luckily for you, I'm not anything like Carol. I already have a car."

"Pat . . ." Carly warned.

"But we do have one thing in common," she said. "I suck at chemistry and biology, too."

Carly couldn't help but laugh.

"Good. A smile. Because you're absolutely gorgeous

when you smile." Before Carly could protest Pat spoke again. "I brought the film from yesterday. We can drop it off before we go to the printers and pick it up on the way back. That way, if there are any good shots, we can always add it to the brochure later," she suggested.

So, just like that, the subject of Carol was closed. As it should be, Carly thought.

"Okay. Tell me where to go."

CHAPTER TWENTY-THREE

"I like the changes," Pat said. She was scanning the brochure as they made their way back to Port Aransas. "It's much more positive."

"Yes. Thank you for so strongly suggesting I rewrite it. And I liked the pictures you picked out. I think the brochure will turn out great."

"Sorry about yesterday, though."

They'd picked up the photos of the egrets after they met with the printers and even Randy couldn't brighten them enough.

"We'll try later," Carly said. "When it's not pouring down rain."

"Not to mention lightning."

"You really scared me, you know. That one was so close."

"Yes, I know. I felt the electricity around me."

"Promise me you won't take a chance like that again,"

Carly said. For some reason, it was important to her that Pat remain safe.

"I promise. And I think you need to pay up on that dinner you owe me. I know a cute little place on the island."

Carly hesitated. It wasn't like she needed to get back to the ranch. And after their little adventure yesterday, she at least owed Pat dinner.

"Okay. Deal," she said.

Pat directed her to The Shrimp Shack and as they stood beside the Jeep, she saw Carly raise her eyebrows. The music was turned up loud and the outdoor patio was crowded with an assortment of people.

"Are you sure it's safe?" Carly asked.

"Perfectly. These are all locals. I'm not sure tourists would dare to venture inside."

"I can't say that I blame them."

Pat led her inside, finding Angel behind the bar. She motioned to a booth and raised two fingers. Angel nodded and reached for two mugs.

"They have the best seafood platter on the island. But if you like po'boys, don't pass that up. Good gumbo, too."

"I take it you come here a lot?"

"She practically lives here," Angel supplied. "I don't think she knows how to cook." She placed two mugs of draft beer on the table, then stuck out her hand. "I'm Angel."

"Carly Cambridge."

Angel raised her eyebrows. "*Dr*. Carly Cambridge?"

Pat actually blushed. She hoped Angel wouldn't repeat the words Pat had used to describe Carly that first day.

Carly noticed Pat's blush and smiled. She leaned her elbows on the table and waited until Pat looked at her.

113

"Something you want to share?"

"No."

"Are you sure?"

"Very."

Angel laughed. "I think you've met your match with this one, Pat. Yell at me when you're ready to order."

She left them alone and Pat sipped from her beer, stalling for time. But Carly didn't give her time.

"Spill it."

"It's no big deal," Pat said. "The first day I met you, I came here for lunch. I may have repeated some of our conversation to her. That's all."

"And you told her what?"

"I don't really remember the words. I may have used 'obnoxious' and 'environmental wacko' in the same sentence."

Carly laughed. "That's okay. I think I used 'obnoxious', too. Along with 'insufferable' and 'jerk' to describe you."

"Now I'm offended. Jerk?"

"Actually, I think that was the first word I used."

They grinned at each other, then both drank from their beer. Carly couldn't remember another time in her life when she enjoyed someone's company as much as Pat's. She irritated her sometimes, sure. But she always made her laugh.

"So, what are you having?" Pat asked.

"No menus?"

"No. I mean, they have them. I think. Surely. I've just never seen one."

"Well, then I'll take your advice and get the seafood platter."

"Excellent. You won't be able to eat it all," Pat warned. She caught Angel's attention and raised two fingers.

"Platter?" Angel called. "Or beer?"

"Both."

"So, you don't cook?"

"Not really, no."

"I don't, either. Of course, living at the ranch, I'm going to have to start. It's not like I can go down the road for take-out."

"You should get in better with Aunt Rachel. Alice is a great cook."

"Alice?"

"Cook. Maid. Companion. She's been with Aunt Rachel for as long as I can remember."

"Rumor has it that Rachel's been married eight times."

"No rumor," Pat said. "She says she falls in love easily."

"And out of love, apparently," Carly said.

"Nope. They're all dead."

"Dead? Natural causes?"

"Well, there was the boating accident. And the hit and run. And one was murdered at his desk. They suspected suicide." Her lips twitched only slightly. "One just disappeared, presumed dead."

"Oh my God. You're joking, right?"

Pat grinned. "Yes. I'm joking. Although, I do think a couple of them have passed away."

"Still, eight," Carly said. She couldn't imagine.

"Most people think she married for money. Her second husband was loaded. But she caught him in a compromising position and pretty much cleaned up. I think she's added to her wealth considerably since then, but really, she's had more money than any of her husbands."

"You have never mentioned parents or siblings. Are you not close? And forgive me if I'm prying."

115

"It's okay," Pat said. "I have parents. They've just disowned me. My very proper Catholic family could not tolerate my being gay."

"How does someone disown a daughter? Do they just not allow you around the family or what?"

Pat sighed. She hadn't told anyone this story in so long. She hardly remembered the details anymore. At least, that's what she told herself.

"I was twenty when I finally accepted that I was gay. I had always been honest with my parents about other things in my life and I didn't think this should be any different. I was on yet another date that my father had arranged with one of his friend's sons when I just got up and left. I'd had enough of the lies. But having a gay child just didn't fit in with my family's corporate image, much less the church. They hauled me off to speak with our family priest, insisting that I could find guidance there, that I could be absolved of this horrible sin. It wasn't pretty," Pat said, remembering that terrible day. "I caused quite a scene. Rule number one: Never embarrass your parents at church. Their next option was locking me away until I could be healed. They already had an appointment at some hospital in Houston. That's when Aunt Rachel sent for me. And I ran to her."

"And they let you go."

"Oh, yes. I'm sure they were glad to be rid of me. Donald Ryan needed an heir and I wasn't likely to give him one. My sister was still in high school at the time. I suppose they focused on her after I left."

Carly's eyes widened. "Donald Ryan? CEO of Gasworks?"

Pat laughed. "Let me guess. Number one on your pollution hit list?"

"Number one on all my lists. He's your *father*?"

"The same."

"So you weren't exactly brought up to love and respect nature," Carly guessed.

"No, it was a resource only."

"So? Wildlife photography? Probably rocked his boat, huh?"

"No doubt. He still calls Aunt Rachel occasionally. I'm sure she gets her digs in where she can."

"Is she a sister of your father or mother."

"Father."

Angel brought over two heaping platters of fried seafood, interrupting their conversation. Pat was thankful. She hated thinking about that time in her life, much less talking about it.

"Are we still on for dinner Saturday night?" Angel asked.

"Of course. What can I bring?"

"Why don't you bring Carly?"

Carly looked from Angel to Pat. Dinner?

"We're having steaks Saturday night. Lannie bought a new grill she's been dying to try out. Why don't you come along with Pat?"

"Oh, I don't know," Carly said, looking at Pat. "She may have someone else in mind."

Pat and Angel looked at each other and laughed.

"No. Pat doesn't have anyone else in mind. Come along. We'd love to have you."

Again Carly looked at Pat and raised her eyebrows.

"I would love for you to come," Pat said. Then she winked and Carly grinned.

"Okay. I accept."

When Angel left, Carly looked at her plate, her eyes wide.

"You weren't joking."

"Always good for lunch the next day."

Conversation ceased as they both shoved plump

fried shrimp into their mouths. They both moaned at the same time.

"Excellent," Carly murmured. Then she snagged a fried oyster and rolled her eyes. She had just found a new favorite place to eat.

Pat watched as Carly picked up a piece of fish with her fingers and bit into it. The pleasure on her face caused Pat to grin. *Beautiful.*

CHAPTER TWENTY-FOUR

Pat went out to the ranch on Friday morning, but found only Elsa and Martin.

"Carly's in town meeting with some bird woman. A Mrs. Davenport. Ever heard of her?"

Pat laughed and Elsa stared at her.

"Yes. And when Carly gets back, I'm sure she'll tell you all about her."

"I know her," Martin said. "A little eccentric."

"A *little?* Have you seen her in one of her outfits?" Pat asked.

"Oh, she's one of those," Elsa said. "Well, Carly wants to round up some local birders. She wants to get them familiar with the ranch so during the fall migration, we'll have enough bodies on hand for a bird count."

"Uh-huh," Pat muttered. God, she hated birders. "What?"

"Nothing. I'm going to walk the length of the bay. See what's out and about this morning. I'll see you two later."

Pat found the usual assortment of pelicans and terns flying along the bay, hunting for food. There was a sandbar not far from the property line and Pat found what she thought was an American Oystercatcher. She got several good shots as the bird totally ignored her. On the other side of the sand bar, where a protected cove had formed, she found two herons. Or where they egrets? Shit. She needed to bring her damn field guide out with her.

Back at the ranch house, there was still no sign of Carly. She was disappointed. They had not spoken since dinner on Wednesday night. She hoped Carly still planned to join her tomorrow. It was then she realized she didn't have a phone number for Carly.

She found Elsa and Martin huddled over the blueprints, talking to one of the workers.

"I'm heading out," she said.

"Okay. I'm sure Carly will be sorry she missed you," Elsa said.

"Listen, does she have a number here? Or do you have her cell number?"

"Well, I know the phone has been installed because her computer and fax are working but I don't have a clue as to the number. I just use her cell. Let me just get you one of her cards."

Pat nodded then walked over to Martin.

"What's up?"

"Dr. Cambridge wanted to extend the kitchen and utility room down here and make a patio out back.

Seems the calculations were a bit off and they want to take out the two oaks in the back."

"What? The two behind the house?" Pat asked loudly, taking a step backwards.

"Yes."

"No!"

"Excuse me?"

"You can't. They're huge. They're beautiful. They're probably a thousand years old. Do you know how slowly trees grow down here? How many storms and hurricanes they have to fight through to get that big?"

"Yes, but she wants the rooms bigger and a patio."

"I'm sure if she knows that she'll lose the trees, she won't do it."

"Do what?" Elsa asked.

"Cut the trees," Martin said.

"Well, I have to agree with Pat. I think she would fire you and the entire crew if she came back here and the trees were gone."

Pat breathed a sigh of relief, not pausing to wonder why she had gotten so worked up over a couple of trees. Well, they were beautiful. But still, it wasn't like she was going to chain herself to them like some nutcase.

"Okay. We better wait," he told the other man. "It's just, you know, she wanted a patio," Martin said to Pat.

"Tell her to sit on the front porch," Pat said. She took the card from Elsa. "Thanks."

She called Carly's cell on her way back to Port Aransas and the island. She got voicemail and she smiled at hearing Carly's voice.

"God, you've got it bad," she whispered. Then, after the beep, "Carly, it's Pat. Just wanted to make sure you remembered dinner tomorrow night. You can call for directions and I'll meet you there or you can come by

the house. We should probably be there by seven. Ah.
. . hope you enjoyed your visit with Mrs. Davenport,
can't wait to hear about it." She paused only a second
before continuing. "By the way, I love the two trees
behind the house. I hope they're still there tomorrow."

CHAPTER TWENTY-FIVE

"Cut the goddamn trees? Are you out of your mind?"

Elsa walked between Carly and Martin and grabbed both of Carly's arms.

"Chica, the trees are fine. Pat was here. She threw some sort of fit and scared poor Martin. He decided to wait until you got back so you could decide, so calm down."

Carly looked from Elsa to Martin.

"Pat was here? She threw a fit? Over *trees*?"

"Yes, Dr. Cambridge," Martin said, still surprised by her anger. "She said they were beautiful, maybe a thousand years old. But you wanted the rooms extended. You said you wanted a patio."

"Not quite," she murmured.

"What?"

"A thousand years old. Maybe five hundred."

"She said we should tell you to sit on the front porch instead," Elsa said.

Carly laughed and both Elsa and Martin stared at her. God, the woman wasn't making it easy, was she? If Pat were here now, Carly might very well hug her.

"So, Martin, we're clear? The trees stay. If we can enlarge the rooms a little, that's fine. My thinking was, eventually with a full staff, we'll need a good-sized kitchen. And the utility room, well that was just for my own needs. We don't have to have a patio right off the house. We can build a small deck under the trees later. I just wanted a place where we could put a table and chairs and have someplace to sit outside. We can figure all that out later."

"Okay."

"And Martin? Don't call me Dr. Cambridge."

"Yes ma'am."

Carly glanced at Elsa. "Help him, will you?"

"Don't worry, chica. I'll have him as disrespectful as I am in no time."

Carly climbed the stairs to her apartment, her hand clutched around her cell phone. Pat's message had made little sense to her. But then, she wasn't really surprised. Why in the world would Pat be talking about the trees? And that she loved them? But she was very thankful Pat had been here. She didn't know what she would have done if she'd come back and they'd been gone.

She went to her desk and pulled out Pat's card. She tried her house first but got no answer. She hung up instead of leaving a message. Pat answered her cell on the second ring.

"It's Carly."

"Hey."

"I hate to be the one to tell you this, but you now have a reputation as a tree hugger."

124

"Oh, please. With my reputation, I doubt anyone would believe you."

"You scared Martin, or so Elsa said."

"I had a brief thought of chaining myself to one of the trees, then I came to my senses," Pat said.

Carly laughed. "And you call me an environmental wacko."

"But seriously, the trees are safe, right?"

"No. We had to cut them this afternoon. I mean, I wanted a patio. I wanted a utility room I could actually walk in."

She heard only silence on the phone. But only for a few seconds.

"You're fucking me, right? Because I'll never speak to you again if you cut the goddamn trees down."

"Yep. Definitely an environmental wacko."

"*Carly?*"

"Your trees are fine, Pat. I wouldn't dream of cutting them down."

"Okay. Good. I'll be able to sleep tonight then. Now, dinner?"

"Yes. But I should meet you there. I may not want to stay as long as you do."

"Okay. Just come to my place first. You can follow me over there."

"Deal." Carly sat down on her sofa, looking out over the bay. "What are you doing, anyway? I hear traffic."

"I'm just off the bridge over Copano Bay. There was a heron or egret or something over here."

"Pat, you really need to get your herons and egrets straight. They look nothing alike."

"They look *exactly* alike. They're just different colors."

"Well, there you go. That's a start. By the way, Mrs.

Davenport says you trespassed onto her property the other week. She's very upset with you."

Pat laughed. "The woman hates me."

"I think she may have a crush on you."

Silence again.

"I'm hanging up now. You've obviously lost your mind."

It was Carly's turn to laugh. She wrapped her arms around herself as she cradled the phone to her ear, a smile firmly in place.

"Okay. Go back to your herons or egrets. I'll see you tomorrow."

Carly laid the phone down beside her, still smiling. God, she didn't know why, but the woman made her laugh. Made her happy. She wished with all her heart that she didn't still have issues because of Carol. If she could just let herself go, let herself forget that terrible time, let Pat into her life, it would be so much easier. She might be willing to give it a chance.

But she couldn't forget. She had nearly lost her life.

CHAPTER TWENTY-SIX

By six-thirty, Pat was pacing back and forth in her living room. The day had been endless. She had started it with her usual run, then went to the taco stand on the main drag for breakfast. And, acting like a tourist, she stopped at the city's birding pond, just in case something interesting was there. She knew she should listen to the hotline, especially during migration, but she couldn't stand to hear Mrs. Davenport's voice for that long. Maybe they had an online version.

She was surprised to see the RV campground filling up. It was only mid-May and the winter Texans had gone back north, but surely, it was too early for the summer crowd.

The birding center was well kept and Pat usually enjoyed her visits there. Native plants and flowers lined the sidewalk and disappeared where the reeds and cattails took over. A wooden walkway parted the reeds and the pond appeared. Pat stopped in her tracks. A hundred Mrs. Davenports were on the platforms and walkways, all with scopes and binoculars.

"Jesus Christ," she muttered. At first, she assumed some news had hit the hotline, but they all appeared to be looking at different things. So, Pat stayed where she was, her binoculars scanning the pond, but finding only a few duck stragglers that hadn't left yet. During the winter, thousands of ducks and shorebirds fed here and she could only identify a handful of them. She was too embarrassed to whip out her field guide in front of the birders. She could imagine them pointing at her and whispering. Maybe she could drag Carly out here in the winter and she could be her living field guide. That thought brought a smile.

She spotted one of the alligators that lived in the pond. She didn't want to think about what they ate. She'd never seen them do anything but lay in the shallows, but surely, they ate. Probably, those cute little ducks.

Home again, she had spent her afternoon doing laundry and cleaning her cluttered house. Then, on impulse, she pulled her Jeep into the sun and washed it. For this, she had donned her bikini top and enjoyed an hour in the sun.

But now, she was getting restless. She should have asked Carly to come early and they could have visited some before going to dinner. She loved Angel and Lannie's company, but she would much rather spend time alone with Carly.

The knock on the door came only a few minutes later. Pat tried to wipe the huge smile from her face before opening it but she didn't succeed.

"Hi," she greeted Carly. Shorts. Good. Her eyes moved up Carly's legs, finally meeting the amused green eyes looking back at her. "Come on in."

Pat was wearing shorts, too. Long, baggy shorts that nearly reached her knees. Carly couldn't resist inspecting Pat, much as Pat had done her.

"Want me to turn around?" Pat teased. "Give you a back view?"

"No, thanks. I've seen you from behind."

Carly walked past Pat and stood in front of the large windows, looking out.

"You've got a great view. I imagine you love sitting on the deck."

"Yes. But I can't take credit for it. Aunt Rachel bought it for me about seven years ago. She wanted to buy that monster on the corner, but I told her I wouldn't have use for four bedrooms."

Carly nodded. "This suits you. Warm, casual. Nothing fancy."

"I think I should be offended."

"I didn't mean it to be offensive. You drive a Jeep. You dress for comfort. There's nothing pretentious about you. It was a compliment."

Pat shrugged. "Okay. I can be *not* fancy with the best of them." Then Pat casually took Carly's hand and pulled her to the door. "Come on. They'll be waiting."

Carly followed Pat through town, ending up on the bay side of the island. The house Pat stopped in front of was small, with close neighbors. But the yard was impeccably neat. Two palm trees, still small, were surrounded with blooming hibiscus. Other flowers crammed the beds on both sides of the porch. The porch itself was littered with pot plants and two very beautiful hanging baskets of bougainvillea.

"I somehow doubt Angel's the one with the green thumb," Carly said.

Pat laughed. "Lannie doesn't allow Angel anywhere near her plants. Come on. You'll like them."

Pat knocked only once then opened the door when a voice called to them. Unlike Pat's house, this one was crowded with furniture and knick-knacks. On one wall was a large framed print and Carly suspected it was one of Pat's.

"Hey girls. Come on in," Angel called from the kitchen. "Carly, I'm glad you came. This is Lannie."

Carly smiled and took the hand of the very tall woman standing before her. Her hair was so blonde, it was nearly white. But friendly blue eyes smiled back at her.

"Nice to meet you," Carly said. "Thank you for inviting me."

Lannie laughed. "It's just nice not to have to try to fix Pat up with someone. She must be very difficult. I can't get any woman to go out with her more than once."

"Thanks a lot, Lannie. I already told her I have no bad qualities. Now what's she going to think?"

"She's going to think you've been lying," Carly said. "Why won't anyone go out with you more than once?"

"She's difficult," Angel said. "Stubborn."

"Tell me something I don't know."

"Are you all quite through?"

Carly laughed, noticing the slight blush on Pat's tanned face. God, she was beautiful. Then blue eyes glanced up and captured hers and Carly couldn't look away. Pat's eyes darkened and Carly feared Pat could read her mind.

"Beer? Wine? A drink? Plain old Coke?" Lannie offered, ending her teasing for the moment.

"I'll have a beer," Pat said. "Carly?"

"That's fine."

"Come on out to the deck," Angel said. "I'm about

to put the steaks on. Later, if you want, we thought we'd start up a card game."

"That's sounds fun," Carly said. "Spades? Hearts?"

"Spades. Pat refuses to play Hearts."

Pat glared at Angel, but Angel only grinned back at her.

"Doesn't work on me, remember," she told Pat.

Carly couldn't resist. "Why don't you like Hearts?"

"I like it just fine. It doesn't like me."

"I don't think Pat's attention span can handle it," Lannie said.

"And I call you two friends," Pat said. "I simply don't like something that requires that much — concentration."

Carly laughed, enjoying Pat's discomfort. She never imagined this unflappable woman would get flustered by the teasing of her friends.

"Let me guess. You hate to lose," Carly said.

"Lose? Please. I get lots of practice. I think it's just the women they insist on pairing me with. Underneath it all, I'm sure I'm a very good card player. They're the ones with the problem."

"I'm a great card player," Carly told her. "So if we lose . . ."

"Well, shit, Carly, is there anything you can't do?"

Carly grinned. "I can't take pictures. That's what I have you for."

Lannie and Angel laughed and Lannie stood behind Pat with hands on her shoulders.

"Pat, I think you have your hands full with this one."

It was Pat's turn to laugh. "I *wish* I had my hands full."

Carly blushed. "I'll get you for that."

"Promise?"

"Oh, I promise, all right," Carly threatened. "A dunking in the bay, perhaps."

But the look in Pat's blue eyes sent chills over her body. She felt as if they were positively caressing her. She accepted a second beer from Lannie without pulling her eyes away from Pat's. She couldn't. They held her.

All Pat wanted to do at that moment was close the distance between them and kiss Carly senseless. If she didn't think that Carly would kill her, she would do just that. But Angel got up to turn the steaks and Carly finally looked away from her.

They moved inside when the steaks were done. Lannie pulled four potatoes from the oven and Angel motioned to the bar.

"We'll eat here. We're really informal," Angel told Carly. "I hope you don't mind."

"This is perfect," Carly said. "Can we help with anything?"

"Yes. Pat, show her where the plates are."

Pat and Carly set out plates and napkins and they all set down to a simple meal of steak, baked potatoes and green beans. Lannie opened a bottle of wine and filled four glasses, then lifted hers in a toast.

"To good friends. And new ones," she said, glancing at Carly.

"Thank you."

The card game started before they had even cleaned up from dinner. Angel said they would get it later, despite Carly's protests.

"I always feel like we should smoke cigars or something," Pat said as she shuffled the cards. She looked across the table at Carly and winked. "I'll apologize now for the many stupid plays I'll make."

Carly leaned her elbows on the table and grinned. "Do you not grasp the concept of Spades?"

"Oh, I grasp it. But I'll want to look at you instead

of the cards and I'll end up just tossing one out and inevitably, it'll be the wrong one."

"I thought it was because you couldn't concentrate?"

"Well, with you sitting there, I won't be able to concentrate."

"You are so full of shit, you know that."

"I'm hurt. It's the truth."

"Is that the same line you use with everyone?"

Angel saved Pat having to answer. "No, she's usually bored to death and never pays attention."

"Ah, well then, I'm flattered," Carly said.

"You should be," Pat told her.

Their teasing continued throughout the game and they lost badly. Angel and Lannie were fantastic players and it was obvious they knew each other's moves. But Carly couldn't remember the last time she'd had so much fun.

"You weren't lying," she told Pat. "You're awful."

"Thanks. You're not so good yourself."

But their eyes met across the table and both softened. That instant, Carly had the strangest desire to reach across the table and kiss Pat, but she managed to control the impulse. Just barely.

"I should be going," she said. "I've had a wonderful time. Thank you both for including me."

"We enjoyed you being here. Come back any time," Lannie offered.

"Let me help with the dishes?"

"Of course not. That's what Pat is here for."

"Yes. It's my job," Pat said. "Let me walk you out."

The evening was warm, the ever-present breeze tossing the fragrance of the flowers around them. Carly felt Pat's presence beside her and suddenly she was frightened. Part of her wanted Pat to take her in her arms and kiss her passionately. But the sane part, however, the part that knew she couldn't handle that, prayed Pat would do no such thing.

"I'm glad you came tonight," Pat said. "I had a great time with you."

"Me, too. It was fun."

The streetlights cast a soft glow around them, adding to the mood. Carly finally gave in and met Pat's gaze but wished she hadn't. Her blue eyes were warm, compassionate, just hinting at the desire that simmered beneath the surface.

Pat stepped closer, leaving little room between them. Carly's hands came up and pressed against Pat's shoulders, stopping her forward progress.

"Oh, God, Pat . . . please don't," she whispered.

"Sorry. But you know I can't help it. Carly. . ."

Carly decided it was the way Pat said her name that melted her completely. Her hands relaxed as she allowed Pat closer.

Pat felt Carly's lips yield under her own as they opened to her — soft, warm, responsive. The hands at her shoulders stopped pushing and relaxed, fingers digging into flesh instead. Pat wanted to grasp Carly's hips and hold her close. She wanted to feel Carly's tongue against her own. But instead she pulled away, leaving Carly as breathless as she was.

Stepping back, Pat said, "Please drive carefully. I'll see you next week."

Stunned, Carly stood and watched her walk away. No woman should be able to do this to her with just a kiss. Her body felt as if it was on fire. It had taken all of her strength not to wrap her arms around Pat and beg for her touch.

"I am in such big trouble," she said under her breath.

Pat closed the door and leaned against it, trying to collect herself.

"What's wrong?" Angel asked.

134

"Nothing."

"Why haven't you told us about her?" Lannie asked. "She's great. How long have you been seeing each other?"

"We're not seeing each other," Pat said.

"You mean you're not . . . involved? Oh, come on."

Pat walked to the bar and sat down. "I think I could be in trouble here," she said. "I think I'm in love with her."

"I thought you weren't seeing each other?"

"We're not. That's why I'm in trouble."

CHAPTER TWENTY-SEVEN

Carly spent Sunday alone. Elsa had called and invited Carly over to watch a movie. Feeling the need to be alone, she used having to work on the brochure as an excuse not to go. She just wasn't up to seeing anyone. There was only one other time in her life that she felt this confused and it was on the day that Carol had packed up their things and moved out.

She knew it wasn't fair to compare Pat and Carol. They were absolutely nothing alike. But that still didn't change the fact that she had sworn off involvement... with anyone... for the rest of her life. But, *damn*, Pat really got to her. And her kiss... it simply wasn't fair. Carly had been afraid she would collapse right there in Pat's arms.

But despite what her body wanted, her mind balked. The stakes were just too high.

CHAPTER TWENTY-EIGHT

Pat was actually nervous as she drove through the gates to the ranch on Monday morning. She had spent nearly all of Sunday recalling how it felt to take Carly into her arms and kiss her. In her mind, it had turned into much more than a kiss. She could practically feel Carly's breasts in her hands, could taste their softness.

"You can't possibly be in love with her. You've hardly kissed her." Then she met her eyes in the mirror and grinned. "And you really need to stop talking to yourself."

Pat resisted the pull of the ranch house and purposefully drove past Carly's Jeep and on to the bay. She was too late for the sunrise, but she would walk the shore again and check out the sandbar. Later, she wanted to check out the egrets. It was sunny. Maybe she could get some shots of the nest today.

She dutifully tucked her field guide into her camera

bag. Not that she thought she would use it. It would take her forever to find the damn bird in the book. It was so much easier to describe it and let some *birder* tell her the name. But later, she was squatted on the sand, watching a group of shorebirds in the small cove behind the sandbar with her field guide lying open across her knees. She sighed and absently brushed the sand off her knees without looking.

She lowered her binoculars for the third time and flipped through the pages.

"Why isn't it in the goddamn book?"

"They're black-necked stilts."

Pat jumped, spilling the field guide and binoculars onto the sand.

"Jesus Christ! Are you trying to give me a heart attack?"

Carly laughed and sat down next to Pat, picking up her book and finding the right page. She pointed at the picture.

"Black-necked stilt."

Pat narrowed her eyes and gave Carly her best glare. It caused more laughter.

"Oh, please. Are you trying to scare me?"

"I hate birders. Have I told you that?"

"I'm sure you have."

"How did you know what page it was on?"

Carly smiled. Sometimes, Pat was so innocent, so bewildered, that Carly just wanted to wrap her in her arms and hold her. And kiss her, she added.

"Pat, all field guides are the same. Every one of them start with the loons. Then water birds and wadding birds, then ducks, then the hawks, then the shorebirds, and all down the line, ending with the sparrows."

"Well, that's just lovely to know. And I'm not even going to tell you what I'd decided it was."

"Please don't say a miniature heron," Carly teased.

"One of these sandpipers here," Pat said, pointing at a picture.

"They don't look anything like sandpipers."

Pat flashed a grin, letting Carly know that she was teasing. Carly grinned back.

"May I ask why you were sneaking up on me?"

Yes, why Carly? Why did you watch her Jeep drive past the ranch house, feeling disappointed that she didn't stop? And why did you follow her? Why are you sitting here now, as if there is nothing better to do? Because you missed her, that's why.

"They're going to start on the marshes today," she said. "I thought you might want to get some shots. If you'd like, you can go with me to the back. I'm going to mark off the other marshes that I want to dig out next."

"You need help, don't you? You're going to make me work," Pat accused.

Carly pulled her knees to her chin and circled them with her arms, watching Pat. Carly decided she had never met a more attractive woman. With her hair pulled through the back of her baseball cap, Pat looked adorable. She met her blue eyes without flinching. Yes, she was going to make her work. But not because she needed help. Only because she wanted to be in Pat's company.

"Yes," she finally said.

"Okay." Pat smiled and then reached out and playfully pulled one of Carly's fingers. "But you'll owe me. There'll be paybacks."

"I don't doubt that for a minute."

They spent the rest of the morning walking the would-be marshes with Pat dutifully holding the rope Carly had staked down while Carly walked to the next marker, stretching it tight. Their conversation was pleasant, although impersonal. Neither of them mentioned last evening. . .or the kiss that they had shared.

Pat left shortly after lunch, which she'd shared with Carly and Elsa. She had prints to pick up and she was ready to put together her layout for the magazine. She left with just a wave, telling them she'd be back later in the week.

Carly felt oddly depressed once Pat had left. Not wanting to bring up last night, she had purposefully kept their conversation light while they worked. She was surprised that Pat, too, seemed to avoid the subject. She should be thankful, she guessed.

Suddenly feeling the need to be alone, she used the excuse of the fresh paint smell to escape upstairs to her apartment, settling at her computer, intent on answering email and working on the mailing list. The printers had promised her the brochure would be ready in two weeks. She already had the mailing labels. It was just a matter of gathering help to put the thousands of labels on the brochures. She could have had the printers do it, but the cost was enormous. She decided, with their budget, to do it by hand. Elsa and Martin would help, of course. And perhaps Pat.

"Are you okay?" Elsa asked from the doorway.

"Yes. Why?" She pulled her eyes away from the email she had scarcely read.

"You've just been kinda quiet."

"I'm fine, Elsa."

"Pat?"

"What about her?"

Elsa smiled and walked into the room, perching on the edge of Carly's desk.

"You like her?"

"I like her fine," Carly said.

"You know what I mean," Elsa said.

"Elsa, don't," Carly warned. "Pat is becoming a friend. That's all."

"So, you're going to hide from this then?"

"Hide? What are you talking about?"

"I've seen the way she looks at you, and whether you like it or not, I've seen the way you look at her."

"I do not *look* at her," Carly insisted.

"Carly, you can't go the rest of your life denying that you could possibly feel something for another person. You had a bad experience. Do you think you're the only one?"

"A bad experience? I almost fucking killed myself," Carly yelled. "Over a *woman*. A woman who *lied* to me for four years and I didn't even *know* it. I will never be put in that situation again."

"So you let Carol ruin your life? That's your answer?"

"I . . . I can't do it, Elsa."

"Pat would be good for you. She *is* good for you. She makes you laugh. I haven't seen you laugh in years, Carly."

Carly stared at Elsa. Was it true? Did she not laugh? No, not really. She told herself she was happy with her life and for the most part, she was. Happy enough, anyway. She was close to her family. She had a handful of very good friends. But Pat . . . yes, Pat made her laugh. Carly raised her eyes to Elsa, not trying to hide the tears that threatened.

"She scares me," she admitted quietly. "She's gotten inside me," Carly said, "and I don't know what to do."

"You have to let the past go, Carly. You know yourself, you've not been really living, just existing. You deserve to be happy."

Carly reached out and took Elsa's hand and squeezed.

"Thank you. You're a good friend."

"Yes, I know, and so are you. That's why it makes me feel good to see you laugh and she's the one who makes you laugh."

"Yes. She is."

"Okay. Well, I'm glad we could have this little chat. I hope you take some of it to heart."

"What if I promise that I'll try? Will that make you feel better?"

"It's a start, Carly."

CHAPTER TWENTY-NINE

Pat stared at the picture. Then she put it aside and flipped through the others, pleased at the lighting. The curlews were fabulous. She picked up the picture again, her eyes softening. *Damn.* She put it face-down in her lap and sorted through the others again, pulling out the ones she wanted to use in the magazine. She had enough. They were good. And she was thankful it was over. Her mind wasn't on nesting shorebirds.

She flipped over the picture again. She couldn't help it.

"Beautiful," she whispered.

The eyes that looked back at her were questioning, just a slight crease in the brow. The mouth was soft, the beginnings of a smile transforming the lips. Blonde hair in permanent disarray as the continuous gulf breeze caught it.

She liked Carly's hair that way, she thought. Breezy, rumpled. And her fingers itched to move into the softness, straightening the windblown locks around her eyes.

For the first time in her life, Pat was scared.

CHAPTER THIRTY

The rest of the week followed the same pattern as Monday. Pat arrived early each morning and drove to the bay. Then Carly watched as Pat drove to the marshes where the digging had begun, watched as she circled with camera in hand. Then she would disappear into the woods, finally stopping at the ranch house before leaving. It was as if Pat were avoiding her. And Carly couldn't even begin to wonder why.

She moved away from the window as Pat approached, pretending interest in the printer that Elsa was setting up.

"If you're going to act like you're helping, at least pick up a cable or something," Elsa said.

Carly stared at her, trying to think of something to say, but she hastily reached for one of the cords when the door opened.

"Hey ladies," Pat greeted.

Carly looked up, twisting the cord in her hand. Her movement stopped however when her eyes roamed over Pat's body. Her tank top was short, leaving her tanned belly exposed and Carly swallowed with difficulty. Her strong shoulders and arms were bare and Carly's greedy eyes took it all in. Jesus, the woman was dangerous.

"Hi Pat. Done already?" Elsa asked.

"Well, actually, I was going to take a look at the egret nest. I thought maybe Carly would want to come," she said.

Carly met her eyes for nearly the first time since Monday. She couldn't look away.

"I would love to," she said.

"But you look busy," Pat said. "Just waiting to plug into something, huh?"

It was only then that Carly noticed that she held the power cord in her hands. Elsa laughed and took it from her.

"I think I can manage," Elsa said. "You run along."

Pat's Jeep was topless again and Carly sat quietly beside her as they drove past the barn. She had not been to see the egrets, fearing she would scare them off. But she trusted Pat. And she was anxious to see if any had hatched and survived.

"You haven't been around much," Carly finally said.

"What do you mean? I've been here every day."

"I guess I mean that *I* haven't seen you much," Carly clarified. "Is anything wrong?"

Pat gripped the steering wheel hard. *Wrong? What could be wrong? I could be in love with you, that's what is wrong!*

"No, I've just been busy. I'm through with my nesting shorebirds, though. I should have more time to spend out here now. In the afternoons, anyway."

"Are you upset with me?"

"No! Why would you think that?"

"Because you've been avoiding me," Carly said. "And you know you have so don't try to deny it."

Shit!

"Is it because of what happened the other night?" Carly asked.

"Maybe. Look, I know I shouldn't have kissed you. You told me you weren't attracted to me. In fact, *not at all* is what you said. So, yes, I feel bad about what happened. I'm sorry. I won't . . . it won't happen again."

Carly closed her eyes, remembering her words that night. So, Pat had actually believed her. Amazing. However, she didn't believe Pat.

"You're so full of shit, Pat Ryan. Why won't you tell me what's bothering you? I *know* you're not upset because you kissed me."

"Look, I can be remorseful. I have it in me."

"Remorseful? Because we *kissed*? I hardly think that merits remorse."

"Okay, fine. You don't want me to apologize, I won't."

"What the hell is wrong with you?"

"You want me to tell you what is wrong with me?"

"I just asked, didn't I?"

"Okay, I'll tell you." Pat stopped at the edge of the pond and killed the motor. She turned in her seat and faced Carly. It was a mistake. The sea-green eyes that looked back at her were wounded, confused. *Damn.* "I'm attracted to you. And the fact that you're not attracted to me hasn't killed this desire I have to kiss you senseless every time I'm around you. That's what is wrong."

Pat grabbed her camera bag and got out, leaving a speechless Carly staring after her. She disappeared into the brush, finally slowing her pace. She would scare off every bird for half a mile if she didn't.

"I *fucking* hate this," she whispered. She hated being out of control and around Carly Cambridge, she was simply out of control. *In love with her?* Christ! *You haven't even slept together. I really think that's a requirement, Pat.*

She knew what had her so freaked. It was the damn picture she'd taken of Carly on the porch that morning. The eyes in that picture totally controlled her. And for the first time in her life, Pat really *wanted* someone and that someone didn't want her back. Or so she'd convinced herself. The kiss the other night may have told otherwise, but Carly's words still haunted her.

Carly stared at the spot where Pat disappeared. So, Pat wanted to kiss her senseless. Lovely. She grabbed the bridge of her nose with two fingers and closed her eyes. She didn't think she could stand it if Pat kissed her senseless. In fact, just the thought of that made her weak. She could not resist Pat Ryan. She didn't know why she was even trying.

Pat finally emerged into the clearing and Carly remembered why they were here in the first place. She grabbed her binoculars, resisting the urge to look at Pat, instead, searching for the egrets. She found them much as they'd been that first day, the male on the ground. The female was not on the nest, she was on a branch above them. Two fuzzy white balls, heads barely showing above the nest, greeted her. So, they hatched.

She finally moved her binoculars to the woman who had been consuming her thoughts all week. She caught her breath. Pat's beauty never failed to move her. The concentration on Pat's face was intense, but her lips looked soft, gentle. As Carly knew they were. Suddenly, Pat's blue eyes were there, staring right at her. She felt her hands trembling but she couldn't look away. *My God, I want her to kiss me senseless.* Mercifully, Pat looked back to the nest and Carly lowered the glasses.

A few minutes later, Pat disappeared into the brush again and Carly tried to relax. But when Pat opened the door and met her eyes, Carly felt her heart rate increase.

"Could you see?" Pat asked. "I could only make out two."

"Yes. They usually lay five to seven eggs in a clutch and they'll hatch several days apart. That's why those that hatch last usually don't survive."

"I don't know how fast they grow, but they didn't look newly hatched."

"They may have hatched sometime this week. They'll double in size in no time."

Pat put the camera bag in the back, then before starting the Jeep, she turned to Carly.

"Look, I'm sorry, I . . ."

Carly stopped her with a light touch on her bare arm. "You have nothing to apologize for, Pat."

"You make me crazy, Dr. Cambridge, you know that?"

Carly looked up and met her blue eyes.

"Yes, I know. And," she admitted, "I lied."

"Lied?"

"When I said I wasn't attracted to you."

To say that Pat was stunned was an understatement. She searched the green eyes that were so close to her own, but they were full of questions, not answers. Finally, the green eyes pulled away and Pat started the Jeep, driving them back to the ranch house in silence.

"Stay for lunch?" Carly offered.

"No. I promised Aunt Rachel I would swing by there."

"Okay."

Carly got out and walked around to Pat's side.

"I was wondering if you were free on Sunday," Carly said.

Pat grinned. "I'm never free, Dr. Cambridge. Cheap, but not free."

Carly smiled. "How cheap?"

"We can barter if you like?"

"My niece's birthday is Sunday. My parents are having a little party. Why don't you come along," Carly offered.

"Meeting the family? Kinda early for that, don't you think? I mean, I haven't even seen you naked yet."

Carly smiled at Pat's teasing.

"And by Sunday, you still won't have."

"But, I've already imagined it anyway."

Carly couldn't resist. "That's okay. So have I."

Pat opened her mouth to speak, then closed it again. What could she possibly say to that?

"So do you want to go or not?"

"Sure. It's a date," she said and backed away.

"Not a date," Carly called after her.

"Think what you want," Pat shot back as she drove off.

Damn the woman. Can't anything be simple with her? It wasn't a date, Carly told herself. She just thought that Pat might enjoy her family. They were friendly, easy to be around. And they would be full of questions. Carly had never brought a woman with her before.

CHAPTER THIRTY-ONE

Carly picked Pat up at one on Sunday afternoon. Pat had on white shorts and a dark blue blouse that made her eyes even bluer, if possible. Her dark hair hung loose around her face, her bangs brushing her eyebrows. She looked absolutely gorgeous. Yes, her family would be full of questions.

"So, all lawyers, huh? This should be fun," Pat said.

"They're very nice. I promise you won't be subjected to a deposition."

"No. But you may be."

Carly laughed. "Yes, you're probably right. I've never brought a . . . friend with me before."

"Well, I promise I'll behave. Now, fill me in on everyone so I won't be completely lost."

"My oldest brother is Mark. His wife is Suzanne and they have three children. Robert is the oldest. We call him Bobby because my father's name is Robert. Haley is ten and Michael is eight. Carl is my other brother.

He's married to Kim and they have two kids, both girls. Brittany is six today. And then Katie, she's two. She's an absolute angel and I adore her."

"And your mother?"

"Katherine. Everyone calls her Kathy."

Pat nodded. It would certainly be different than anything she was used to. Her own upbringing had been so formal. She never recalled a backyard birthday party.

"Are you nervous?" Carly asked.

"Past that. Terrified is more like it."

Carly laughed. "Somehow I doubt there is anything that could terrify you, Pat."

"You terrify me."

Carly glanced quickly at her then away. The softly spoken words echoed in the Jeep and Carly reached over and squeezed one of Pat's hands.

"I don't mean to terrify you. I'm just trying to survive here."

Pat opened her hand and entwined their fingers, feeling the gentle pressure that Carly returned.

"Yes, I know. Maybe that's what terrifies me. One of us may not survive."

Carly relaxed, allowing Pat to hold her hand. It felt nice. Occasionally, Pat's thumb would caress her skin, then stop, as if Pat just then realized what she was doing.

When they crossed the bridge into Corpus, Carly turned down Bayside Drive, past the monster homes that lined the bay. Her parent's home was no different.

"Damn," Pat murmured.

"Yes, I know."

"You grew up here?"

"No. They've only been here about five years. Our home was a little more modest than this. But please don't judge them by this house," Carly said. "They are really down-to-earth. But when my grandfather died, they could afford this. Putting three kids through law school and med school wasn't cheap," she said, feeling the need to defend her family.

"Hey, Donald Ryan, remember. I know what pretentious means. And I wasn't for one minute judging you or your family."

"I'm sorry. This is just a bit much, I know. It's so different from where we grew up. All the homes here just scream the word 'snob'. But they are really very nice."

"Now who's nervous?" Pat asked.

They parked on the circle drive behind a Lexus and a Mercedes. Carly's black Jeep looked totally out of place. She wondered if Carly ever regretted her decision not to follow the rest of the family into law school. No, she doubted that thought ever crossed her mind. Carly loved her job with a passion few could match. And she could not picture Carly dressed in a business suit, sitting behind a desk in a stuffy office. Carly was totally at home trudging through the marshes, trying to save what she loved.

"What are you thinking about?" Carly asked as they walked to the front door.

"I was trying to picture you in a business suit in a lawyer's office," Pat admitted.

"And?"

"And in my mind, you were wearing shorts and your hair was windblown and the sun was shining on your face and you were absolutely beautiful."

Their eyes met and Carly smiled warmly at Pat. Beautiful, huh? No, beautiful was this woman standing next to her.

"Thank you," Carly whispered. Her eyes dropped for a brief second to Pat's lips. She turned away before she did something really stupid. Like kiss her.

The outside of the home looked much like Pat's parents house. Once inside, however, the difference was enormous. This was definitely a home. Family pictures were everywhere and there was a warmth that had always been missing in Pat's home. Love. That was the difference.

They followed the laughter out to the patio where the extended deck held six adults and an assortment of children.

"Come on. They're very friendly, I promise."

"Aunt Carly! About time."

A blonde headed girl raced up and threw herself at Carly. It could have been her own daughter, Pat thought.

"Happy birthday, Brittany."

"Where's my present?"

"What makes you think I got you a present?" Carly teased.

"Because it's my birthday and you're supposed to bring presents. That's what mommy said."

"Oh. Well, I did. It's inside with the others."

"Good. Who's this?" she asked, pointing at Pat.

"This is my friend, Pat."

"Hi Brittany," Pat said.

Carly laughed at Pat's nervousness. She doubted the woman was ever around children.

"Come on. Let me introduce you."

Pat nodded, then reached for Carly's arm.

"Please don't leave me alone," she whispered.

"Not for a second. I promise."

Introductions were made and Pat finally relaxed when Carly shoved her into a lawn chair. The oldest boy, Bobby, offered her a glass of iced tea and before she knew what was happening, a small child was climbing into her lap.

"What the hell?" she murmured.

Carly laughed and took Katie into her own lap.

"She's never met a stranger," Carly explained. "How's my angel?"

Pat smiled as she watched the child snuggle against Carly. She looked up and found Katherine's eyes on her. She smiled at Carly's mother, then looked away. She wondered what they must all think.

"How's the ranch going, Carly?"

"Good, Mark. The ranch house is completely finished, finally. We started digging the marshes out this week. That will take the rest of the summer. I got your check, by the way. That was very generous. Thank you."

"I know how important this is to you. I've been shamelessly soliciting donations for you, too. Send some of your brochures over to the office. Clients are always looking for a tax write-off."

"I don't care what their reason is," Carly laughed. "I'll take it."

"I just now made the connection with your name," Mark said to Pat.

Pat cringed. She didn't want to talk about her father. But that wasn't the connection he was talking about.

"I have one of your prints in my office. Whooping crane at sunrise. I love them. I hope they find the ranch eventually. I would love to see one close up."

"They are beautiful. I know the print you're talking about. That's the closest I've ever been to one. I had to practically bribe the rangers at Aransas to let me out into the marshes."

"Do you ever go out on the tour boats?"

"I've been a few times, but you can't really get close enough, not for a good photo, anyway."

"Pat just enjoys the company of the other birders, don't you?" Carly teased.

"*Other* birders? You know as well as I do that title does not apply to me."

"You're not a birder?" Mark asked.

Pat rolled her eyes and Carly laughed.

"Yes, she is. Her identification skills are just a little lacking," Carly said.

Pat glared at her, which only caused Carly to laugh more.

"That doesn't work on me and you know it."

"I'm not a birder," Pat hissed.

"Careful. You don't want to offend Mark."

Mark looked confused at the banter between the two women and Carly took pity on him.

"Pat's afraid she'll end up like Mrs. Davenport, all dressed up in her birding outfit, hat and all. So, she refuses to be labeled as a birder."

Pat smiled sweetly at Carly, but murmured, "You'll pay for this."

"Can't wait."

They both forgot about Mark. Green eyes locked on blue and Carly felt her heart pound against her chest at all those blue eyes promised.

Later, when the hamburgers were ready, they all stood around the picnic table, fixing their own. Carly's mother pulled her aside, motioning with her head to Pat.

"Where did you find her? She's gorgeous."

Carly smiled. "We're not seeing each other. We're just friends. Besides, I didn't find her. She's working with me."

"Sure."

"Sure, what? Really. We're not," Carly insisted.

But her mother only smiled at her and nodded. "That's nice. Keep telling yourself that."

"What do you mean?"

"I think she needs rescuing," her mother said. "Katie seems to like her, too."

Katie was perched on Pat's lap, reaching for her hamburger. Pat held it out of her reach, then Katie grabbed a fistful of dark hair. Carly covered the smile on her face and walked over.

"I see you've been captured," she said to Pat.

"Yes, this little monster has about six arms."

Their eyes met and Carly thought Pat looked adorable with her hair in disarray and one sticky hand still wrapped around a fistful.

"Let me save you, sweetheart."

Pat nearly dropped her plate.

"Thank you. I thought you'd never ask."

"I was talking to my niece."

Carly snatched the child out of Pat's lap, then gave Pat a slight wink.

"You'll pay for that, too," Pat told her.

"I don't doubt that I will. Isn't that right, sweetheart?" she cooed to Katie.

Pat's eyes never moved far from Carly, even when her father came over to make conversation. Pat wondered what they all thought of her, what Carly had told them. They were all pleasant enough, friendly actually. And her mother showed particular interest in her. In fact, she enjoyed their company. Whereas Mark was serious, Carly's brother Carl was the jokester. The kids seemed to flock to him and Pat noticed that Carly's personality was a combination of both her brothers. One minute serious, the next teasing.

She had a sudden feeling of loss. She looked around her, seeing all the happy faces, the love, and she deeply regretted her own lack of family. They had never been this close, even when her mother pretended that they were.

Carly noticed the frown, the pensive look on Pat's face. She went to her immediately.

157

"Hey, how are you holding up?"

"I'm good," Pat said.

Carly didn't believe her but she didn't press. Instead, she sat down next to her.

"We should probably get going," Carly said. "There's a couple of board members coming out to the ranch tomorrow."

"Board members?" Pat asked.

"From Habitats For Nature," Carly explained. "They want to take a look at the construction."

"So, you have bosses, too," Pat said.

"Yes. Habitats For Nature has several projects going on right now. They get generic donations, but each project solicits their own to be earmarked directly. The success of the ranch depends on how well I market it."

"So they'll be looking at the construction as well as your bank account?" Pat guessed.

"Yes. And it's pretty thin right now. But once we get the brochures out we should be fine. And then of course, with the local contributions I hope to get, that should put us in the black."

"When will the brochures go out?"

"They'll be ready next week. I hope," Carly added. "So, are you ready to call it a day?"

"Whenever you are," Pat said. She glanced around, looking at the happy family and she felt the depression settle more firmly around her. She had no place here.

The trip back was made almost in silence. Carly made several attempts at conversation, but Pat's comments were minimal. She finally gave up.

"Are you okay?" Carly asked when she pulled up behind Pat's Jeep.

"Yes, fine," Pat said. "I really enjoyed meeting your family. They all seem very nice."

"They are. I'm glad you went with me."

Pat got out and slammed the door, looking in from the passenger's side at Carly.

"Me, too. Drive carefully. I'll be out sometime this week."

Carly caught her eyes for only a moment before Pat looked away. She couldn't understand what could be wrong.

"Okay. See you later," she said. She watched Pat walk up the stairs before backing away.

As she sat on the ferry, Carly tried to think of what could be wrong with Pat. Did someone say something to her? Had her mother cornered her? Surely Pat would have said something. But the look in her eyes was almost haunted, painful. And it bothered Carly all the way to the ranch.

CHAPTER THIRTY-TWO

Pat made herself a drink and took it to the deck, listening to the waves as they crashed against the shore. For the first time in so long, she felt totally alone. Seeing Carly with her family showed her all that she didn't have. She had Aunt Rachel. That was all. She had no family. She had no mother and father and sister. They were there, somewhere. But not anywhere where she was welcome.

A few years ago, she'd tried to contact her sister. The conversation had been brief. Her father had threatened Melissa so Pat couldn't really blame her. Melissa told her that she wasn't a part of their life anymore.

Pat downed her drink in one swallow, then held the glass against her chest. The stars were out and she leaned her head back, watching them. God, but she hadn't felt this way in so long, she hardly knew how to handle it.

She went inside for another drink, then stared at the phone as it rang. It would be Carly, she knew. She could tell by the look in her eyes as she drove away that Carly was worried about her. Pat thought about not answering it. But she reached for it with one hand as the other poured coke into her glass.

"Are you okay?"

"Sure. I'm fine," Pat said quietly. She walked out to the deck, again sitting in the lonely chair in the dark.

"You seemed upset. What's wrong?" Carly asked.

"I'm sorry," Pat whispered. "Just sometimes, I miss having a family, having someone in my life."

"Oh, Pat. I didn't mean for this outing to upset you. I just wanted you to meet my family. And I wanted them to meet you."

"Carly, I really enjoyed the day. Your family is very nice and I liked spending time with you. I'll be fine. It just . . . made me realize what I've never had."

CHAPTER THIRTY-THREE

When Carly hung up the phone, she had a strange sense of loss. Pat was obviously upset, despite her words. And Carly wished she were there. She wanted nothing more than to hold Pat, to comfort her. That scared her. It was one thing to be insanely attracted to the other woman. It was totally another to want to offer comfort — and love.

Even as she fell asleep, her thought were on Pat, wondering if she would find any peace tonight.

CHAPTER THIRTY-FOUR

Carly felt totally underdressed as she escorted three men in suits around the ranch. They were, however, impressed with the progress she'd made on the ranch.

"Dr. Cambridge, everything is ahead of schedule. You've done a fabulous job here," Mr. Kaplan told her.

"Thank you, but we've been blessed with great weather. This marsh will be finished in a week or so, then we can start planting. They should be through with the rest by the end of summer. In two or three years, the marshes will look almost natural."

"Is this a freshwater marsh?"

"No, actually it's called brackish. It's too close to the bay to be freshwater. See where they dammed the bay there," Carly said, pointing towards the mound of earth the bulldozer had yet to move. "Once we plant the native coastal grass, we'll move the dam and let the water from the bay back in. It'll flood this whole area here," she said, motioning to where they were standing. "The other marshes will be freshwater. But this will be the largest. This is where we hope the whooping cranes will winter."

"Have you had contact with Aransas? I'm sure they're concerned with losing some of their birds," he said.

"Yes, they are. But as long as we offer protected habitat, they're all for it. Politics aside, we are all working for the same cause," she said.

Their tour lasted another hour and by the time they walked back to the ranch house, it was nearly noon. She hoped Elsa had lunch ready.

She did. The table in the kitchen was crowded with take-out from a local restaurant in Rockport. Seafood salad and fresh shrimp, along with pasta and garlic bread. She nodded at Elsa, thanking her silently.

While the men filled their plates, she whispered to Elsa. "Have you heard from Pat?"

"No."

"Where's Martin?"

"Out at the barn."

"Doing what?"

"He talked them into redoing the shed. No extra cost."

"How in the world did he manage that?"

"He's persuasive, what can I say?"

Carly stared at Elsa, then grinned.

"Something I should know?"

"Well, he's *very* persuasive. Is this a good time to tell you that I think I'm in love with him?"

"What?" Carly hissed. "How in the world did this happen? And why didn't I know about it?"

"Dr. Cambridge, this is delicious," Mr. Kaplan said. "Local seafood?"

"Yes. This is from a restaurant in Rockport, right off the marina."

"Well, my compliments."

"Thanks." Carly glanced at Elsa and rolled her eyes. She was ready for the suits to leave.

And they did as soon as the last shrimp was eaten. Carly and Elsa were watching their rental car leave as Pat's Jeep approached. Only Pat wasn't alone. Rachel Yearwood got out, her normally perfect hairdo windblown beyond recognition.

Carly watched her step gracefully from the Jeep but her eyes went to the other woman, the one with the shorts and tank top and ever-present baseball cap.

"*Mira, que mujer tan bonita*," Elsa murmured.

"What?"

"What a beautiful woman," Elsa whispered, translating.

"Si," Carly agreed.

"Dr. Cambridge, so good to see you again," Rachel greeted.

"Hello, Rachel. What brings you out this way?"

"Pat's been describing the ranch and I wanted to see for myself," she said. "I hope you don't mind."

"Of course not. You're welcome any time." Carly slid her eyes to Pat and smiled, pleased to see that the normal sparkle was back.

"She threatened me," Pat said. "Don't let her fool you."

Carly grinned and turned to Elsa. "This is my assistant, Elsa Sanchez. Elsa, this is one of our donors, Rachel Yearwood, Pat's aunt."

"Pat's told me about you. Pleased to meet you," Rachel said.

"What's she told you?" Elsa asked.

"She said you were feisty. I hope she wasn't kidding. I like feisty."

Elsa looked at Pat and laughed. "Thanks." She took Rachel's arm and led her to the porch. "Come on inside. I'll show you around."

Carly walked up to Pat and lightly grasped her arm. "Okay?"

"Yes, thanks."

"I was worried about you," Carly admitted.

"Don't be. I'm fine. I had half a bottle of rum and things seem much better today. Except for the slight headache."

"If I'd known it would upset you, I wouldn't have ever asked you to go with me," Carly said. "I'm sorry."

"I would never pass up a chance to be with you. I just got a little bummed. But I'm fine. And really, I had a good time. I enjoyed meeting your family. You're very lucky."

Carly read between the lines and her heart broke for this proud woman. She had so much to offer. For the life of her, she couldn't understand why Pat's family had deserted her. Especially for something that was totally out of Pat's control.

Without thinking, Carly took the step necessary to reach Pat. She touched Pat's lips lightly with her own. Then she turned and walked to the house.

"Wait! You can't do that and just walk away," Pat called.

"Sure I can."

"No, you can't."

Carly turned and shrugged. "Yes, I can." She then disappeared into the house.

Pat still stood beside her Jeep, speechless. Carly had kissed her. And it had been so quick, Pat hadn't had time to react. To kiss her back. *Damn.*

She walked inside, finding the three women engrossed in conversation over some bird. She rolled her eyes. Get birders together and they never shut up.

"Mrs. Davenport claims they've nested on her property for years," Rachel said. "Oh, Pat, there you are. Tell Dr. Cambridge about the ruddy turnstones."

Pat met Carly's amused eyes and gave a half-smile.

"And what should I tell her?" Pat asked. "They had four young to start with. The last time I was there, only two were left. I suspect Mrs. Davenport abducted the other two and sold them on the black market."

Rachel's eyes widened and Elsa stared. Only Carly laughed outright.

"Patricia!"

"*Patricia?*" Carly murmured.

"Okay. We can blame owls if you like," Pat said. "But I still suspect Mrs. Davenport."

Carly laughed again, loving Pat's sense of humor.

"You are so bad," she said.

"You've not yet seen bad, Dr. Cambridge," Pat replied as her eyes locked on Carly's.

"Why don't I show you the Visitor's Center," Elsa offered to Rachel. "I'm sure these two can find something to argue about."

"I would love to see it. And what about the egret nest Pat's been talking about? She said they've hatched."

"No," Pat said. "They're nervous. We don't want to scare them. No visitors."

Carly was surprised at Pat's possessiveness over the nest, but she agreed. If they wanted to build a colony, they couldn't chance disturbing the first nesting pair.

"Well, then I'll settle for the Visitor's Center. Ms. Sanchez, if you would?"

"Thank you," Carly said to Pat when the door closed.

"It's ours," Pat said, referring to the nest. "No one else needs to know where it is."

Carly nodded, resisting the urge to go to Pat. At that

moment, she wanted nothing more than to wrap her arms around the woman and hold her.

"But, there is the little matter of what you started outside — and didn't stay to finish," Pat said.

"I thought I had finished," Carly said.

"No. You barely got started."

Pat took a step towards her and Carly stood her ground, swallowing nervously as Pat neared.

"Why did you kiss me?" Pat asked quietly

"I would hardly call that a kiss," Carly said.

"You're right, of course. You want to try again?"

Carly got lost in Pat's eyes. She was actually drowning, she realized. Her feet refused to move, even as Pat drew nearer.

"You have no idea how much I want you to kiss me again," Pat murmured.

"Yes, I do," Carly whispered.

They were but a breath apart, their bodies moving together without thought. Carly closed her eyes, wanting Pat's kiss like never before. She simply could not resist this woman. She realized she no longer had control of her feelings.

But just as their lips met, just as Carly felt the softness of Pat against her, just as she opened her mouth to Pat, Martin called to her.

"Dr. Cambridge, do you . . . *Madre Mia! Perdoname.*"

"*Shit.* Can I not get a break here?" Pat whispered.

Carly turned scarlet and moved away from Pat, putting a safe distance between her and the woman she could no longer resist.

"Martin, it's okay. What?" she asked sharply.

"Ah, the ah, the. . ."

"Martin?"

"The shed. Do you want water and electricity run in there?"

"Yes, if it's possible. We'll use that for rehabilitation, if we need it," Carly said, all business now. "And I'm sure at some point, we will." She moved farther away from Pat. She seemed to have her body under control again. At least for the moment. "I'll go with you and have a look."

Pat finally found her voice. She walked over to Martin and playfully punched his arm.

"Thanks a lot," she murmured. "Perfect timing."

Carly glanced once at Pat and returned her smile, then followed Martin out the kitchen door. They walked the short distance to the barn and adjoining shed.

"I thought you couldn't speak Spanish. What the hell did you say in there?"

"I'm really sorry, Dr. Cambridge," he said. "I never would have just barged in on you like that if I'd known. . ."

"It's Carly. And I'm sorry, Martin. I'm sure this must be a shock to you. I never discussed my personal life with you. Actually, I didn't plan on having a personal life to discuss," she said.

"No, it's not that. Elsa told me already. I just. . ."

"Elsa told you what?" Carly asked.

"She. . . she told me about you and Pat," he said, now embarrassed himself.

"About me and Pat? What exactly did she tell you?" She would kill Elsa later, she decided.

"She just said. . . look, it's none of my business. I'm sorry. I'll be sure to knock next time," he said.

"You will not knock, Martin. That's our office. I will try to keep my personal life out of it."

Jesus, she couldn't believe Martin had walked in on them. And she regretted it. Not because Martin had seen, but because of what he'd interrupted. She doubted she and Pat would have another moment alone today. Perhaps it was best. One kiss would lead to another and soon, she would be in over her head. And she definitely was not ready for that kind of intimacy with Pat. Oh, her body was ready, of that she was certain. But her mind was still locked on the past.

CHAPTER THIRTY-FIVE

The morning was beautiful, cloudless. Carly stood at the edge of the bay, watching the sun rise out of the water. She wanted to enjoy the morning while she could. Soon, she would be stuck inside. The brochures were in. Elsa was picking them up for her and they would spend the afternoon affixing labels. Thousands of labels. She hoped she could persuade Pat to help, too. Pat had been out every day, but she was busy following the contractors around. They hadn't had a moment alone all week. Either Elsa or Martin seemed always to be around. She wondered if Pat regretted it as much as she did.

Then she smiled. She had cornered Elsa, demanding to know what she'd told Martin. Elsa denied saying anything, then Carly had threatened to tell Martin that Elsa was in love with him.

"*Dios mio*," Elsa had stated. "I'll kill you."

Elsa finally spilled everything, including the night she and Martin had spent together.

"You *slept* with him?" Carly demanded. "With my Martin?"

"He's not *your* Martin. And yes, I told you, I couldn't resist him."

"Elsa, you are so weak."

"Yes, I am. But unlike you, I won't run from a possible love life."

"I'm not exactly running anymore. I can't seem to resist Pat either," she told Elsa.

And that was true, she admitted. She couldn't resist her. She didn't want to. Each night, when she crawled into her empty bed, she wondered what it would be like to make love with Pat. And each morning she woke still wondering.

"What are you doing?"

Carly jumped, putting a hand to her chest.

"Jesus! Why must you *always* do that?" she demanded.

"I don't always, Dr. Cambridge. You want me to start honking my horn when I drive up? Or perhaps those bells you mentioned?"

Carly turned around and looked at Pat. Earth tones today. Tan shorts and dark brown sleeveless shirt. Beautiful.

"So, catching the sunrise?" Pat asked.

"Yes. We're going to be stuck inside today. The brochures are ready."

"Good. Did they send you an advance? Did they turn out?"

"I haven't seen them. Elsa drove to Corpus to pick

them up. We're going to start on the labels as soon as she gets here."

"Need help?" Pat offered.

"Yes, actually. I was hoping you wouldn't mind."

"Can I sit next to you?" Pat teased.

"You can sit anywhere you want."

"Anywhere? Careful. I might just want to crawl into your lap."

Carly laughed.

"I doubt my lap would hold you."

Pat loved it when Carly laughed. Her whole face lit up, making her more beautiful, if that was possible. Without thought, she raised her camera, capturing Carly with a smile still on her face.

Carly pretended to be annoyed. She normally hated having her picture taken. But there was something about the way Pat looked at her, the way she held the camera with such poise.

"What makes you think you can do that?"

Pat grinned. "Because I'm the one with the camera."

The smile that Carly flashed caused Pat's heart to stop. She slowly lowered the camera, her eyes searching and finding Carly's.

"Jesus, you are so beautiful," she whispered.

Carly watched as Pat stepped closer, but she was powerless to move. Her eyes dropped to Pat's lips, knowing without a doubt that she could not say no to this woman. When she raised her eyes again, there was no doubting the look in Pat's blue ones. She reached for Pat even before Pat stopped walking. Their mouths fought for control.

Carly whimpered when Pat's tongue moved past her lips and danced with her own for the first time. She needed no encouragement from Pat as her lower body molded itself to the other woman. And God, it felt so good to be held and kissed this way. She crushed Pat to her, her arms holding Pat tightly against her body.

They drew apart, their breathing ragged. Carly opened her eyes, looking into Pat's. So blue. She wanted to drown there. She pulled Pat's mouth to hers again, softer, gentler now. The fury of their first kiss was absent as they explored each other with gentle tongues.

Finally, Carly pulled away, separating herself from Pat.

"You drive me absolutely crazy, you know that, don't you?" Carly asked.

"You could pretend you're smashed and I'm a stranger and you won't know my name in the morning," Pat suggested quietly.

"You know I can't do that. You're not a stranger and I'm not going to use you to satisfy my . . . hunger."

"Please, use me," Pat whispered.

Carly reached out a hand and touched Pat's face.

"I would never."

"Then, let's try it the normal way. I don't want a house from you or a car or biology homework. I just want you."

"I can't do that, Pat. I almost lost it. Over *her*," she said, disgusted. "I can't take a chance again. Not with you. I couldn't survive."

Pat wondered if she could survive the rest of the day after the kiss Carly had just given her. But she smiled. She couldn't be angry with Carly because it was right there in her eyes. Love. Carly could fight it for awhile and Pat was content to let her try. But she knew Carly would never win. It was there in her eyes. And love would win.

So she took Carly's hand and tugged her along.

"Come on. Let's go see your egrets before we have to work."

"That's it?" Carly asked. "You have nothing else to say?"

"What?"

"I think you enjoy making me crazy," Carly accused. She never thought Pat would just let it go. Not after their little kissing scene.

"Oh, please. I'm the one that needs a cold shower here."

Carly stopped.

"I need one, too, Pat."

Pat grinned.

"Oh, and now you're just being mean, teasing me like that."

Carly laughed. God, she liked this woman. Pat could drive her emotions from one end to the other, all in a matter of seconds. She liked Pat's sense of humor. Pat enjoyed baiting her, teasing her, making her so angry she wanted to throttle her, and then she would have her laughing the next instant. But it was her kisses that drove her totally over the edge.

And over the edge of the nearest cliff is where she wanted to toss Pat after nearly three hours of label sticking.

"Jesus Christ, are you sending this to every goddamn birder in the country?" Pat asked for the third time.

"You have the attention span of a five-year-old," Carly said.

"Five? Earlier you said ten."

"Earlier I still had a sense of humor."

Both Elsa and Martin laughed, but Pat gave them her best glare and they stopped immediately. This caused Carly to laugh.

"Oh, please, you two. Don't humor her."

"Dr. Cambridge, for cheap labor, you're taking an awful lot of liberties with me," Pat said.

"You're right. I am. I forgot you *willingly* volunteered for this project."

"I volunteered to photograph this project. Perhaps I should capture *this* on film. It just reeks of environmental abuse. How many trees died for this?"

"Recycled paper. None."

"I hate you," Pat murmured.

"No you don't."

"I can pretend to."

"Will you two stop?" Elsa finally asked. "You're making me crazy. *Dios mio!*"

Carly and Pat both looked at her and laughed. Then they looked at each other and their laughter turned to smiles.

CHAPTER THIRTY-SIX

Pat watched the weather forecast in disbelief. Tropical storm? It was barely June. And the bright sunshine outside did little to change her mind.

"Additional strengthening is expected in the next twenty-four hours. We'll have an update at ten. Stay tuned."

Well, it was still far out in the gulf. Maybe it would turn and Louisiana could worry about it. Pat hated storms. She hated the buildup, the preparations, the boarding up of her house. And she especially hated it when she went through all of that and the damn storm hit hundreds of miles away. But still, she never took a chance, not after that first time. She had lived on the coast too long for that.

Her phone rang immediately. It would be Aunt Rachel. It always was when a storm formed.

"Did you hear?"

"Yes. I heard."

"You'll stay here, of course. Alice has already called. They'll be here tomorrow to start securing everything."

"Aunt Rachel, it's still in the Caribbean. It'll be days before they even know which way it's going."

"You can't be too careful," she said.

"You get like this every time the first one forms. By November, you hardly care."

"And bring your own liquor. I'll not have you stranded here for days and expect to share mine."

Pat laughed. It was another standing joke between them. Aunt Rachel laughed, too.

"But seriously, don't take any chances, Pat. Board your house when the time comes. I don't want to worry about you."

"You'll never let me live that down, will you? That was *years* ago," she said. In fact, it was the first year she'd lived on the Gulf. She'd lost nearly everything, all because she didn't believe the forecast. She'd escaped with her cameras and made it to a bar on the bay side. She'd had a wonderful time as a handful of locals watched the storm rage around them.

"No, I won't. And perhaps you should check in with Dr. Cambridge. I'm sure she could use some help out there. To think they just finished with the construction. It would be such a shame to lose all that in a storm. Why, remember Carla?"

"I wasn't even born when Carla hit. How old do you think I am?"

"Old enough to have heard my stories a hundred times."

"Okay. I'll check in with Dr. Cambridge," Pat said.

"You like her, don't you?" Aunt Rachel said unexpectedly.

"Of course I like her."

"Good. She's gay, you know. Elsa told me."

"Elsa told you?"

"Well, I asked her," Aunt Rachel admitted. "I thought that perhaps she was, but you never know nowadays."

"Don't meddle," Pat warned. "She's fragile."

"Fragile? She is no such thing. She can handle you."

Pat laughed. "But I'm not so sure I can handle her."

CHAPTER THIRTY-SEVEN

"Yes, I heard," Carly said. "I don't fucking believe it, but I heard."

"We've got plenty of time. Don't worry," Elsa said.

"It'll flood the marsh and we've not planted. I'm not worried about the structures. The Visitor's Center is sound. The ranch house is far enough from the bay. And there's the barrier island. But the storm surge. We'll be starting over with the marsh."

"Calm down. You're sounding hysterical."

"I *am* hysterical. This could set us back months," she said.

"Open a bottle of wine," Elsa suggested.

"I've done that."

"Well, then try drinking it."

And Carly did just that. She pulled one of the chairs

out onto the front porch and sat watching the bay as the water shimmered in the moonlight. It was a crystal clear night, belying the storm that was hiding far in the distance. It was quiet and she breathed deeply, inhaling the scent of the bay. In the six months she had been here, she'd grown to love this piece of property. And in the few weeks that she'd actually been living here, she'd grown accustomed to the peaceful bay. The gulf could turn angry and the bay was always at its mercy.

She thought of the marsh, nearly ready for the planting of the native coastal grasses and reeds. Even a minor storm would flood it. It could take weeks to drain. But she didn't want to think about that. She could not control nature.

She could hear the phone ringing upstairs. She'd not brought it down with her and she didn't relish running up the stairs to catch it. Then, a short time later, her cell phone rang. It was still strapped to her waist.

"Hello."

"Am I interrupting?"

"You're only interrupting my worrying," she said.

"It'll be okay."

"I'm worried about our egrets," she admitted.

"They've seen storms before."

"Not the babies."

"Where are you?"

"On the porch. Watching the bay. You?"

"On the deck. Watching the gulf."

Carly smiled. "And is it doing anything?"

"Still coming towards me. I guess that's a good sign."

"Will your house be okay if a storm hits?"

"Well, I guess I'm glad I didn't have it painted," Pat

said. "But yes, I'll board it up, as usual. Will you need some help out there?"

"Yes. I'll need you to be here," she said without thinking.

"Then I'll be there."

Carly cradled the phone against her shoulder as she twirled the wine in her glass. She glanced up and looked at the moon, only half full.

"I can always count on you, can't I?"

"Yes. Always."

"You're very good for me, you know. You make me laugh. Elsa said that I haven't laughed in years. I think she may be right."

"I hope to always make you laugh, Carly."

"I missed you today. I thought maybe that the labels yesterday scared you off. We finished, you know."

Pat laughed. "I had a meeting with the magazine guy today. We were writing captions for my pictures. I think I impressed him by actually knowing the names of all the birds."

"You'll be a birder before you know it."

"Carly, stop threatening me."

"Oh, you're so full of shit, Pat. You pretend to detest all of this, but you're just a naturalist at heart."

"I'm offended."

"No, you're not. I think you love this as much as I do."

"If you tell anyone, I'll deny it. I have a reputation, you know."

Carly smiled. There was a storm brewing, a storm that could ruin what she'd worked so hard for, and yet she smiled. Pat did that to her.

"I'm really glad you called. I think maybe I can sleep now," she said.

"I'll be out tomorrow. We'll know about the storm then. We've got time," she said.

"Yes. A another day, at least."

"Don't drink the whole bottle," Pat said.

Carly laughed. "How did you know?"

"I heard you pouring. Red wine, right?"

"Yes. And it's too late. The bottle is empty."

"Well, I'll bring aspirin tomorrow."

CHAPTER THIRTY-EIGHT

Pat stared at her TV and shook her head. Tropical Storm Adrian was now Hurricane Adrian. And they had a sixty-percent chance of getting hit.

"Further strengthening is expected."

"Great. Shit."

But the clouds moving in from the south didn't lie. The gulf was churning. Pat had known this just from her run this morning. She didn't need the news to tell her.

She took her coffee out to the deck, watching the waves as they crashed on shore. Her neighbors were already busy. She could hear the pounding of nails all around her. Normally, she would wait. At least one more day. It could move east, towards Galveston. But she had seen the radar. The entire gulf was shrouded in clouds. The first bands of rain were expected by nightfall, but the storm was still another day away.

For once, she wouldn't wait. She would board up her house and move inland. Aunt Rachel would need help. Carly would need help. With that, she went to her storage room and drug out the sheets of plywood that were neatly stacked against the wall.

CHAPTER THIRTY-NINE

Carly paced as she watched The Weather Channel. The storm was huge. It would grow by midday to a category two. It was barely daylight, but she could tell the bay was restless. There were no pelicans. No gulls or terns. They had already moved inland.

She knew the construction workers would be there soon to move their equipment. And Elsa and Martin were on their way. The Visitor's Center was equipped with storm shutters. It wouldn't take long to secure it. And the ranch house was safe. It had survived worse storms, even without the added equipment. There really wasn't much that she could do. The marsh was on its own, she knew. But she did worry about the egrets. They weren't ready to fly. In just a few more weeks, maybe. But not yet.

She busied herself with breakfast. She doubted Elsa

or Martin would take the time. And they would have a busy day. She was just finishing the eggs when she heard them drive up.

"Come on up here," she called from the stairs. She didn't pause to wonder why they had arrived together.

"I see you're bribing us with breakfast," Elsa said. "I assume we'll be doing manual labor today."

"Yes. And lots of it. We've got to move the pallets of grass and reeds into the barn," she said. "Not to mention boarding up the Visitor's Center and this place."

"You hardly slept," Elsa accused.

"I slept. I had a bottle of wine."

"Well, you can stay at my place tonight."

"No. I'm staying here. It's perfectly safe," she said.

"You are not staying here alone," Elsa said.

"Yes, I am. I live here. And I want to be here."

"Martin, tell her she can't stay here," Elsa said.

"Dr. Cambridge, really, there's nothing you can do here. We'll come back as soon as it's over."

"Thank you both for your concern, but I'll be perfectly fine here. It's not like it's a major storm. This house has seen much worse than Adrian. And Martin, if you call me Dr. Cambridge one more time, I'll deck you," Carly threatened.

"You're as stubborn as a mule," Elsa said, but she let it drop.

They were still struggling with the pallets of grass when Pat drove up. The construction workers had literally ignored them as they rushed to move their equipment to the other side of the barn. They were hand-loading yet another pallet onto Martin's truck when Pat walked up.

"Damn, talk about manual labor," she said. "Don't they have like machines to do this?"

187

"Yes they do," Carly said. "And the machines unloaded it last week and left."

"Well, good thing I'm here. You know how much I love moving things with you guys. Why the hell are you moving it anyway? Surely a little rain can't hurt this."

"A little rain wouldn't hurt it," Carly said. "A flood would kill it. And it would be thousands of dollars down the drain."

"Elsa, where are those burly men when you need them?" Pat asked.

Elsa and Carly laughed.

"There's only Martin, and he's as burly as we get. Well, besides you, of course," Elsa teased.

"I'm not sure if I should be offended or not," Pat said as she lifted a section of the grass.

It took them three more loads to move the rest of the grass and reeds. By then, the lunch hour had passed and the clouds were dark.

"Let's take a break," Carly said. "Then we do the Visitor's Center."

Lunch consisted of cheese sandwiches, all that Carly had in her fridge. She suddenly realized that if she were stuck there for more than one day, she would starve to death.

"No wonder you're so skinny," Elsa said. "Not only can you not cook, you don't know how to shop for food."

"If I weren't so tired, I would argue with you," Carly said.

"I think it's great," Pat said as she bit into her sandwich.

"I take it you don't cook either," Elsa said.

"Take-out. I know all the best places."

"Did you get your house boarded up?" Carly asked.

"Yep. Anything less than a ten-foot storm surge and I'm good."

"Are you staying with Rachel?"

"I suppose. I haven't talked to her today. She's busy preparing. She really gets into this."

"Well, she's lived here for years. I'm sure she's used to it," Carly said.

"Yes. But she likes the excitement."

"I could do without it."

Pat put her sandwich down and looked at Carly.

"It'll be okay, Carly. You'll see."

Carly nodded, but she couldn't help glance at the TV in the other room. It didn't look very promising.

By the time they'd put the last sheet of plywood on the ranch house, they were all exhausted. The rain had not yet started, but the dark clouds were swirling over the bay.

"I'm starving," Elsa said. "Why don't we get cleaned up and have dinner somewhere?"

Carly was about to protest, but Pat agreed.

"There's a great little place in Fulton. Best gumbo around."

"The Sandpiper," Martin said. "Yes. I could go for a bowl of gumbo. And fried shrimp."

"I could eat a seafood platter this big," Elsa said, spreading her hands apart.

"We'll meet you there. About seven?" Martin suggested.

"That's fine. That'll give me time to swing by Aunt Rachel's and get cleaned up."

"You're welcome to use my shower," Carly offered. "I assume you have clothes. Your Jeep looks packed."

"I have some clothes and my camera stuff. But I should really check on Aunt Rachel. Thanks for the offer, though."

189

Elsa and Martin went ahead, but Pat stopped at the stairwell.

"Do you know where it is?"

"I can find it. Fulton is not that big," Carly said.

"I assume you intend on staying here, then?"

"Yes."

Pat paused, then met Carly's eyes.

"Want some company?"

Carly was about to decline. Surely Rachel would want Pat with her. But so did she.

"I would love company," she finally said.

Pat smiled. "Great. We'll have a hurricane party. Of course, that means we'll have to shop. I've seen your refrigerator."

CHAPTER FORTY

By nine, Carly and Pat pushed their way through the local grocery store with the hundreds of others who were stocking up. They managed to get the last bottle of water on the shelf. It always amazed Carly how crazy people became when a storm approached, as if they would be stranded for weeks. Of course, she and Pat were doing the same thing.

"It's really hard to shop for food when I'm so stuffed," Carly said. She had eaten an entire seafood platter and two bowls of gumbo. "Nothing looks good."

But Pat was having no problems. Their basket was loaded with chips, bread and turkey slices and several cans of soup.

"Sandwiches and soup," Carly murmured. "We're pathetic. You would think at least one of us could cook."

"Frozen pizza?" Pat asked.

"We'll probably lose power."

"Isn't the generator hooked up yet?"

"No."

"Okay. Sandwiches and soup. Works for me."

They stood in the endless line waiting to check out and Pat snatched up a pack of batteries.

"I know the flashlight in my Jeep is dead. Need any?"

"No. I have a new one," Carly said. In fact, Martin had put several around the ranch house.

"So, Elsa and Martin seem quite friendly," Pat said suddenly. "Are they seeing each other?"

"I guess that's what you'd call it. They're very secretive though. If I hadn't had to practically beat it out of Elsa I would only be speculating."

"Well, I like them both. I hope it works out."

Carly nodded. She did, too.

"How was Rachel? I assume she wanted you to stay with her?"

"She did. But I told her you were staying at the ranch alone and she insisted I stay there with you. To protect you, of course."

Carly smiled. "Do you think I need protection?"

"I may be the one who needs protecting," Pat said. "You may try to take advantage of me."

Carly laughed. "Yes, I may."

Pat knew she was teasing, but there was still an underlying tension between them. She wondered if Carly would allow her to share her bed or make her use the sofa. The sofa, Pat decided. There was no possible way they could sleep in the same bed and actually sleep. At least, that's what she thought. Carly may not have a bit of trouble.

The rain hit just as Pat was locking up the gate. She followed Carly's Jeep to the ranch house and they unpacked the groceries and Pat's clothes quickly, but were soon both soaked.

"We should really put our Jeeps in the barn," Carly suggested. "It's only going to get worse."

"This is just the first rain band. There'll be breaks," Pat said. "Come on. Let's put the TV on and see what's happening."

After they changed into dry clothes, Carly made them both hot chocolate and they sat on the floor, leaning against the back of the sofa. Only the recliner faced the TV, but she decided to join Pat on the floor.

Adrian was now a category three hurricane. She flicked her eyes to Pat. It still had another day in the gulf to strengthen.

"Total rainfall may exceed twenty inches along the coast. We're now seeing the first bands of rain come ashore, but the eye is still more than two hundred miles south-southeast of Corpus Christi. Hurricane warnings have been posted from St. Charles, Louisiana south to Brownsville, Texas. The highest probability of landfall is between Galveston and Corpus Christi . . ."

Carly let the voice fade as she watched Pat's face. She was worried, Carly could tell. They were perfectly safe here — but their land, that was another story.

"We should move the Jeeps at first light," Pat said. "Are you sure we have everything secured? Any lawn chairs laying around?"

"No. Martin put them up. And yes, I think we have everything secured. We'll be fine here. Won't we?" she asked.

Pat gave her a reassuring smile. "Sure. It'll be fun. Imagine the shots I can get."

"If you think for one minute that I'm going to let you go out when it hits, you're sadly mistaken," Carly told her.

"I'm just kidding. I'm really a wimp."

"Somehow I doubt that." She watched Pat sip from her chocolate. "You know, I've got something stronger than that, if you want."

"Yeah? Like what?"

Carly smiled. "If I listed my entire liquor cabinet to you, you might think I was a bartender in another life."

"Okay. How about something simple? Rum or bourbon and coke? That'll do."

Pat handed over the rest of her hot chocolate and turned back to the TV, watching the radar image that was up. They were in for a lot of rain. Even if the storm moved east, like she was hoping, they would still be hit. The entire gulf was covered by the storm.

"Doesn't look good," Carly said.

"No."

Pat looked up and took the drink Carly offered, then smiled as Carly sat down beside her again. This was nice. It was also the first time they had spent any significant time totally alone.

"What would you be doing if you weren't here?" Carly asked.

"Tonight?"

"No. I mean, what do you normally do in the evenings?"

"Oh. You mean, in my previous life before I agreed to become your photography slave?"

Carly grinned. "Yes. Before you became my slave."

Pat leaned back, and sipped from her drink. It beat the hell out of the hot chocolate. What would she be doing? Nothing nearly as much fun.

"I used to go to The Brown Pelican, a local dive on the island. Their great claim to fame is pool tournaments."

"Are you any good?"

"Of course. I've won my share. Some of the guys there think we're best buds. They always think they can outdo me with tequila shots. Something I'm very proud of," she said sarcastically. She sounded pathetic, she knew.

Carly watched the expression on Pat's face change. She wondered why Pat was embarrassed.

"Do you date much?"

"Date?"

Carly smiled. "You know, women . . . go out, that sort of thing."

"No, not really. I never met anyone I wanted to spend that much time with," she said. "Or maybe they just didn't want to spend time with me. Because, you know, I've been called arrogant, obnoxious and a jerk, among other things."

"Of all the things I wish I could take back, I would take back calling you a jerk," Carly teased.

"But arrogant and obnoxious fit?"

"Okay. I'll take back obnoxious, too."

Pat nodded. "Okay, I can live with that."

"How old are you? You never said."

"Carly, you know you're never supposed to ask a woman her age. Surely you know that."

"I'll say thirty-five."

"Are you trying to offend me? I don't look thirty-five."

"Tell me."

"I'm thirty-six," Pat finally said, causing Carly to laugh.

"Is this where I'm to say that you don't look anywhere *near* thirty-six?"

"That would be the proper thing to say. Especially if you're trying to win points with me. And I would say you don't look a day over twenty-five. See how that works?"

"You are so full of shit," Carly said.

"That's because I know you're thirty-two."

"Let me guess. Elsa?"

"Of course. She loves to talk."

"Yes, I know." Carly glanced at Pat, watching the smile leave her face. She seemed depressed, and she hated to use that word to describe Pat. She was always so upbeat about everything.

"You've had some sort of relationship, surely. Why won't you tell me?" Carly asked again.

Pat shrugged. "I really haven't. At first, I was young and out there, you know. And please don't call me conceited, but. . ."

"You had your pick of women?" Carly guessed. And why not? She was beautiful. She could imagine a younger Pat walking into a bar, scanning the crowd for a woman willing to go home with her, just because of her looks.

"Something like that. That's when I realized that women could care less about me or my personality, they just wanted to be seen with me. And God, that sounds conceited," she admitted. "I'm sorry."

"You're very attractive, Pat. That's not something you can hide — or deny. You shouldn't have to apologize for your looks."

"No, but I've always had a hard time believing women when they came on to me."

"So you tried your best to be obnoxious and arrogant and see who would run from you and who wouldn't?"

"Well, it was a strategy, at least. But honestly, I've been physically attracted to women over the years, but not really emotionally. I just never met anyone that I wanted to get to know on a more personal level — other than just the physical part. And that's why Angel and Lannie were teasing me. They've tried to set me up with plenty of women and I never bring the same one around twice."

Carly smiled sadly, wondering at the loneliness this woman has endured most of her life. Not only from her parents, her family, but also from not having the intimacy of a relationship. And sadly, she could relate. It had been so many years since her disastrous relationship with Carol ended and she was no better than Pat. But at least she had her family.

"But you know, I can't really lump you in that category," Pat said. Carly looked up and Pat immediately captured her eyes. "I'm attracted to you physically, of course. You know that. But you're the first person I've really wanted to spend time with. You're the first person that I've felt . . . connected to."

"I won't deny that I'm attracted to you, Pat. In fact, I'm happier when you're here than when you're not." She swallowed hard, her voice catching, but she didn't pull her eyes away. "But I don't know what you want from me," she finished in a whisper.

"I want your heart," Pat said softly.

"I can't give you that, Pat. I won't ever be able to give you that. I might give you some, but I would have to keep some back, for myself. Pat, I nearly didn't make it after Carol. But you, with you, I don't think I could recover."

"I'm sorry, but I want all of it," Pat said. "Every bit of your heart. But that's okay. Because I want to give you all of mine. And I've never given mine away before."

Carly felt tears gather in her eyes and she blinked them away. She reached out and took Pat's hand, pulling it into her lap.

"You say things like that, and I want so to believe you," she whispered.

"Carly, if there's one thing you can believe, it's that I'll be honest with you. Always."

"You scare the hell out of me, you know. I don't seem to have any defense for you."

Pat moved until she was facing Carly, their knees brushing. Her eyes still held Carly captive and she reached out, brushing the blonde hair away from her face.

"Please don't kiss me, Pat," Carly whispered even as her eyes dropped to Pat's lips. "I'm too weak."

"It's not like I have a choice, Carly."

The lips that touched hers were so soft, so gentle that Carly whimpered. She felt her hands slide up Pat's arms to her shoulders, felt herself pull Pat closer. Suddenly their kiss turned hungry, mouths opening, tasting. Carly didn't try to control the hunger inside of her. She had wanted to kiss Pat this way for weeks. She wouldn't deny herself now.

But it was Pat who pulled away first and Carly felt the loss immediately. She looked at Pat, her eyes questioning.

"If we don't stop now, I'm going to drag you into your bedroom and I don't think you're ready for that," Pat said.

"Why must you always leave me wanting a cold shower?"

"Because I want to make love to you like no one ever has," Pat breathed. "And I want you to be sure. I don't want you to tell me this was a mistake in the morning. And because I want you to give me your heart."

"You're asking the impossible. I can only give you my body."

"Then we're going to be taking cold showers."

Carly smiled at that and leaned forward and touched Pat's lips again, this time gently, without the hunger that was simmering just under the surface.

"So you really are trying to drive me crazy," she murmured. "I should have known."

Pat stood up and pulled Carly to her feet. She wanted to hold her. She drew Carly into her arms, holding her with all the tenderness she had never offered another soul. She felt Carly melt into her, felt her arms slide around her shoulders, felt the lips that moved over her neck. She moved her head, taking Carly's lips again. The fire between them ignited and she felt Carly's hips press into her own. She grasped Carly's hips, holding her firmly against her and she moaned. God, she wanted this woman. Never in her life had she wanted someone like this. Before she could stop herself, her hands slid to Carly's waist, then higher, cupping Carly's breasts.

"Oh, God, what are you trying to do to me?" Carly whispered into her mouth. She wanted her. She could feel her own wetness and she opened her legs, pressing against Pat's thigh, so afraid she would have an orgasm right then. And would it be so bad, she thought.

Pat wanted to let go. It would be so much easier than trying to control her desire. But if she had Carly tonight, there were no assurances that she could have her again tomorrow. And Pat knew she wanted a thousand tomorrows with this woman. But what she felt was close to pain as she pulled away from Carly.

"You're dangerous, Dr. Cambridge. I can't seem to control myself when I'm around you."

"I could hate you right now, Pat Ryan," Carly whispered. "Because you know exactly how much I want you and you won't take it."

"We both know you don't hate me."

"I can't let myself love you, Pat."

But Pat smiled. Carly's eyes didn't lie. The hardest part would be convincing Carly that she was capable of giving . . . and accepting love.

"Let's call it a night, huh? We're going to have a busy day tomorrow."

"How the hell can you just change gears like that?" Carly accused. "You're driving me crazy and I think you enjoy it," Carly accused.

"Yes. Obnoxious, I know."

"You know, of course, that you'll pay for this," Carly told her.

Pat laughed and bent down and picked up their drinks. She handed one to Carly and drank the last of hers. Yes, she would pay. Gladly.

"Do you have a pillow or something that I can use out here?" Pat asked.

"You don't have to sleep on the sofa. My bed is plenty big enough for the both of us," Carly offered.

"You're joking, right? It's all I can do to be in the same house as you. Don't tempt me with a bed."

"So when Lannie called you stubborn, she wasn't kidding."

"I'm not stubborn. Jesus, Carly, I'm trying to be a saint here."

"And you're succeeding."

CHAPTER FORTY-ONE

The continuous pounding against the shutters made for a sleepless night. Pat was constantly tossing on the small sofa, trying to get comfortable. Finally, she gave up. Four-thirty. *Great.*

She walked down the hall to Carly's bedroom. The door was opened, but the soft glow of the nightlight in the hallway wasn't enough for her to see Carly's face. But she imagined how she would look in sleep. She'd been imagining it for weeks. She quietly closed the door and crept back into the living room.

The Weather Channel was having continuous coverage and after starting coffee, she settled down to watch. Landfall was predicted by late afternoon and already the storm surge was hitting. The nighttime pictures they showed of Corpus, Port Aransas, and Galveston were frightening. The only encouraging thing she heard was that the strike probability was now north of them. They would be spared the brunt of the storm.

She was on her third cup of coffee when Carly stumbled in. Her hair was a tousled mess and she wore plaid boxers and a wrinkled white T-shirt. Pat was certain she'd never seen a more beautiful sight.

Carly rubbed her eyes with one hand and murmured, "Coffee?"

Pat grinned. "Not a morning person?"

"No. It's best you find out now."

"Like that matters. You look gorgeous, by the way."

"Rule number one. Don't talk to me until I've had coffee."

"I guess I should warn you now. I'm a morning person. Actually, I'm a chatterbox in the morning. Unfortunately, I seldom have anyone to talk to. Maybe that's why I have a penchant for talking to myself."

"Shut up."

Pat laughed and watched as Carly shuffled into the kitchen. She heard coffee being poured then a quiet sigh. Ah, her first sip. Won't be long now.

Carly came back and this time her eyes were opened. When Pat opened her mouth to speak, Carly held up her hand.

"Don't."

Carly sat in the recliner and sipped her coffee, her eyes on the TV. Pat watched her, saw her stretch slightly as she moved her shoulders, then her neck. Finally, nearly ten minutes later, Carly turned and looked at her.

"What ungodly hour did you get up?"

"Four-thirty."

"I knew you were insane."

"Couldn't sleep. I think I'm longer than your sofa."

"Christ, why didn't you just come to bed with me?"

"I thought we'd already covered that?"

"Trust me. Once I'm asleep, I'm asleep."

"Yes, I know. You also snore."

"I most certainly do not snore!"

"Not like big burly man snores, but yes, you snore. It's very cute."

Carly stared at her, contemplating tossing the rest of her coffee on Pat's head. She smiled slightly. It was a pleasant thought.

"Don't even think about it."

"Too late. And if you spread nasty rumors about my snoring, I'll take you out into the bay and drown you."

"You're vicious in the morning."

"Yes. And don't ever forget it."

"Do you like to make love in the morning?"

Carly choked on her coffee and Pat laughed.

"Do I look like I like to make love in the morning?"

"You look like you could be extremely aggressive," Pat said. "Could be fun."

Carly couldn't help the smile that crossed her face. Even in the dreaded morning, Pat could make her laugh.

"How about a weather update?" Carly suggested, changing the subject.

"It's category four, just barely. Winds are at 135. Gusts at Corpus were already 80."

"Jesus Christ. What's the prediction?"

"More strengthening today, but it's moving faster, which is a good thing. It's also turned a bit to the north."

"Galveston?"

"Between here and there."

"Category four is very dangerous. But a category five?"

"It won't reach that. It's so large, when the outer bands hit land, it'll stop strengthening."

"Do you think we should leave?"

"If we were on the island, sure. Port Aransas has been evacuated. Galveston Island, too. But, we've got the barrier island and the bay between us and the storm. I think we'll be okay. Besides, our Jeeps would get beat to hell out there."

Carly looked back to the TV, watching as a reporter stood in the early morning dawn near Corpus Christi Bay as the water from the bay washed above the jetty.

"I hope my parents are okay," she said.

"Were they going to leave?"

"Dad said they were going to wait until today. Both my brothers live inland." Then she looked at Pat. "Do we need to check on Rachel?"

"No. She's boarded up. She'll be okay."

Carly nodded. "Let's make some breakfast. I can do eggs."

"Yes. We should probably cook while we still have power."

Pat sat at the table and watched as Carly opened the package of bacon they'd bought last night. Pat couldn't remember the last time she'd had a real breakfast cooked for her, other than Alice. This was nice, she decided. The smell of frying bacon had a soothing effect on her and she was content to sit and watch Carly as she moved about her kitchen. She was bent over now, head stuck inside the refrigerator. It was a nice view.

"Bacon, eggs, toast?" Carly asked.

"Sounds great."

Carly pulled out a jar of what used to be some sort of jam. Pat smiled at the frown on Carly's face.

"Guess it's only butter on the toast. I'm not really certain what this has turned into," she said as she tossed the jar into the trash. "Don't know why I even packed that." Then she looked up. "What time is it, anyway?"

Pat turned her wrist. "Almost six-thirty."

"I hate it all boarded up like this," Carly said. "I'm going to be crazy by the end of the day."

"I know. I hate not being able to see what's going on out there. But we should move our Jeeps as soon as we eat."

"There are two oil lamps down in the kitchen. Remind me to bring one up here. With the shutters closed, it's going to be dark as hell when the power goes out."

"Candles?"

"Yes. I have some." Then she paused. "You're not going to suggest we fill the bathtub up with water, are you? I never understood that."

"I think that precaution is still from the old days when utilities could be out for weeks after a storm hit."

"Have you been through many?" Carly asked.

"A few tropical storms but only one hurricane. The first year I lived at the beach house and I was totally unprepared. I did get new furniture out of the deal."

"But your house is safe now?"

"Category four? I don't know. The storm surge alone will probably have water up to my deck. But the structure, the roof . . . I don't know."

"I'm sorry. You're worried about it, aren't you?"

Pat nodded. "But I don't have a lot there. I keep all of my prints and negatives at Aunt Rachel's and some of my equipment."

Carly took the bacon out to drain on paper towels and cracked four eggs into the pan.

"Do you have any inventory? I mean, do you sell over the Internet?"

"No. I've got a deal with a place in Corpus that produces my prints and does the framing for the large ones that I market locally."

"Why don't you have your own gallery? Surely, you've got enough material."

"I've actually been thinking about that for awhile

now. There's an old T-shirt shop in Rockport that Aunt Rachel's heard is going to come up for sale by the first of the year. She wants me to get it. But owning a gallery means more work and I'd have less time out in the field."

"And that's why you hire a good manager," Carly said. "Why have other galleries sell your work and make a profit when you can do it yourself?"

"I know. Flip those already, would you?" she said, pointing to the eggs.

"Sorry. I normally do scrambled."

Pat put bread in the toaster while Carly filled their plates.

"Juice?"

"You have some?"

"Yes. Two days to expiration. You're just in time."

They sat across from each other at the table and ate in silence. Carly looked up from time to time, watching Pat. For the first time that morning, she allowed her thoughts to revisit last night. She shouldn't have. Her skin tingled, her breasts ached. She closed her eyes, remembering Pat's urgent hands as they touched her. She suddenly found it difficult to breathe and when she opened her eyes, Pat was watching her. She dove into the blue eyes but said nothing. Finally, Pat's hand reached out and covered hers.

"I'm thinking about it, too," she whispered.

Carly blushed. God, was it that obvious?

"You have no idea how long it took me to get to sleep last night," Carly admitted.

"At least you got to sleep. And trust me, all the squirming I did had nothing to do with the size of the sofa."

"Well, it's your own fault."

"Yes, I'm a glutton for punishment."

"I think you may be," Carly said. She got up and

took her plate to the sink, then reached for Pat's. She was going to be absolutely crazy by the end of the day if they were stuck inside. "Let's move the Jeeps. I need to get outside."

But Pat grabbed her arm as she walked past, pulling her close.

"Don't . . . please?" Carly whispered when their eyes met. "I still haven't recovered from last night."

But Pat lowered her head anyway. She couldn't help it. But her kiss was light, brief. She hadn't recovered, either.

"I'm sorry."

"It would be so easy to fall in love with you."

"Yes, I know. It's my glowing personality," Pat said.

"Please don't make me."

"It's too late. And you know it," Pat said quietly.

"Yes. That's what scares me."

"I want to do a lot of things to you, Dr. Cambridge, but scare you is not one of them."

"Well, it's too late for that, too."

Pat smiled warmly then backed away.

"Come on. Let's get our Jeeps in the barn."

The wind was ferocious but not nearly as fierce as it would be later in the day. Already, small branches from the oaks were breaking off, littering the ground. The pounding rain of the night before had slacked some, but the swirling clouds only promised more.

Both Jeeps fit easily inside the barn and they closed the double doors with Pat on the outside pushing against the wind. Then, with the hoods of their rain jackets pulled over their heads, they ran back to the ranch house. Carly looked back once, a frown creasing her brow, then she closed the door.

"What?" Pat asked.

"They'll never make it," she said.

"The egrets?"

"Yeah. I'm sure the parents have already headed inland. The babies are on their own."

"You want to try and get them?" Pat asked.

Carly shook her head. "Our Jeeps barely made it to the barn without blowing over."

"We could walk."

"No. It's too dangerous. I just have to keep telling myself that this is nature and these things happen."

"I'm sorry, Carly."

"Come on. Let's go get dry. I could use a shower," she said as they climbed the stairs. "You?"

"Yes. You want to go first?"

"No. Go ahead. I think I'll call Elsa and check in."

Pat took her time, then searched everywhere in Carly's bathroom for a blow dryer. She finally stuck her head out.

"Blow dryer?"

"Sorry. I don't use one," she called.

No wonder her hair always looked wind blown. It *was* wind blown. She gathered up her things and walked back out to the living room, wet hair and all.

"Sorry about that. I haven't used one in years."

"It's okay. It'll dry soon enough."

Carly was again on the floor, watching the never-ending weathercast. Beside her was a tall drink that looked suspiciously like a Bloody Mary.

Pat raised her eyebrows.

"I thought it was a good day to stay inside and drink," she said.

Pat nodded. "And mine would be where?"

"In the fridge. I left the Tabasco on the table. I wasn't sure how spicy you liked them."

Pat came back with her glass, sat down beside Carly and they watched TV in silence. It wasn't long before the rain started in earnest again and they listened as it pounded against the shutters.

"I really hate this," Carly said. "I hate that the marsh will be flooded, that trees will be lost. And I hate it about the egrets."

"I know," Pat said. "Listen, it's still manageable out there. Why don't I just go out and get them?"

"It's too dangerous, Pat. You can hear yourself that the wind is picking up by the minute. Limbs will be snapping off and blowing around. It would be insane to go out."

"I can stick to the woods," she said.

"You can't penetrate the oak mottes and you know it."

"Look, I like the damn little birds, too. They're ugly as hell but . . . they're *ours*," she said. For some reason, she equated the safety of the egrets with the fragileness of their new relationship. If the egrets died, she was irrationally afraid that she and Carly would have no chance either.

Pat's words touched Carly. She knew Pat had become fond of the nest. She'd seen her sneak off with her camera on numerous days, but Pat never said anything. Carly thought maybe she would be embarrassed over the attention she was giving them. But still, it was too dangerous.

"You could get hurt," she said. "I would never forgive myself. They're just birds."

"They're not just birds, Carly."

The romantic part of Carly wanted to say, yes, go save them. But the sensible part said it was totally irresponsible to try. But Pat's eyes were so sure and confident — as fierce as the storm raging around them.

She wanted to believe her. She wanted to believe that it was worth the risk to try and save them.

"Okay. But only if I go with you."

"No way. You're not going out. No offense, but I'm bigger and stronger than you are." She was already getting to her feet and Carly followed.

"I don't think you should go out alone, Pat. What if something happened?"

"Then it shouldn't happen to both of us."

"That's just crazy."

"Maybe. But you're staying here."

"You are so fucking stubborn," she said to Pat's retreating back. She was already headed down the stairs.

"I thought obnoxious and arrogant."

"Those, too."

Pat grabbed her rain jacket off of one of the chairs and slipped it on. She looked at her bare legs, wishing she'd put jeans on. But she was too impatient to run back up the stairs. They both looked up as a limb slammed against one of the shutters, shaking the window.

"This isn't a good idea," Carly said.

Their eyes met and Carly walked to Pat, slipping her arms around her without thinking. She kissed her cheek, then moved to her lips, kissing her gently, then with more urgency.

"If you let anything happen to you, I'll never forgive you," she whispered.

"Don't drink all my Bloody Mary while I'm gone."

"Pat, please don't do anything foolish. If it's too bad, just come back. Please?"

"I promise. Now, what am I supposed to put the little monsters in?"

"Shit. I didn't think. Wait," she said and ran back

up the stairs. She came back carrying a pillowcase. "Put them in here. It's the best I've got."

Pat nodded, then bent and kissed Carly hard.

"I'll be back."

"Watch your head," Carly called after her as Pat sprinted out into the storm. Suddenly, Carly wanted to call her back. She wanted to tell her it was foolish. She wanted to take her upstairs where it was safe. But Pat was already to the barn and Carly watched as she disappeared around the corner.

"Please be safe," she whispered.

CHAPTER FORTY-TWO

A gust of wind nearly picked Pat up off the ground. Frantically, she latched on to the nearest tree branch, wrapping her arms around it just to stay upright. The trees that lined the road were bending with the force of the wind. Buffeted about by one blast after another, she understood what a bit of dandelion fluff must feel like. She stayed as close to the woods as possible, as the line of trees absorbed most of the force of the wind, using anything she could to hold herself up against the fierce onslaught. Squinting up into the rain, she saw a very angry, turbulent sky. For an instant, she felt real fear, then she shook it off, not allowing herself the luxury of panic.

She would be safer inside the oak mottes, but as Carly had said she couldn't penetrate the brush. She knew this because she tried, scraping her face, arms and legs in the process. Disoriented and exhausted, though she figured she hadn't yet covered thirty or forty feet, she trudged on. It seemed she'd lost time, as if the minutes had blown past her along with the flying debris. Had it been hours? She couldn't see the pond, couldn't see beyond the end of her nose. Then, behind her, the sizzle of lightening and a loud pop of thunder spun her around. She watched as an oak was split in half and fell to the ground, not twenty feet from where she'd just passed.

"Well, fuck me," she shouted, and the wind quickly carried her words away.

She knew the closer she got to the pond, the more exposed she would be, but she pushed forward anyway. A violent gust knocked her off her feet with such force she suddenly understood how wind could demolish buildings. Her breath came in short gasps and her body felt pummeled, as if the wind had a grudge against her personally. She had just been tossed as if she were a rag doll. She got to her knees, fighting to reach the woods. It was then that she realized this was a fucking stupid idea.

"Too late," she muttered. She would be lucky if the damn egrets were still alive anyway. The nest may have already been blown to the ground. A tree could have fallen on them. "Shit, shit, shit."

She pressed on, finally seeing the pond through the torrential rain. Not much farther, she thought. But again, a gust caught her, tossing her forward.

"Whose bright idea was this? It was yours." Then she laughed, another sign that she was out of her mind. "You've really got to stop talking to yourself."

At last, she reached the cover of woods. The nest wasn't too much farther, provided the path was still clear. She was amazed that even the wind seemed to have a hard time penetrating the mottes. She could at least hear herself think, but she'd rather the thoughts running through her mind remain silent. How the hell was she supposed to make it back, *against the wind*, when she could barely hold herself up?

She pushed through the brush, ignoring the branches that scratched at her face and legs. At the clearing, she looked for the nest. She couldn't find it.

"Fuck," she whispered, rain rushing into her open mouth.

She took a deep breath, then ran towards the trees, falling down when her foot caught a downed branch. She got back up and fought against the wind, pulling herself to where the nest should be. It was there, covered now with a broken limb from a neighboring tree. She pulled the branches back and there, staring at her, were two of the ugliest looking birds she'd ever seen.

She laughed.

She reached under her shirt where she'd stuffed the pillowcase and pulled it out. Before the startled birds knew what was happening, she grabbed them both and shoved them inside. They gave little resistance. She tucked the birds against her stomach and turned, heading right back into the wind.

And she couldn't move. The force of the wind blew her backwards and she landed on her ass with a thump.

"Son of a bitch," she muttered, got back up on her knees and crawled into the brush.

The roar around her sounded like a train and she had a sudden urge to begin chanting prayers from her childhood.

"A little late for that now," she told the birds.

She crawled through the brush, stopping when she reached the road. It looked endless. It was also cluttered with branches and limbs.

"Okay, here goes."

She clutched the birds to her chest and bent over

as low as she could get, fighting against the wind. The wind was winning. For every step she took forward, the wind blew her two steps back. The rain stung her face, small pellets pounding against her skin. It was nearly impossible for her to see. But she kept on, falling to her knees but getting back up again. As her hand plunged into the mud, she thought . . . jeans, should have worn jeans.

A red blur in the distance told her she might not be that far from salvation.

"Just make it to the barn. A few more steps."

It was in slow motion that she saw the oak limb flying through the air. Then, with a quick jerk of her head, she realized she had been hit. She dropped like a rock.

"Stars . . . you really do see stars," she murmured.

CHAPTER FORTY-THREE

Carly paced, then opened the back door, looking for Pat. Then she repeated the routine, only this time she took two steps out into the rain before she went inside and started pacing again.

"Stupid. It was fucking stupid to let her go out," she said over and over again. She'd heard it from Elsa who had spent ten minutes yelling at her over the static on her cell phone.

"Have you completely lost your mind?" Elsa had yelled. "You shouldn't even be at the ranch, much less out in the goddamn woods!"

"Don't you think I know that? She's stubborn, in case you haven't realized."

"She loves you. She's getting the birds for you in case you're too stupid to realize that."

"It was her idea to go out," Carly said.

"And you didn't stop her."

Carly was almost thankful they had lost the connection. But she knew Pat was going for the egrets as much for herself as for Carly. Pat pretended indifference, but Carly knew it was breaking her heart to think of the egrets out there on their own. She had seen that in her eyes. But still, it was insane to try and save them. The trees were barely able to withstand the force of the wind. How in the hell would Pat be able to? Carly checked her watch. Too long. Pat had been gone for ages it seemed.

It would be her fault if anything happened to Pat. And, God, how could she live with herself? Pat had gotten inside her. She had reached out and taken something that Carly swore she would never give. And she couldn't bear the thought of losing Pat before they'd really had a chance — a chance at something special.

She went to the door again and nearly made it down the back steps when a fierce gust knocked her down and stole her breath. She blinked the rain out of her eyes, at least she told herself it was the rain, and then went back inside.

CHAPTER FORTY-FOUR

Pat opened her eyes, ignoring the pain shooting through her cheek, her face. She was on her back, the rain and wind lashing at her. She had no idea how long she'd been there. The pillowcase was still on her stomach and it was warm against her. Rolling over, she felt light-headed, but she shook it off. She had to get back. Now. She sat up, shaking the rain from her face, feeling, she was certain, her brain as it banged against her skull.

She couldn't walk against the wind, that much was certain. So she crawled. She could feel the scrapes on her knees as they dug into the wet earth, but she pushed on. Limbs were breaking and crashing around her and she had a brief moment of humor as she realized she could very well be in a disaster movie. Only in the movies, it was all for play. The wind roaring around her was nothing to play with.

One small step at a time, she crawled, hands sinking into the muddy ground. She tried in vain to ignore the sheets of rain that plummeted her face. She squinted, looking into the angry sky, seeing for the first time in her life, sheets of rain, blowing horizontal, so fierce she could hardly see the ground in front of her.

For one crazy instant, she panicked. Had the storm hit full force? Was she *outside* in the middle of a goddamned hurricane? She shook her head, no . . . they still had hours before landfall.

"Focus," she murmured. "Focus."

It was then she noticed the chill traveling slowly down her body. Her teeth chattered and she wiped frantically at the rain against her face. She was blown down, face against the wet earth. She looked up, blinking several times as she tried to get her bearings. There was nothing but the wind and rain.

She felt movement against her stomach as the birds stirred.

"Hang on. We're almost there."

Through the murky blur of the storm, in the distance she saw a sight that flooded her with relief . . . the hulking shape of the barn.

"Thank God," she breathed.

It was still a long way off but in her heart, she knew she would make it. She was soaked through and through, chilled to the bone, but it didn't matter. She had the birds. And soon, they would all be safe. She tucked her head against her chest and crawled on, ignoring the constant pain in her cheek as she fought against the rain.

As she crawled around the corner of the barn, the back door to the ranch house flew open and Carly was standing there, shielding her eyes against the wind and rain. Then she was running towards her and Pat finally relaxed.

"Made it," she said. "Never doubted it for a minute."

Then Carly fell to her knees in front of her, her eyes wide as she saw blood running down Pat's face.

"Jesus Christ," she whispered, but her words were carried away with the wind. "Can you make it to the house?" she yelled.

"Piece of cake," Pat yelled back with a grin. But it hurt to smile and she squeezed her eyes shut for an instant.

Carly grabbed her arm and pulled her to her feet, struggling against the wind towards the house. They fell once, both face down and muddy. Then Carly pulled them up, dragging Pat along with her. Finally, the door slammed shut and the sudden silence startled Pat.

"Oh my God. You're hurt. Sit down."

"I'm okay," Pat said. "Here." She lifted up the pillowcase, now as wet as she was, and handed it to Carly.

"You found them?"

"Safe and sound. Or they were," she said as she collapsed into a chair and wiped the blood away from her eye. She shivered.

Carly opened the pillowcase and peeked inside, meeting two pairs of wild eyes.

"I can't believe you did this," she said. She glanced at Pat and grinned. "My hero."

She went to the box she'd prepared, just in case. Carefully lifting the birds from the bag, she settled them inside, and then covered it with a towel. She would tend to them later. Right now, someone more important needed her.

She cupped Pat's face gently, her frown deepening as she saw the deep cut above Pat's right eyebrow.

"What happened to you?"

"I think it was a baseball bat," Pat said. "I'm certain Sammy Sosa was swinging it."

Carly touched her cheekbone and Pat pulled away. "It hurts," she said.

"You'll be lucky if it's not broken." Then she lightly touched Pat's lips with her own. "I was . . . I was so scared," she admitted. "I didn't know what to do."

"How could you think I wasn't coming back?" Pat asked. "I haven't seen you naked yet. You think I'd miss out on that?"

Carly closed her eyes, then bent and kissed Pat again, her lips lingering this time.

"Okay, enough of that mushy stuff," Pat said. "I'm bleeding to death here."

"I'm sorry." Carly stood back. "Sit up there," she said, pointing to the counter. "I'm going upstairs for my bag. Don't move."

Pat did as she was told. The throbbing in her face was nearly unbearable, but it beat the constant roar of the storm. She glanced at her watch, surprised to see that over two hours had passed since she'd left the ranch house. No wonder Carly had been frantic.

She heard her running back down the stairs, then she reappeared with what looked like a medical bag in her hand.

"Jesus, Pat. At least take your rain coat off," Carly said. She moved to Pat, sliding the wet jacket off her shoulders. "You're absolutely soaked. What did you do? Take a dip in the pond?"

"I may have. I don't really remember," Pat murmured.

Carly frowned. Pat's face was flushed, cool. She seemed to be in shock.

"You probably have a mild case of hypothermia. Lift your arms up," Carly instructed quietly. Pat did and

221

Carly pulled her wet T-shirt over her head, leaving Pat in only her sports bra. Carly raised her eyes, meeting Pat's. Now was no time to stare, she knew, but Jesus, the woman was beautiful. She threw the wet shirt into the sink, then opened her bag.

Pat cringed as Carly dabbed at her cut. It burned and she squeezed her eyes shut against the pain.

"I'm sorry. I know it hurts but I've got to clean it. You need stitches."

"Stitches? No."

"Yes."

Carly spread Pat's legs and stood between them, wiping at the cut. The bleeding would not stop. She put pressure on it and held it, seeing the pain in Pat's eyes. Then she felt Pat tremble, felt the pressure as Pat's legs tightened around her hips.

"What? Too hard?"

"Why are you doing this to me?" Pat whispered.

"I'm trying to stop the bleeding. I know it hurts."

Pat suddenly gripped Carly's hips and pulled her tightly into her opened legs. Carly gasped at the intimate contact.

"No, this is what you're doing to me," Pat murmured. She leaned forward and captured Carly's lips. Despite the pain in her face, the ache between her legs was greater.

Carly melted into the kiss, letting Pat hold her close. But she pulled away finally. This was not the time or place to start this.

"Behave," she said. She dabbed at the wound again, pleased that the bleeding had nearly stopped. "I need to close this." She reached into her bag again and pulled out a suture. She ignored Pat's gasp.

"That's for dogs, right?" she asked.

"Well, I *was* training to be a vet," Carly said.

"Maybe you shouldn't use that on me. Right?"

Carly nearly laughed. It was at times like this that she just wanted to take Pat in her arms and hold her. Not kiss her. Just hold her.

"Be quiet. You're such a baby," she said.

"Surely you have something to deaden it," Pat said.

"I didn't think you'd need it."

"Of course I need it! I'm not completely insane."

This time Carly did laugh.

"Will you hold still? I put a topical on it. I don't have anything else."

"Dr. Cambridge, and I use that term lightly, because I'm not a dog," Pat said. "But I'm really a wimp when it comes to pain."

"You could have fooled me." Carly dabbed again at the wound and this time Pat didn't pull away. "See. Can't even feel it."

"I'm sure I'll feel a needle and thread."

"Suture," Carly said. "But maybe I should just put a butterfly on it. It's not a clean cut and I'm a little out of practice. It may leave a scar. We can take you to a doctor tomorrow."

Pat met her eyes, then took her hand and brought it to her lips. She closed her eyes as she kissed Carly's palm.

"That's okay. I don't mind a scar. Years from now, it'll give us something to talk about. I'll remind you of how you tried to kill me, all for a couple of egrets. And we'll have hundreds of egrets out here then, just because of these two little guys. So I won't mind a scar, Carly."

Carly stared at her, again diving into her eyes. She reached out and touched Pat's face gently.

"Sometimes, you say things . . . you just take my breath away."

CHAPTER FORTY-FIVE

Carly settled Pat into her bed, freshly showered, now in dry shorts and a clean T-shirt. She could tell Pat had discarded her sports bra and had to pull her eyes away from her breasts, moving instead to Pat's face. She had given her a pain pill and Pat was nearly asleep. The bruise on her cheek was more pronounced and there was a slight discoloration under her eye. She was damn lucky. Actually, the egrets were damn lucky. They would surely be dead by now.

"It was a stupid thing to do," Pat murmured.

"Yes, it was."

"But I would do it all over again."

"I'm sure you would."

"The bed smells like you."

Carly smiled as Pat drifted off to sleep. She watched her for a minute, then walked downstairs. She needed to check on the egrets.

They lost power just as she lifted the towel from the box.

"Great."

She fumbled along the counter, trying to find the flashlight she'd set out. Then she flashed the beam around the kitchen, going to the cabinet where she'd stashed the oil lamps. She lit one, illuminating the kitchen with a soft glow.

The egret chicks were wet but seemed okay. They shied away from her, seeming alert but wary.

"It's okay. I won't hurt you," she murmured softly to them. She covered the box again. They would be okay until morning. She would worry about feeding them then.

She jumped as something hit the house, rattling the windows. Another tree branch, no doubt. She moved the flashlight to her watch. It was nearly four. The storm was moving over them. The last weather report she'd heard had the eye hitting closer to Galveston but still too close for comfort. The winds were probably at least one hundred-twenty as it were.

She pulled out the second lamp and set it on the counter. She would use it in the morning. She took the lit one and carefully climbed the stairs, trying to ignore the pounding of the shutters as they banged against the house. The worst was upon them. It could only get better.

She made a sandwich, wishing she had made Pat eat something before she slept but the woman was nearly exhausted. Carly finally admitted to herself how scared she'd been. After one hour had passed, she'd been frantic. After two, she had been ready to bolt out the door in search of the other woman.

What she felt for Pat was certainly more than simple attraction. She wouldn't say she loved her, well, that she was in love with her. She wouldn't say that. She couldn't.

But yes, she loved her. Sitting at the table alone, she squeezed her eyes shut. She wasn't *in* love with her. That would be crazy. But the thought of losing Pat before they'd even had a chance to explore this new relationship hurt her deeply. And whether Pat would admit it or not, she had been in great danger out there. What if the limb that hit her had been larger? What if it had hit her square in the face?

"She could have been killed."

Carly felt the ache deep in her heart. Pat could have been killed.

She got up quickly from the table, pushing her chair back. She filled a glass with ice and closed the freezer quickly. Hopefully, the power wouldn't be out for long. Not that she had a lot in the freezer that would spoil. She found a bottle of rum and poured a generous amount into her glass. Then she added Coke, walked into the living room and sat in the recliner in the dark.

She listened to the wind and rain, sipping from her drink occasionally while trying not to think of the woman sleeping in her bed. Because if she did, she would completely lose herself. She ached to go to her. She wanted nothing more than to crawl in beside Pat and hold her. And that scared the hell out of her.

She didn't know how long she sat here. Long enough for her drink to empty. But she was surprised when Pat appeared in the shadows, her silhouette outlined by the lamp in the kitchen.

"What are you doing up?" Carly asked.

"Hungry."

Carly sat up, moving to her. She took her hand and pulled her into the kitchen, into the light. Her cheek was swollen and discolored and Pat's eyes were hazy.

"We lost power?"

"Yes. Hours ago," Carly said.

"I guess that's why I'm hot," Pat said. She nearly

collapsed into a chair, the effects of the pain pill still obvious.

"How do you feel?"

"Okay," Pat lied. Actually, her face throbbed but, she wouldn't tell Carly that. She could see the worry that was still etched across her face.

"Why don't I believe you?"

"It hurts a little," Pat finally admitted.

"Sandwich? That's about all I can offer."

"That would be great."

Carly quickly made a turkey sandwich, then went back for cheese when Pat requested it.

Pat found she could only chew on her left side and even then, each bite hurt. She ate silently and drank some water that Carly had poured from the jug.

"Have you eaten?" Pat asked.

"Yes. Earlier."

"It hasn't slowed, huh?"

"No. And I'm actually thankful for the shutters. At least I don't have to watch."

Pat didn't answer. She couldn't seem to gather her thoughts. Finally, she pushed her plate aside. She had only been able to eat half of the sandwich.

"I think I'm going to go back to bed," she said.

"Yes. You should." Then Carly looked at the half-eaten sandwich. "Hurts to chew?"

Pat only nodded.

"Would cold soup be better?"

"No."

Carly stood and walked to Pat, pushing her head back to get a better look at her wound. It was puffy and red. She felt her face, finding no fever.

"Do you need something for the pain?"

"No. I'm okay for now. I'm still kinda out of it."

"Okay. Come on."

227

Carly grabbed the flashlight with one hand and Pat's arm with the other and led her back into the bedroom. She pulled the covers back and pointed. Pat obediently laid down, leaving her long legs on top of the covers. She was hot, Carly knew, but she dared not open the shutters, even on the north side of the house. She perched on the edge of the bed near Pat.

"Close your eyes," she said. When Pat did, she pointed the flashlight onto her face, making sure the sutures were still tight. Then she inspected the rest of Pat's body, seeing for the first time the scratches on her legs and the small cuts on her knees. "I should have cleaned these, too. Why didn't you tell me?" Carly asked, running her finger lightly over Pat's knee.

"I forgot about them," she said. She reached out and took Carly's hand, squeezing it. Then she shut her eyes. Her face was throbbing again, but she still felt drowsy. "Why don't you lay down, too? You must be tired," Pat murmured.

"Yes. I am. Go back to sleep. I'll be back in a little while."

"Okay." She felt Carly get up and move away from her, but she was too tired to open her eyes. She shifted on the bed, trying to find a cool spot.

Carly walked back into the kitchen, putting Pat's plate in the sink along with the two glasses. She was tired, but didn't think she'd be able to sleep with the storm still raging outside. She couldn't very well wander around the dark house. She pulled the T-shirt away from her body, just now noticing how warm it was getting inside. By morning, it would be stifling. But then, they should be able to open the shutters and let in some air inside.

She finally blew out the lamp and took her flashlight into the bathroom. She brushed her teeth and splashed her face with cold water. She should at least try to get some sleep. Tomorrow would be a very busy day.

Pat was sound asleep, but Carly very nearly dropped her flashlight. Pat was apparently hot. She had discarded her T-shirt.

"You're not making this easy, are you?" she whispered. She was — simply beautiful and Carly's hungry eyes moved over her exposed body. She ached to touch it.

But she turned the flashlight off, moving to the other side of the bed. She lay down next to Pat, trying not to wake her. But she, too, was hot. She sat up and pulled her own T-shirt off. Finally, the rhythm of the storm lulled her to sleep and she let herself drift off, thoughts of the nearly naked woman beside her filling her dreams.

CHAPTER FORTY-SIX

Carly woke to moaning beside her and she turned in the darkness, listening as Pat nearly whimpered in her sleep. Carly reached for the flashlight, seeing the pain on Pat's face. The swelling was worse.

"Pat," she whispered.

Pat opened her eyes, then shut them again. The throbbing in her face was too much.

"What is it?" Carly asked. "Are you in pain?"

"Throbbing," she murmured. "Hurts like a son of a bitch."

"Let me get you a pain pill."

"Yes. Please."

Carly swung her bare feet to the floor, hurrying to the kitchen for water and her pills. She guessed Pat's cheekbone was fractured. That would account for the swelling. She hoped it was nothing more serious.

She walked back to the bedroom with the flashlight

tucked under her arm, holding out the water in one hand and the pill in the other.

"Can you sit up?"

Pat opened her eyes and lifted up, fighting against the pain. Then her heart clutched in her chest.

"Jesus Christ, are you trying to kill me?"

"What?" Then she followed Pat's gaze to her breasts. She had not put her shirt back on. She stood beside Pat in nothing but her boxers. Pat finally raised her eyes to Carly's, a look of hunger in the blue depths.

"I was hot," Carly said. "I'm sorry."

"Suddenly, the pain is gone," Pat whispered.

"No, it's not. Now take this."

Pat took the pill and water from Carly, her eyes never leaving the exposed flesh before her. Carly was absolutely beautiful. Her small breasts were shadowed, but Pat could see the aroused nipples. She wanted her mouth there. She wanted to feel them swell against her tongue.

She handed the glass back to Carly as her eyes roamed over the perfect body before her.

"Please come here," she whispered.

"Pat, you're in pain. Lay down."

"Yes. I'm in pain and it's below the waist."

The beam of the flashlight moved across Pat's body and Carly allowed her eyes to follow it, settling on the swell of breasts that begged for her touch. She simply couldn't resist. Putting the water on the small table beside the bed, she turned the flashlight off.

"Please come here," Pat said again, quietly.

"Don't start something you don't intend to finish," Carly said. "Not this time."

"I want to make love with you."

In the total darkness, Carly moved to her voice. Pat's arms found her, pulling her down beside her on the bed. Flesh met flesh and Carly was lost. Mouths met and mated, tongues danced, and hands touched. Carly moaned when Pat's hands found her breasts, cupping them both. She forgot about Pat's injury, forgot everything she had ever vowed. She wanted her. She wanted to make love to her. She pushed Pat onto her back, straddling her. Pat's hips came up and met her and Carly groaned.

"Am I hurting you?" she asked.

"No," Pat whispered. Her face ached but didn't compare to the ache between her thighs. And if she weren't so tired, so drugged, she would already be inside Carly. But her movements were slow, her hands soft upon Carly's skin.

Carly bent down again, and her mouth and tongue moved across Pat's bare skin, finally finding her nipple. Pat arched into her and Carly's mouth closed over the erect peak, sucking it hard into her mouth. She felt Pat's hands slide over her back, moving inside her boxers and cupping her hips, pulling her more firmly to her.

Her hips pressed into Pat, undulating against her. God, she wished there was some light. She wanted to look at Pat, to see her eyes. Then she felt Pat's body relax, felt her hands still. She pulled away slightly, moving her mouth back to Pat's. But the lips that met hers barely moved.

"Pat?"

"Can't move," she murmured. "It's your fault. You made me take the pill."

With an exasperated sigh, Carly let her head fall to Pat's chest. The fucking pain pill. Pat was out.

"I'm not believing this," she whispered. "I'm really not fucking believing this."

But Pat didn't answer. Her even breathing told Carly that she was asleep. Carly rolled off of Pat, her body still on the verge of exploding.

"You will so pay for this," she whispered to the sleeping woman. She lay on her back, staring into the blackness, barely hearing the storm. She had been ready to give herself to this woman, to take everything Pat could offer.

Her breathing finally slowed and she again gained some control over her body. Rolling onto her side, facing Pat, she couldn't see her, but her hand reached out, touching bare flesh. She found her breast, her hand closing around it. She felt Pat stir, felt Pat move towards her. She smiled. It was enough. For now. She rested her head on the pillow, so close to Pat. She closed her eyes, her hand still upon Pat's breast, and she slept.

CHAPTER FORTY-SEVEN

Carly woke to silence. The shutters were no longer banging, there was no rain hitting the house. And Pat was still asleep. Carly untangled herself from Pat, both their bodies damp with perspiration. It was stifling. And it was dark. She got up and moved to Pat's side of the bed, finding the flashlight she'd discarded earlier. She moved out into the hallway before turning it on.

It was later than she'd thought. Nearly six. She moved into the kitchen and opened the window, reaching for the latch that held the shutters. She opened one and smiled as the cool breeze hit her face. The storm had passed. She moved around the apartment, opening all the shutters, letting in light and fresh air.

She wished there was coffee. She couldn't function without coffee. She settled for a shower instead. There was no hot water, but it didn't matter.

Later, as soon as it was light enough, she walked downstairs. In the kitchen, she lit the oil lamp and lifted the towel that covered the box. The egrets were huddled together and they both opened their mouths wide when they saw movement.

"Hungry?" Carly asked. The only thing remotely suitable she found was a can of tuna. It would have to do until they could get into town and buy some fresh fish. She fed them the small bits of tuna, pleased that they ate so easily. But they probably hadn't had food since early yesterday morning, if then. She covered them again, then opened the back door.

The sun was barely up, but there was enough light for her to see the thick clouds that still swirled overhead. And it was a mess. Limbs and branches lay scattered around, but the two old oaks behind the house looked intact. Pat would be pleased.

Carly walked around the house and towards the Visitor's Center. She nodded. It looked fine. She began moving some of the branches that had blown against the entrance, then gave up. There were too many for her to even begin to make a dent. And she doubted that even with Elsa and Martin's help they would be able to clean up the mess. She would have to hire someone. Or gather volunteers from town.

Then, with a heavy heart, she walked around the front and to the marsh. It was flooded, as she knew it would be. It looked like a small lake. She was mentally planning how they could drain it. It would have to be pumped into the bay. There was too much salt water in it for them to dump it into the woods. It would damage the oaks and probably kill the shallow-rooted brush if they did that, which of course, would have been the easiest solution.

Then she turned a complete circle, looking all around her. It could have been a lot worse. It *should* have been, she realized. The wind had been so strong. She could see a few uprooted trees and she knew that they had suffered the brunt of the storm. But the structures looked intact. Of course, she hadn't been to the old barn. She was surprised that it was even still standing this morning.

She walked back to the ranch house, seeing for the first time the damage to the roof. The corner section was torn. She was surprised that they hadn't had water in the living room upstairs.

When she went back inside, Pat was standing in her kitchen, freshly showered. Her wet hair was slicked back from her face. She had on long, baggy shorts which didn't cover the scratches on her knees.

"Let me see," Carly said, pulling Pat towards the window and the light. The swelling had gone down some, but the bruise was deeper now. Her wound appeared to be healing. There was no infection that she could tell. "How's the pain?" she asked.

"Bearable," Pat said. Her eyes searched Carly's. She remembered her dream from last night. It had seemed so real. Carly had come to her in the night, had covered her body with kisses. When she woke this morning, she still felt the lingering touch upon her breasts.

"What?" Carly asked as she met Pat's eyes.

Pat smiled slightly, but shook her head.

"Nothing. I was just remembering my dream," she said.

"Dream?" Carly saw the wistful look in Pat's eyes. So, Pat thought it had been a dream. *Great.* "Going to tell me about it?"

"Oh, no. It's too early to get you pissed off at me. Besides, there's no coffee."

"I won't get pissed off. I promise. Now tell me about your dream."

Pat swallowed, embarrassed. She shouldn't have said anything. But did it matter? Carly already knew how Pat felt about her. Surely she assumed that Pat had delicious fantasies about her.

"We made love," Pat said quietly. "Or, you made love to me," she clarified. "I don't remember participating."

Carly smiled. "Maybe that's because you fell asleep."

Pat's eyes widened.

"Wasn't really a dream, Pat."

"You made love to me?" Pat whispered. "You made love to me and I don't even remember it?"

"Trust me, we never really got that far."

"So, you just took advantage of me in my weakened state? You drugged me then had your way with me?" Pat teased.

"Yes. And had I known you were going to start something and not finish it, *again*, I would have only given you . . ."

"I'll finish it now," Pat interrupted. "I feel great. Not a bit sleepy."

"Sorry. The mood's passed."

Carly turned away, but Pat pulled her back around.

"You can't just tell me that you had your hands on me last night and expect to walk away."

"As I recall, you're the one that usually walks away."

Pat smiled shyly, meeting Carly's eyes.

"Was I enjoying it?" she asked.

"Oh, yeah."

"Were you?" Pat asked seriously.

Carly remembered the throbbing ache of her body, the way she'd pressed her hips into Pat, wanting release. The wanton way she'd straddled Pat, Pat's breasts in her mouth, Pat's hands on her own breasts. She felt the flush creep up her face. Was she enjoying it? God, yes.

"The next time you fall asleep on me while making love," Carly threatened quietly, "I'll dump you into the bay."

Pat grinned. "I have no intentions of ever getting dumped into the bay."

"Good. Because believe me, you'll pay for last night."

"Had you in a state, did I?"

"Yes," Carly admitted. "You did. And you don't even remember doing it."

"I remember you touching me. I just thought it had to be a dream."

"No. I'm just sorry you fell asleep."

Their eyes locked and Carly let Pat pull her the short distance towards her, the fire in her eyes mesmerizing Carly.

Carly moved into her arms, pressing against Pat, loving the way Pat's body felt next to her own. She lifted her head and met Pat's mouth, gentle and unhurried. She didn't want to respond, not now. Not when there was so much to do. But her body wouldn't listen. Pat's hands moved over her back, sliding to her hips and Carly moaned into Pat's mouth. It was too hard to fight these feelings and she let herself go. Her mouth opened, meeting Pat's tongue with her own. She remembered the softness of Pat's skin under her hands, sliding them under Pat's shirt now, feeling the warm smoothness under her fingers.

"I want you so much," Carly murmured. "You can't keep doing this to me."

Pat didn't answer. She couldn't. Carly's hands had found her breasts.

No bra. Carly moaned as her hands touched the soft swell of Pat's breasts, the hard nipples pressing into her palms. No time? They had all day. The cleanup would have to wait. Pat's hands at her hips pulled her closer still and Carly parted her legs, feeling Pat's hard thigh move against her. Their mouths were hungry and tongues dueled. Carly let herself go. She lifted Pat's shirt, her mouth immediately replacing her hands on Pat's breasts.

"Oh, God," Pat murmured. Her head fell back, her eyes closed against the pleasure of Carly's mouth at her breast.

Ringing interrupted their passion. Carly paused. Her cell phone. *Jesus, not now.*

"Please don't answer it," Pat whispered and she brought Carly's mouth back to her own.

But the ringing continued.

"It'll be Elsa or Martin," Carly said. "They'll be worried if I don't answer." She pulled away from Pat and snatched up the phone on the table. She paused to breathe, trying to gather herself, before answering.

"Good morning," Elsa said cheerfully.

"Morning," Carly said, trying to keep her voice even.

"What's wrong? You sound like you were running."

"I . . . ran up the stairs to catch the phone," Carly said, smiling at Pat who chuckled beside her.

"I assume you made it okay, then. Pat got back safely with the egrets?"

"Yes. How are things in town?"

"Power's out, but that was expected. Galveston got hit hard, but I think Port Aransas made it through okay."

"Good," Carly murmured. She couldn't think. Pat had moved behind her, pulling Carly against her body. She felt Pat's mouth move under her hair, wet lips moving over her neck. She trembled.

"We're coming out there. The roads are clear."

"Good." Then Pat's hands moved around her, cupping her breasts from behind and Carly only barely stifled a moan. She closed her eyes and leaned back against Pat, losing herself as Pat caressed her breasts.

"Are you okay?"

"Mmm," Carly breathed. Then she opened her eyes, trying to focus on Elsa. "Yes. We're fine," she said. Pat

239

was pressed hard against her and Carly let her hand fall, resting against Pat's thigh. She rubbed it gently. Then Pat's hand covered her own, moving it firmly, sliding it to the heat between Pat's legs.

The phone fell to the floor as Carly felt the wetness that soaked Pat's shorts. She turned in Pat's arms, facing her now and her mouth was immediately captured by Pat's.

"Carly?"

Carly ignored the tiny voice from the phone. Her hands moved over Pat, sliding to her hips, then down, cupping Pat intimately, again feeling the heat.

"Jesus, you're so wet," she murmured into Pat's mouth. "I'm going to go crazy if I don't get my hands on you."

"Carly?"

"*Christ!*" Carly pulled away again, picking up the phone. "I'm sorry. It fell," she said. "What is it?" she asked impatiently.

"What the hell is wrong with you?" Elsa demanded.

"Nothing. I'll see you when you get here."

"Fine. Do you need anything?"

"No! Wait, yes. Fish," she said as Pat's mouth found hers again.

"Fish?"

"For the egrets," she murmured before she disconnected. She tossed the phone on the table and grabbed Pat's hand, pulling her towards the bedroom. She pulled her shirt over her head, then reached for Pat's.

"Hurry. They're on their way."

Pat stared at Carly's exposed breasts. She was beautiful. Then she remembered last night. Remembered how Carly's breasts had looked in the shadows. No, it wasn't a dream. She went to Carly, pulling her into her arms, their mouths meeting again.

"We could wait," Pat offered. "There's not enough time. I don't want to hurry through this, Carly."

"I swear, if you stop this now, you'll be in the bay before they get here," Carly threatened. Her hands went to Pat's shorts, and she unbuttoned them, sliding the zipper down in one motion. She didn't care that Elsa and Martin were coming. She didn't care that they wouldn't have time to savor this. She wanted Pat. She *needed* her. Now.

Pat let her shorts fall and she stood nearly naked, watching as Carly's eyes darkened at the sight of her. No, they couldn't wait. Her own hands reached for Carly's shorts, pulling them down.

"Beautiful," she whispered. Her eyes rested on the only piece of clothing still covering Carly. Then her hands slipped inside the waistband of her panties, urging them downward.

Carly closed her eyes as Pat exposed her. Her chest rose and fell with each breath. Then she reached out, pushing away the last bit of clothing covering Pat, leaving her as naked as Carly was.

"My God," she murmured. She moved back to the bed, pulling Pat with her. Then Pat was covering her body and Carly opened her legs, surging up to meet Pat as she felt her weight upon her. Their kisses were slower now, not hurried. Pat's tongue traced Carly's lips before slipping inside. Carly took her, sucking her tongue, swallowing the groan that mingled with her own.

"Please touch me, Pat," Carly whispered. "Please."

Pat lifted up, supporting her weight with one arm and the other hand moved over Carly's breasts, then downward, touching damp curls. Carly's hips rose to meet her and Pat slid her fingers into her.

"Oh. . . *yes*," Carly breathed. She jerked up hard when Pat entered her and her hips moved, meeting Pat's thrusts. It had been too long. Carly had forgotten the feeling of another's touch upon her. Then she groaned loudly as Pat's mouth found her breast. Her nipple ached as Pat's tongue swirled around it, finally sucking it into her mouth. Carly's hips arched again and her own hands moved over Pat's warm flesh, into her still damp hair and held her close against her breast.

Pat was lost in the sensation of Carly's wetness. She felt the muscles contract against her fingers and she pulled out again, meeting each thrust of Carly's hips. She knew Carly was close to climaxing and with her thumb, she touched her swollen clit. That was all it took. Carly cried out, her hips moving hard against Pat's fingers. Pat left Carly's breast, moving to her mouth and catching the last of Carly's screams. Finally, she felt Carly's body relax against the bed, felt Carly's arms pull her tight.

Carly closed her eyes as she held Pat against her. Pat's fingers were still inside her. Carly squeezed her legs tight, holding them. It was too fast. Much too fast.

"Thank you for not making me throw you in the bay," Carly whispered. "But I still haven't had my hands on you. And I so want to touch you."

Pat rolled over, pulling Carly with her. Carly settled between her thighs, her mouth finding her breast before Pat could speak. Pat's hands slid up Carly's back. She couldn't remember a time when she'd wanted another's touch like she now wanted Carly's. Carly moved her mouth back to Pat's, kissing her lightly.

Carly leaned on her elbows, looking at Pat. Her eyes were closed. Carly smiled and pressed into her, feeling Pat's wetness as it coated her stomach. Her hands itched to touch her and she moved between them, wondering at how many years it had been since she'd touched someone like this. The few affairs she'd had were never like this. They were just a quick release then forgotten. With Pat, she would never forget.

Like silk through her fingers, she touched her. Pat moaned, her eyes opening and finding Carly's. Carly closed her own as her fingers slipped inside Pat. So warm. So wet.

"I had forgotten how it felt," she whispered. She pulled out, finding Pat swollen and she moved over her, teasing her. When Pat's hips moved against her, she entered her again, feeling Pat clutch her hand tightly between her thighs.

They both heard the car door slam at the same time. Pat whimpered as Carly pulled away from her.

"I don't believe this," Pat whispered. She pulled Carly's hand back to her, pressing it hard between her thighs. "Don't you dare leave me like this."

"Sweetheart, I'm so sorry," Carly murmured. She kissed Pat hard, part of her wanting to ignore Elsa and Martin and finish what they'd started. She let her fingers slide through Pat's wetness again. It wouldn't take long, she knew.

"Hello?" Elsa called from downstairs.

"*Christ!*" Carly rolled away from Pat, nearly laughing at the pained expression on Pat's face.

"I just can't catch a break, can I?" Pat murmured. Then she too got up, taking her clothes from Carly's outstretched hands.

"You deserve it for all the times you made me wait," Carly said. She pulled her T-shirt over her head then went to Pat and held her. "And you were right. We needed hours for this." She kissed her, letting her lips linger. And that was all it took. Her desire flared again and she groaned as she pulled away from Pat. "I can't keep my hands off you, you realize that, don't you?" She took Pat's hand and brought it to her lips, kissing it softly. "I want to make love to you. And I want to take hours doing it, until you're begging me to stop."

"You can't just tell me something like that and walk

away," Pat said. She reached for Carly and pulled her against her, kissing her hard.

"You guys up here?" Elsa called again.

"Get dressed," Carly said as she pulled away. "I promise I'll make it up to you."

She closed the door after her and Pat lay back down on the bed. So close. She had been so close. But she smiled. It didn't matter. It was enough to remember how it felt to be inside Carly, how it felt to bring her to orgasm. And later, tonight perhaps, they would have time to explore each other at leisure. Pat ached to know how Carly would taste. She groaned, imagining her mouth between Carly's thighs.

CHAPTER FORTY-EIGHT

"What's going on?" Elsa asked when Carly met her on the stairs.

"Just . . . getting dressed," she said. It wasn't a lie. "How were the roads?"

"Good. A lot of trees down. We saw a barn that was completely lost out off 39."

Carly nodded. "Fish?"

Elsa held up a bag.

"Where's Pat?"

"She's . . . ah . . . she'll be down in a minute. Why don't you help me feed the egrets," Carly suggested. "Where's Martin?"

"He went to check on the barn." Elsa followed Carly back down the stairs, finally taking her arm to stop her when they entered the kitchen. "What's going on? You're acting strange."

"I'm not acting strange. I'm just . . . tired. Didn't sleep much last night, with the storm and all."

"Uh huh."

"Really."

"And how did Pat sleep?"

"She slept fine. In fact, I gave her a pain pill and she was out."

"A pain pill? What happened?"

"She got hit in the head with a limb."

"*Dios mio!* I told you it was too dangerous to be out. *Estupido!* She could have been killed!"

"Don't you think I know that?"

"What's all the yelling?" Pat asked from the doorway.

"Jesus! Look at you . . . *porbrecita*," Elsa murmured with a shake of her head. She walked to Pat, gently touching her bruised cheek. "Stitches? You let her give you stitches?"

Pat met Carly's eyes and smiled, still seeing the lingering desire there.

"She didn't exactly give me a choice," Pat said. "In fact, she tied me down and had her way with me."

"I most certainly did not. If I'd had you tied down, I'd have stitched your mouth shut as well."

"Well, I see nothing's changed with you two," Elsa said.

Pat and Carly exchanged glances again, then Carly lifted the towel off the egrets. Twin mouths opened immediately.

"I know you're hungry. Tia Elsa brought you some lunch," she cooed.

"*Dios mio*, they're ugly," Elsa said as she peered into the box, looking at two fuzzy white birds with abnormally large heads. In fact, most of their body consisted of long black bills. Then she looked at Pat. "You risked your life to save *them*?"

246

"Yes, I did. They were just so helpless out there. They would have been killed."

"*You* could have been killed," Elsa said.

Pat shrugged. "But I wasn't."

She watched as Carly cut the fish into small pieces, then smiled as the hungry birds snatched it up. She touched the bruise on her cheek. Yes, it was all worth it.

"Where's Martin?" she asked.

"Outside checking the damage."

"I think I'll join him," Pat said. "Been cooped up long enough. Besides, I want to get some shots," she said, holding up her camera.

Carly grabbed her arm as she walked past.

"Be careful. Don't do any bending or lifting," Carly said. "Your cheek, it'll just start throbbing again."

"Are you threatening me with another pain pill, Dr. Cambridge?"

"No. We certainly can't have a repeat of last night," she teased.

"No, we can't." Pat flicked her eyes to Elsa who was listening to their every word. She stepped closer to Carly and whispered, "Because I want my mouth on you tonight."

Then she walked away, leaving a stunned Carly staring after her. Carly squeezed her eyes shut against the vision of Pat lying between her legs, bringing her to orgasm with her mouth. *Dios Mio.*

She knew Elsa was watching her as she went back to feeding the egrets. Knowing Elsa, it wouldn't last long.

"Oh my God," Elsa said.

"What?"

"You had sex."

"What are you talking about?" Carly said, trying to sound offended.

"You're blushing. You never could lie worth a damn."

Carly raised her eyes, intending to deny it, but when she met Elsa's amused eyes, she smiled and nodded.

"Well?"

"Well what?"

"Details," Elsa demanded.

"I will not. And not one word in front of Pat. I mean it."

"You are so cute." Then her eyes widened. "Oh, God! When we drove up? When you didn't come down?"

"Yes. Are you happy now?"

"Yes. I'm happy now." Elsa walked over and hugged Carly hard. "I knew she was the one," Elsa said.

"The one? I think that's a bit premature, Elsa."

"No. She makes you laugh. She makes you happy. And you probably don't even know it, but Pat's eyes light up each and every time she looks at you."

"Elsa, if I tell you something, you promise you won't overreact?"

"Me?"

"Yes, you."

"I promise."

"Pat doesn't intend for this to be a . . . passing affair. In fact, she wouldn't even sleep with me unless I knew what the stakes were," she said. "I could fall in love with her, Elsa. It would be so easy. But what if it ends? I'm not sure I could manage again."

Elsa smiled sweetly at her. "You're already in love with her, Carly."

Carly hung her head. "If I don't say the words, I can still believe that I'm not," she said quietly. "It hurts. Just the thought of losing her hurts."

"You've just begun. Why are you insisting that it will end?"

"Because that's what happens with me," she said.

"It happened once," Elsa reminded her.

"And I can't go through it again. I promised myself I would never let anyone get inside me again."

"It's too late, Carly. She is inside you."

"Yes, I know she is."

CHAPTER FORTY-NINE

"Hey, Martin," Pat greeted. He was walking around the barn, checking for damage.

"Pat." Then, "Good God, what happened to you?"

"Oh, had a run-in with an oak limb," she said. "But I'm okay."

"Elsa said you were out trying to rescue the egrets," he said. "Is that when it happened?"

"Yes. Foolish, I know. But we'd gotten kinda attached to them."

"Dr. Cambridge made you go out?"

"No, no. It was my idea. Not her fault." Then Pat looked at the old barn. "Any damage?"

"Lost a section of roof on the back side, but other than that, it looks okay."

"You think it's too wet to take your truck out and start on the limbs?" she asked.

"Probably. But we can at least pick them up around the house and the Visitor's Center. Those we can lift anyway. Tomorrow I'll take the chainsaw out and start on the trees."

"What are we going to do with it all? Burn it?"

"The branches, yes. But the trees and larger limbs, we can sell to one of the firewood places. Won't get much for it, but at least it won't go to waste."

"Maybe they would come out and cut it," Pat suggested.

"Normally, yes. But after a storm like this, they'll have more business than they can handle."

They walked back to the house just as Elsa and Carly walked out.

"Well?"

"Just lost part of the roof. That can be easily fixed. I see the ranch house had a problem with the roof, too," Martin said, pointing.

"Yes. But I think it's superficial. I don't believe we had any water inside."

"Well, Pat and I were just discussing starting on the downed limbs. At least around here and the Visitor's Center."

Carly looked around. It seemed an impossible job. The ground was literally covered with limbs and branches. But they had to start somewhere.

For the next several hours, they loaded Martin's truck time and again, but they had hardly made a dent. Pat was helping, despite Carly's objections. She had wandered around with her camera for awhile, but then she insisted on helping. And now, she could see the pain in Pat's face, but she still refused to stop. Carly finally went to her and touched her arm lightly.

"Why don't you stop? I can see you're in pain."

"I want to help," she said stubbornly.

"Yes, I know. But I have plans for you tonight. What good will you be if I have to give you a pain pill?"

"Dr. Cambridge, are you planning on having your way with me?"

"Yes, I am. And I want you fully awake."

"Then maybe I should lie down now and rest up, huh?"

"I think that's a wonderful idea."

Pat captured her eyes, seeing the simmering desire that Carly didn't try to hide.

"You look at me like that and I just want to drag you inside with me," Pat whispered.

"Martin and Elsa might object," Carly said.

"I don't think Martin or Elsa would even know," she said, motioning with her head. Martin and Elsa were locked in an embrace on the other side of his truck.

Carly shook her head and smiled. It appeared Elsa had finally found her Mr. Right.

"Go inside and rest," Carly said. "You should probably call Rachel, too."

"Yes. I'll check in with her."

"Are you okay, really?" Carly asked.

"It's throbbing again," Pat admitted. "But nothing like last night."

"It's from all the bending over," Carly said. She reached out and touched Pat's face, feeling for a fever. But her skin was cool. She met Pat's eyes, again wanting nothing more than to drown in them. She pulled Pat to her and touched her lips lightly.

"Now you've done it," Pat whispered. She pulled Carly into her arms and kissed her, her mouth opening to Carly, meeting her tongue with her own.

Carly dropped the limb she was holding and wrapped her arms around Pat's shoulders, pulling her close. She simply could not resist this woman.

"Excuse me! I thought we were working here," Elsa called.

Carly pulled away guiltily. She had forgotten they were not alone. And the night could not come soon enough.

"Go inside before I really embarrass myself," Carly urged. "You're not safe."

"Don't work yourself to death, Carly. I have some plans of my own tonight."

Carly watched her walk away, her stride so confident and sure, her back straight. She was magnificent to look at, but it was her personality that Carly had fallen in love with. Her outside beauty was just a bonus.

Did I just say that? In love? Yes.

"Not trying to keep it a secret, huh?" Elsa said as she walked up to her. Martin drove off with another load.

"I can't seem to keep my hands off her," Carly admitted.

"Well how could you? She's a goddess."

Carly smiled. Yes, she was. And she was *her* goddess.

"And I saw you sucking face with Martin."

Elsa blushed. "Sucking face? That is so gross."

Carly laughed. "Martin seemed to be enjoying it."

"Yes, he was."

"So, are you going to tell me what's going on with you two?"

"We're . . . seeing each other," Elsa said.

"I gathered as much. What else?"

"Well there's no wedding planned, if that's what you're getting at."

"Are you in love with him?"

"I think I am," Elsa admitted. "He, however, has said no such thing."

Carly saw the sadness in Elsa's eyes and she squeezed her arm.

"Give him time," Carly suggested.

"It's ironic, isn't it? The first man I've met that I think could be husband material and he's only interested in sex."

Carly tried to think of some advice to give, but she had none. What did she know about it?

"Give him time," Carly said again. "Martin is an honorable man. Maybe he thinks all you want is sex."

"It's not like we jumped into bed the first time we went out."

Carly raised her eyebrows but said nothing.

"Okay, maybe the second," Elsa admitted. "But I liked him."

"And maybe that's why he thinks that's all you want," Carly said gently. "Maybe he's afraid you'll run if he suggests more."

"You really have no clue about men, do you? It's the man who runs when the woman mentions the "L" word. Besides, he's been married before. He's probably scared to death of me."

"What I just saw was not scared to death," Carly said.

They heard Martin's truck approach and they went back to picking up limbs, Carly's thoughts on her two friends. She wanted Elsa to be happy. She had been single for as long as Carly had known her, dating several men but never finding the one that she wanted. At least she had not settled on anything less.

Her thoughts suddenly went to Carol, trying to remember how their relationship had even started. How they had ended up moving in together. She had been so blind to everything. She had never had a relationship before, not even with a man when she still thought she was straight. Her studies were always more important.

She never gave thought as to why she didn't find any of the boys in her high school attractive. And even in college, she had buried herself in books and studying, she never thought about dating. Her friendship with Carol was just that, nothing else. But suddenly, Carol had offered her more and she took it, finally realizing why men had never attracted her. She had no concept of what a perfect mate should be. There was only Carol.

It happened so fast, she hadn't had time to analyze it. She had simply wanted to make Carol happy. But no matter how much she spent on her, how much she helped with Carol's studies, it was never enough. Carol always wanted more. And Carly tried to give it to her. A house. A new car. She never stopped to consider her own wants and needs.

She should be thankful Carol had only used her for four years and then moved on. What if she had stuck around longer, continuing her affair on the side? Would Carly have ever known?

And now Pat was offering her something again. Friendship, love. It felt so different with Pat. And Carly admitted that it also felt right. Pat didn't want anything from her except friendship and love in return. There was no underlying agenda. She wasn't using her for personal gain. Pat just wanted . . . her. Nothing more. And Carly so wanted to give herself to Pat. But she was still afraid. She knew that she wouldn't survive if Pat ended up hurting her. If she gave herself to Pat, that would be it. There would be no going back. Could she trust Pat with her life?

"Yes."

CHAPTER FIFTY

"So, you didn't blow away?" Pat asked.

"About time you checked on your old aunt. I could have been blown to San Antonio by now."

"I've been busy," Pat said.

"Yes, I figured. Have you slept with her yet?"

"I can't believe you just asked me that! We were stranded. We barely survived the storm and you're thinking about sex."

"Does that mean yes?"

"I'm not going to answer you."

"That means yes. I'm so happy for you. About time you got laid."

"Aunt Rachel!"

"Oh, please. Give an old woman a little excitement."

"Okay. I'll give you details when I see you," Pat

said with a smile. "Now, how are things at your place?"

"Only lost one tree. That old oak at the edge of the property. I'll have a better view of the bay now, at least."

"Do you need help? Or has Alice called your 'crew' in again."

"Yes, they've already taken the shutters off and cut up the tree."

"I assume you're still without power?"

"Yes, but they've restored it on the north side. Alice is going to run out and pick up dinner. That is, if she can get in. There are only two restaurants open."

"Okay. Well, I guess I'm going to stay here again tonight," Pat said. "I'll make a run to the island in the morning."

"And how is everything there, Pat? No major damage?"

"No. Just trees."

"Very well. I hope you'll come by tomorrow when you're in town."

"I will. I'm sure I'll be starving by then. Let Alice know."

Pat tossed her cell phone down and stretched out on the sofa. Her face was throbbing and she'd swallowed a couple of ibuprofen. Hopefully that would help. No way was she taking a pain pill. Not when Carly had plans for her.

She grinned as her eyes closed. It had happened so fast, really. Her gentle courting had been rebuffed easily by Carly. At least on the outside. But Carly's eyes didn't lie. And the storm had thrown them together, giving them a chance to be alone. A chance to explore their feelings. She wondered if Carly had accepted what was happening between them yet. Physically, yes. That was obvious. But emotionally, she wondered if Carly was still trying to keep her distance.

"Doesn't matter," Pat murmured. "I can see it in her eyes."

And that was how Carly and Elsa found her later, stretched out on the sofa and sound asleep.

"Look at that, she's adorable," Elsa whispered.

"Yes, she is," Carly agreed. She let her eyes linger on the long legs that were crossed at the ankles. Then she moved to Pat's face, noting how peaceful she looked in sleep, even with the bruise.

They went into the kitchen and made sandwiches. Carly left Pat's on the table, wrapped in foil. The others, they took downstairs to join Martin. Carly grabbed one of the bags of chips on her way out.

"I should really feed the egrets," Carly said.

"Eat first," Elsa said. "You must be starving."

"So must they. Go on out. It'll just take me a minute."

She unwrapped the fish and turned her face away. It was already beginning to smell. She wished she had thought to ask them to bring some ice. But she was lucky she had even remembered the fish. The two birds were indeed starved. They took the fish easily from her hands and she knew she needed to get them outside soon. She couldn't just keep them in the box indefinitely. Maybe Martin could rig up some sort of cage for her.

Martin had pulled the lawn chairs back out and they sat under the oaks and ate. The sun had finally broken through the clouds and the day seemed almost normal.

"It's so nice out," Carly mused. "Hard to believe that yesterday a storm was raging."

"Yes. I can't believe the sun is out." Elsa said.

"I really appreciate you coming out today. It would have been a great day to stay inside and lounge around."

"Not without electricity and AC," Elsa said. "Besides, we've got to get this cleaned up sooner or later."

"Speaking of that, Martin, will you call around and see about getting the large limbs picked up? I know you said something about firewood."

"I'll call, but they will be swamped with offers. We may have to move it ourselves."

Carly shrugged. "Oh well. We can haul it out back for now. It won't hurt anything. I just don't want to spend a lot of time on that. We need to get the marsh drained and planted. And I'm sure it will be at least a week before it's dry enough for them to get their equipment back out."

"How will we drain the marsh?" Martin asked.

"I'll have to hire someone from one of the rigs. We'll pump it back into the bay," she said.

"And the cost?" Elsa asked.

"Outrageous. I don't even want to think about it. But it's got to be done."

They rested a bit longer, then went back to work. Carly swore her back would never be the same after bending over all day. The only thing that kept her spirits up was knowing that later, after a shower, she and Pat would be alone.

It was nearly four when Carly called a halt to their labor. They would be totally exhausted tomorrow if they didn't stop.

"Let's call it a day, guys," she said.

"I won't argue with that," Elsa said.

They were still working around the Visitor's Center, but they had made good progress. Carly then saw a familiar figure walking towards them. And a freshly showered one, if the wet hair was any indication.

"Damn, you're a slave driver, Dr. Cambridge. I doubt they'll even come back tomorrow," Pat teased.

"I doubt I'll even be able to get out of bed in the morning," Elsa complained.

"And I doubt this will be the reason," Carly said with a smile. Elsa blushed, then looked at Martin, hoping he hadn't heard.

"How was your cold shower?" Carly asked Pat.

"Refreshing. You ought to try it."

"What are you saying?"

"I should have brought my camera out. This would make a great shot for the next brochure."

"I told you before, I will not be in the brochure."

"And I told you before, people want to know who is spending their money. In their mind, they see old Mrs. Davenport and they hesitate. But if they saw you, they'd think you were totally sexy and would open up their wallets."

"You are so full of shit," Carly said.

"It's true."

"I think it's a good idea," Elsa said.

"Oh, no. Not you, too? I will not be in the damn brochure."

"Can I still take your picture?" Pat asked.

"No, you may not. And you must be feeling better. Your mouth has not stopped moving since you've been out here."

Pat grinned. "Well, that's a good thing, right?"

Carly blushed and walked past Pat, playfully hitting her stomach as she passed.

"Do I even want to know what that was all about?" Elsa asked.

"No," Carly tossed over her shoulder.

CHAPTER FIFTY-ONE

When Carly stepped out of the bathroom, clad in clean shorts, a T-shirt and wet hair, she found Pat in the kitchen, making them sandwiches.

"I'm going to hate sandwiches by the time this is all over with," Carly said.

"Me, too. I'm thinking a bowl of gumbo would hit the spot."

"And fried shrimp," Carly added.

"I'm starving."

"Me, too."

Pat pointed to the table. "I made you a drink. Bourbon. But there's no ice."

"I don't care." Carly settled at the table and lifted the glass, then paused. "I should really go feed the egrets."

"I did it. The fish smells like hell, though. I

doubt we'll be able to stand touching it in the morning."

"I'll need to go into town anyway. I've got to get something to keep them in," she said.

"Pet store?"

"No. I'll go to one of the vets in town and borrow a cage."

"You think they'll make it?"

"Yes. There're old enough. Another two weeks, maybe, then we can let them go."

"You think the parents will come back?"

Carly shrugged. "Maybe. I hope so. It would be nice, wouldn't it?"

"Yes." Pat looked at her damp hair, already nearly dry and reached across the table to brush it away from Carly's face. Their eyes met as Pat's fingers brushed across Carly's cheek. "Why are we making small talk?"

"Because I thought it would be uncivilized if I just dragged you back to the bedroom right away."

"Is that what you want to do?"

Carly blushed. "I've thought of little else all day."

Pat nodded. "Me, too."

"Do you find it amusing?" Carly asked.

"What?"

"That I can't seem to control myself around you. That I can't keep my hands off you," she said quietly.

"Amusing? No, I find it to be exciting, refreshing," Pat said. "In case you haven't noticed, I can't exactly keep my hands off you, either."

"I never thought this would happen to me, Pat," Carly admitted. "The first day I met you, I knew you were dangerous. I tried so hard to keep you away."

"I know. But I didn't want to be kept away."

"I still can't promise you anything, Pat."

"Can't or won't?"

"Please don't make me," Carly whispered. "I'm scared of what I feel for you."

"You know I'm in love with you, don't you?"

Carly squeezed her eyes shut and looked away. "Please don't say that."

"Is it easier for you to pretend that I'm not? That way, it can just be sex between us? No real ties?"

"I'm scared you'll hurt me," Carly admitted.

"So I shouldn't tell you that I want to wake up with you for the rest of my life?"

"Oh, Pat," Carly whispered. She took Pat's hand and squeezed it, finally meeting her eyes. "You don't know what you're asking of me."

"Yes, I do."

They sat quietly at the table with hands clasped between them for long moments, their eyes meeting then pulling away. Finally, Pat stirred.

"You know what I'd like to do?"

"Hmm?"

"Catch the sunset," Pat said. "There's this great little spot on Goose Island that looks out over Copano Bay. I think we can make it in time," she said.

CHAPTER FIFTY-TWO

Pat turned down the dirt road, ignoring the 'Private Property' sign. The road escaped the oak mottes and ended right at the bay. They both got out and stood in front of Pat's Jeep, eyes turned to the west as the sun hovered over the bay.

Then Pat pulled Carly in front of her and leaned against the Jeep, holding Carly lightly from behind. Carly's hands came up and covered Pat's at her waist and she sighed contentedly. They said nothing, just watched as the sun dipped lower in the sky, turning the bay a brilliant orange. Then, as the sun touched the water, a rosy red replaced the orange, shimmering in the waves, only to be replaced by a gentle pink glow where the sun had been only moments before.

For the first time that Pat could remember, she

didn't itch to hold her camera. She was holding all that she needed. Carly.

"That was beautiful," Carly whispered.

"Yes, it was."

They remained that way, looking out over the bay as the pink faded from the sky. Finally, Pat moved, turning Carly in her arms to face her.

"Yesterday, a storm was raging . . . today, we're blessed with a beautiful sunset. No matter what happens, the sun still comes and goes as planned, doesn't it?"

Carly nodded, her eyes locked on Pat's.

"You know, it's funny. All these years, I had given up on finding someone. I mean, I'm thirty-six. I figured I was destined to be alone. It's not that I never looked, you know. I did. But I was always looking for someone that could be there for me. I always imagined the perfect someone that would be a part of my life. I never really considered what I would be to them. It was always about me.

But I find myself wanting to be the perfect someone for *you*. I want to be your hero. I want to be your rock. I want to be there for you to lean on. I find what I need is to be needed — by you. To be *trusted* by you. Everything I imagined in my life before seems so shallow compared to what I feel in my heart for you, Carly. I never thought I could truly love someone. It wasn't a part of my life. But I so want to love you, Carly."

Carly let her tears fall. She no longer cared if Pat saw them. She reached out a gentle hand and touched Pat's face, surprised to find dampness there as well. Her heart broke. This wonderful, proud woman loved her. How could she deny that? How could she possibly run from this?

"You're just a romantic fool, aren't you?" Carly whispered.

"Yes."

Carly leaned forward and kissed Pat, softly, gently, without the raging passion that normally consumed them. This kiss was totally about love . . . and the joining of souls.

"Take me home, Pat. I want to make love to you. I *need* to make love to you."

CHAPTER FIFTY-THREE

Carly placed the oil lamp on the table beside them. She was actually nervous. This was no longer about sex. It was about love.

Pat stood beside her, fully clothed, as was she. Pat, too, seemed nervous. Carly went to her and wrapped her arms around her and held her. Just held her, this woman who wanted to be her hero, her rock. Carly's heart swelled with love, so much so that she was sure it would burst in her chest. She wanted to cry . . . she wanted to laugh. She wanted to make love to this woman.

She finally pulled away, finding Pat's mouth. The slow kiss quickly turned hungry as their bodies pressed together and hands moved freely over the other.

"You have no idea how much I want you right now," Carly murmured into Pat's mouth. She pulled Pat's shirt from her shorts and found warm skin, her hands moving up to her breasts. She pushed her bra aside, cupping her breasts, fingers moving over nipples.

Pat moaned, finally stepping away and pulling her shirt and bra over her head. Then Carly's hands found her again as their mouths joined and mated.

"Take it off, please," Pat murmured, tugging at Carly's shirt.

"No, no, no. It's my turn," she whispered. Her hands went to Pat's shorts, sliding them down her legs impatiently. "Lay down. Let me make love to you. Please?"

Pat trembled at the desire she saw in Carly's eyes. She obeyed without question, sinking onto the bed, her eyes never leaving Carly's. Then Carly pulled her own shirt off and Pat reached out a hand to touch her.

"No. It's my turn," Carly said again. She finished undressing, then went to Pat, kneeling down before her. She slowly slid Pat's panties over her hips and down to her ankles, tossing them on the floor with the rest of her clothing.

"You're so beautiful . . . it should be a crime," Carly murmured as her hands moved gently over Pat's body. "So beautiful. I can't believe you want to give this to me," she whispered.

"Please come here," Pat whispered. She pulled Carly on top of her, settling her weight between her legs. "You say I'm beautiful, when you have no idea how breathtaking you are."

Then there was no time for words as their mouths joined again. Pat's hands strayed, moving over Carly's body so fervently, but Carly grabbed them both, holding them captive over Pat's head. Carly's mouth dipped lower, finding Pat's breast, sucking her nipple inside. She feasted, knowing she would never get enough.

Pat arched into her, loving the feeling of Carly at her breast. Her hands ached to touch her, ached to be inside her, but Carly still held them tightly. Then Carly pressed her hips into Pat, rubbing against her intimately and Pat surged up to meet her, rising off the bed as they touched.

Carly finally released Pat's hands, moving down her body, tasting every inch of her. She wanted to be between her thighs, she wanted to taste the most intimate part of Pat.

Pat threw her head back in surrender as Carly moved down her body. Her hips arched, searching, wanting Carly's mouth on her.

Carly spread Pat's legs, seeing her glistening curls in the shadows of the oil lamp. She closed her eyes and groaned, knowing she would never be the same if she took Pat this way. It no longer mattered. Pat had already taken her heart.

Pat cried out when Carly's mouth found her. She clutched at the bed sheets, her eyes squeezed tight against the pleasure. Then Carly's tongue moved through her wetness, finding her swollen and ready. Carly's lips took her inside, sucking hard against her and Pat rose off the bed, her hips unable to remain still. Then Carly slowed, her tongue again moving through her, finally plunging inside her.

"Oh, dear *God*," Pat murmured. Her hands reached out and grabbed Carly's head, holding her firmly to her as her hips undulated against her mouth.

Carly was delirious with pleasure as her mouth feasted on Pat. So wet, so sweet. She felt her own wetness soaking the bed, felt the throbbing ache between her own thighs. Her tongue pulled out of Pat and Carly's lips found her again, sucking her hard. She struggled to hold Pat down, her hands pressing against Pat's hips as she held her legs apart. Then she felt Pat still, heard her breath catch and hold, then Pat rose up again, one last time, screaming out her pleasure as she climaxed against Carly's mouth.

Pat laid back, pulling Carly up her body, knowing Carly needed her own release. She felt as Carly straddled her thigh, felt her wetness coat her as Carly ground into her hard. Pat's hand moved between them, finding Carly wet and ready. She touched her, stroking her as Carly pressed against her thigh.

Carly felt Pat's hand on her and she reached for it, grinding against her fingers as she sought release. She bent her head low to capture Pat's lips and she came instantly, crying out into Pat's mouth.

She finally collapsed on top of Pat, letting her weight settle over her. She felt Pat's arms come around her, gently caressing her back as her lips moved over her face.

Carly finally pulled away, resting her weight on her arms. She met Pat's eyes and she smiled. Then she bent her head and kissed her softly, gently.

"Oh, Pat . . . I love you," she whispered, so quietly, she wasn't sure Pat had even heard her.

"And I love you with all my heart," Pat whispered back. "I want to love you for the rest of my life."

"Yes. I think I'd like that."

Pat kissed her again, then quickly rolled over, pinning Carly beneath her.

"You know what I'd like? I'd like to make love to you for the rest of the night," she murmured, her lips trailing kisses over her breasts, then finally lower, to where Carly needed her the most.

CHAPTER FIFTY-FOUR

"I think that was taken in my front yard," she told Rachel. "In fact, I'm certain it was. I wonder why it's not mentioned in the caption?"

Pat glared at Mrs. Davenport as she made her way around the Visitor's Center, looking at the framed prints that adorned the walls.

"It was taken here," Pat insisted.

"You probably don't even know what it is."

"I most certainly do. It's a . . ." *Shit!* What was it again? Sandpiper something or other. *Oh, goddamn it!* They all looked alike.

"As I suspected, you have no idea. It's a long-billed dowitcher. They often winter in my yard, by the pond. And this looks suspiciously like it."

"It was taken at the pond out here," Pat said. "Not in your damn yard."

"Now, Pat," Aunt Rachel said. "Is that any way to talk to Mrs. Davenport? After all she's done for you?"

Pat looked appropriately chastised as she glared at the old woman. It wasn't enough that four of the prints mentioned Mrs. Davenport's pond. Now she wanted to claim credit for others.

"I apologize. The ones I took at your pond are farther down the hall there," she said as sweetly as she could.

She let them walk off without her, rolling her eyes at the old woman's outrageous outfit. She glanced around the crowded Visitor's Center. It would be opened to the public next week, but today they had invited the local birders who had helped them throughout the last year and a handful of donors who had contributed large sums of money to this project, Mrs. Davenport included.

She walked to a window, looking out at the bright sunshine. The old road to the bay was now paved, as was the road to the new marshes. And the marsh looked good, she had to admit. The native grasses they had planted had taken hold, as had the reeds. She spotted two white birds and she smiled. Their egrets, no doubt. They had released them back at the pond and she and Carly both cried when the parents returned. They had spent nearly every evening out there watching the four birds, watching as the parents taught the young to fish. The two young had finally moved to the marsh, but the parents stayed at the pond, hopefully to nest again.

She turned back to the room, scanning the crowd. She found Elsa and Martin talking quietly in one corner. She smiled as she caught the sparkle of Elsa's engagement ring. She moved away from them, her eyes searching, finally finding Carly as she talked to three men in suits. Board members. And they looked completely out of place among the birders.

Carly glanced up, feeling Pat's eyes on her. She smiled warmly at her lover, then excused herself. She hadn't talked to Pat since early that morning.

"Hi, love," she whispered. "Having fun?"

"Mingling with birders . . . my very favorite thing in the world," Pat teased.

"I've missed you," Carly said. "Have you been showing Mrs. Davenport around?"

"God, yes. Much more of this and I'll need therapy. I'm convinced the woman is trying to drive me insane."

"You may be right. She certainly enjoys baiting you."

"How much longer?" Pat asked, glancing again at the suits.

"Not long. I'm sure they'll be heading back in an hour or so."

"Well, that's too long," she murmured. "I haven't kissed you all day." She took Carly's hand and pulled her behind the counter and into the storage room. She shut the door firmly behind her.

"Well, this is subtle," Carly teased. "I'm sure no one has a clue."

"Hush," Pat said, silencing Carly with a kiss.

Carly melted into her embrace, her fingers sliding into Pat's silky hair. When Pat grabbed her hips and pulled her against her, Carly felt the now familiar stirring of desire. It had been nearly a year and she still couldn't keep her hands off this woman. She let her hands slip lower, cupping Pat's breasts. Pat moaned into her mouth and Carly squeezed gently.

"Don't tempt me," Pat threatened. "I just wanted to kiss you."

"Then you shouldn't have touched me," Carly whispered into her mouth. She pushed Pat against the counter, her hands moving lower, resting on the heat between Pat's thighs.

"Carly, don't," Pat said, but her hips moved against Carly's hand anyway. God, this woman could drive her to the edge in seconds.

"But I want to." She unbuttoned Pat's shorts and slipped her hand inside, finding the wetness she knew would greet her. "Always so wet for me." She slid her fingers against Pat, moving through silk to reach her goal. "I love you so much, Pat," she whispered.

Pat met her thrust as Carly slipped inside her. She tried to stifle her groan but couldn't. Her hips moved faster now against Carly's hand. She pulled Carly into her arms, settling her lips against Carly's mouth, trying to muffle the sounds of pleasure that she could no longer keep in.

Carly's wet fingers found her clit, swollen and ready. Pat jerked against her, her teeth biting gently into her neck and Carly was lost. She groaned as she moved faster over Pat, stroking her to orgasm. She felt Pat arch and her mouth went to Pat's, catching her screams.

They stood leaning against each other, both breathing heavily. She finally pulled her hand away, moving under Pat's shirt and wiping the wetness against Pat's skin. Like always, she wished they had more time.

"Please let me touch you," Pat whispered, her hands sliding to Carly's waist. "I know you want me to. I know how wet you are."

Carly tilted her head back as Pat's lips moved over her neck. Yes, she was wet. Yes, she wanted Pat to touch her. But there was no time.

"No. I've got to get back," Carly said, stopping Pat's hands before they went inside her shorts.

"That's not fair. You can't just do that to me and then walk away."

"Of course I can." Carly kissed her quickly, the pulled away.

"Carly . . ."

"Hmm?"

"I love you, you know."

Carly stopped at the door, a soft smile on her face. Then she walked back to Pat and kissed her again, gently this time.

"I love you, too. I'm so glad you came into my life," she whispered.

Pat smiled softly.

"When we run everyone out of here, we'll turn the phones off, right?"

"If that's what you want."

"It is. Because tonight . . . no interruptions. You're mine."

Carly reached out and touched Pat's face. "I'll be yours forever."

About The Author

Gerri lives in the Piney Woods of East Texas with her partner, Diane and their two labs, Zach and Max. The resident cats Alex, Sierra and Tori round out the household. Hobbies include any outdoor activity, from tending the orchard and vegetable garden to hiking in the woods with camera and binoculars. For more, visit Gerri's website at: www.gerrihill.com

THE NEXT WORLD by Ursula Steck. 240 pp. Anna's friend Mido is threatened and eventually disappears . . .   1-59493-024-4 $12.95

CALL SHOTGUN by Jaime Clevenger. 240 pp. Kelly gets pulled back into the world of private investigation . . .   1-59493-016-3 $12.95

52 PICKUP by Bonnie J. Morris and E.B. Casey. 240 pp. 52 hot, romantic tales—one for every Saturday night of the year.   1-59493-026-0 $12.95

GOLD FEVER by Lyn Denison. 240 pp. Kate's first love, Ashley, returns to their home town, where Kate now lives . . .   1-1-59493-039-2 $12.95

RISKY INVESTMENT by Beth Moore. 240 pp. Lynn's best friend and roommate needs her to pretend Chris is his fiancé. But nothing is ever easy.   1-59493-019-8 $12.95

HUNTER'S WAY by Gerri Hill. 240 pp. Homicide detective Tori Hunter is forced to team up with the hot-tempered Samantha Kennedy.   1-59493-018-X $12.95

CAR POOL by Karin Kallmaker. 240 pp. Soft shoulders, merging traffic and slippery when wet . . . Anthea and Shay find love in the car pool.   1-59493-013-9 $12.95

NO SISTER OF MINE by Jeanne G'Fellers. 240 pp. Telepathic women fight to coexist with a patriarchal society that wishes their eradication.   ISBN 1-59493-017-1 $12.95

ON THE WINGS OF LOVE by Megan Carter. 240 pp. Stacie's reporting career is on the rocks. She has to interview bestselling author Cheryl, or else!   ISBN 1-59493-027-9 $12.95

WICKED GOOD TIME by Diana Tremain Braund. 224 pp. Does Christina need Miki as a protector . . . or want her as a lover?   ISBN 1-59493-031-7 $12.95

THOSE WHO WAIT by Peggy J. Herring. 240 pp. Two brilliant sisters—in love with the same woman!   ISBN 1-59493-032-5 $12.95

ABBY'S PASSION by Jackie Calhoun. 240 pp. Abby's bipolar sister helps turn her world upside down, so she must decide what's most important.   ISBN 1-59493-014-7 $12.95

PICTURE PERFECT by Jane Vollbrecht. 240 pp. Kate is reintroduced to Casey, the daughter of an old friend. Can they withstand Kate's career?   ISBN 1-59493-015-5 $12.95

PAPERBACK ROMANCE by Karin Kallmaker. 240 pp. Carolyn falls for tall, dark and . . . female . . . in this classic lesbian romance.   ISBN 1-59493-033-3 $12.95

DAWN OF CHANGE by Gerri Hill. 240 pp. Susan ran away to find peace in remote Kings Canyon—then she met Shawn . . .   ISBN 1-59493-011-2 $12.95

DOWN THE RABBIT HOLE by Lynne Jamneck. 240 pp. Is a killer holding a grudge against FBI Agent Samantha Skellar?   ISBN 1-59493-012-0 $12.95

SEASONS OF THE HEART by Jackie Calhoun. 240 pp. Overwhelmed, Sara saw only one way out—leaving . . .   ISBN 1-59493-030-9 $12.95

TURNING THE TABLES by Jessica Thomas. 240 pp. The 2nd Alex Peres Mystery. *From ghosties and ghoulies and long leggity beasties* . . .   ISBN 1-59493-009-0 $12.95

FOR EVERY SEASON by Frankie Jones. 240 pp. Andi, who is investigating a 65-year-old murder, meets Janice, a charming district attorney . . .   ISBN 1-59493-010-4 $12.95

LOVE ON THE LINE by Laura DeHart Young. 240 pp. Kay leaves a younger woman behind to go on a mission to Alaska . . . will she regret it?   ISBN 1-59493-008-2 $12.95

UNDER THE SOUTHERN CROSS by Claire McNab. 200 pp. Lee, an American travel agent, goes down under and meets Australian Alex, and the sparks fly under the Southern Cross.   ISBN 1-59493-029-5 $12.95

SUGAR by Karin Kallmaker. 240 pp. Three women want sugar from Sugar, who can't make up her mind.   ISBN 1-59493-001-5 $12.95

FALL GUY by Claire McNab. 200 pp. 16th Detective Inspector Carol Ashton Mystery.   ISBN 1-59493-000-7 $12.95

ONE SUMMER NIGHT by Gerri Hill. 232 pp. Johanna swore to never fall in love again—but then she met the charming Kelly . . .   ISBN 1-59493-007-4 $12.95

TALK OF THE TOWN TOO by Saxon Bennett. 181 pp. Second in the series about wild and fun loving friends.   ISBN 1-931513-77-5 $12.95

LOVE SPEAKS HER NAME by Laura DeHart Young. 170 pp. Love and friendship, desire and intrigue, spark this exciting sequel to *Forever and the Night*.   ISBN 1-59493-002-3 $12.95

TO HAVE AND TO HOLD by Peggy J. Herring. 184 pp. By finally letting down her defenses, will Dorian be opening herself to a devastating betrayal?   ISBN 1-59493-005-8 $12.95

WILD THINGS by Karin Kallmaker. 228 pp. Dutiful daughter Faith has met the perfect man. There's just one problem: she's in love with his sister.   ISBN 1-931513-64-3 $12.95

SHARED WINDS by Kenna White. 216 pp. Can Emma rebuild more than just Lanny's marina?   ISBN 1-59493-006-6 $12.95

THE UNKNOWN MILE by Jaime Clevenger. 253 pp. Kelly's world is getting more and more complicated every moment.   ISBN 1-931513-57-0 $12.95

TREASURED PAST by Linda Hill. 189 pp. A shared passion for antiques leads to love.   ISBN 1-59493-003-1 $12.95

SIERRA CITY by Gerri Hill. 284 pp. Chris and Jesse cannot deny their growing attraction . . .   ISBN 1-931513-98-8 $12.95

ALL THE WRONG PLACES by Karin Kallmaker. 174 pp. Sex and the single girl—Brandy is looking for love and usually she finds it. Karin Kallmaker's first *After Dark* erotic novel.   ISBN 1-931513-76-7 $12.95

WHEN THE CORPSE LIES A Motor City Thriller by Therese Szymanski. 328 pp. Butch bad-girl Brett Higgins is used to waking up next to beautiful women she hardly knows. Problem is, this one's dead.   ISBN 1-931513-74-0 $12.95

GUARDED HEARTS by Hannah Rickard. 240 pp. Someone's reminding Alyssa about her secret past, and then she becomes the suspect in a series of burglaries.
ISBN 1-931513-99-6 $12.95

ONCE MORE WITH FEELING by Peggy J. Herring. 184 pp. Lighthearted, loving, romantic adventure.   ISBN 1-931513-60-0 $12.95

TANGLED AND DARK A Brenda Strange Mystery by Patty G. Henderson. 240 pp. When investigating a local death, Brenda finds two possible killers—one diagnosed with Multiple Personality Disorder.   ISBN 1-931513-75-9 $12.95

WHITE LACE AND PROMISES by Peggy J. Herring. 240 pp. Maxine and Betina realize sex may not be the most important thing in their lives.   ISBN 1-931513-73-2 $12.95

UNFORGETTABLE by Karin Kallmaker. 288 pp. Can Rett find love with the cheerleader who broke her heart so many years ago?   ISBN 1-931513-63-5 $12.95

HIGHER GROUND by Saxon Bennett. 280 pp. A delightfully complex reflection of the successful, high society lives of a small group of women.   ISBN 1-931513-69-4 $12.95

LAST CALL A Detective Franco Mystery by Baxter Clare. 240 pp. Frank overlooks all else to try to solve a cold case of two murdered children . . .   ISBN 1-931513-70-8 $12.95

ONCE UPON A DYKE: NEW EXPLOITS OF FAIRY-TALE LESBIANS by Karin Kallmaker, Julia Watts, Barbara Johnson & Therese Szymanski. 320 pp. You've never read fairy tales like these before! From Bella After Dark.   ISBN 1-931513-71-6 $14.95

FINEST KIND OF LOVE by Diana Tremain Braund. 224 pp. Can Molly and Carolyn stop clashing long enough to see beyond their differences?   ISBN 1-931513-68-6 $12.95

DREAM LOVER by Lyn Denison. 188 pp. A soft, sensuous, romantic fantasy.
ISBN 1-931513-96-1 $12.95

NEVER SAY NEVER by Linda Hill. 224 pp. A classic love story . . . where rules aren't the only things broken.   ISBN 1-931513-67-8 $12.95

PAINTED MOON by Karin Kallmaker. 214 pp. Stranded together in a snowbound cabin, Jackie and Leah's lives will never be the same.   ISBN 1-931513-53-8 $12.95

WIZARD OF ISIS by Jean Stewart. 240 pp. Fifth in the exciting Isis series.
ISBN 1-931513-71-4 $12.95

WOMAN IN THE MIRROR by Jackie Calhoun. 216 pp. Josey learns to love again, while her niece is learning to love women for the first time.   ISBN 1-931513-78-3 $12.95

SUBSTITUTE FOR LOVE by Karin Kallmaker. 200 pp. When Holly and Reyna meet the combination adds up to pure passion. But what about tomorrow?   ISBN 1-931513-62-7 $12.95

GULF BREEZE by Gerri Hill. 288 pp. Could Carly really be the woman Pat has always been searching for?   ISBN 1-931513-97-X $12.95

THE TOMSTOWN INCIDENT by Penny Hayes. 184 pp. Caught between two worlds, Eloise must make a decision that will change her life forever.   ISBN 1-931513-56-2 $12.95

MAKING UP FOR LOST TIME by Karin Kallmaker. 240 pp. Discover delicious recipes for romance by the undisputed mistress.   ISBN 1-931513-61-9 $12.95

THE WAY LIFE SHOULD BE by Diana Tremain Braund. 173 pp. With which woman will Jennifer find the true meaning of love?   ISBN 1-931513-66-X $12.95

BACK TO BASICS: A BUTCH/FEMME ANTHOLOGY edited by Therese Szymanski—from Bella After Dark. 324 pp.   ISBN 1-931513-35-X $14.95

SURVIVAL OF LOVE by Frankie J. Jones. 236 pp. What will Jody do when she falls in love with her best friend's daughter?   ISBN 1-931513-55-4 $12.95

LESSONS IN MURDER by Claire McNab. 184 pp. 1st Detective Inspector Carol Ashton Mystery.   ISBN 1-931513-65-1 $12.95

DEATH BY DEATH by Claire McNab. 167 pp. 5th Denise Cleever Thriller.
ISBN 1-931513-34-1 $12.95

CAUGHT IN THE NET by Jessica Thomas. 188 pp. A wickedly observant story of mystery, danger, and love in Provincetown.   ISBN 1-931513-54-6 $12.95

DREAMS FOUND by Lyn Denison. Australian Riley embarks on a journey to meet her birth mother . . . and gains not just a family, but the love of her life.   ISBN 1-931513-58-9 $12.95

A MOMENT'S INDISCRETION by Peggy J. Herring. 154 pp. Jackie is torn between her better judgment and the overwhelming attraction she feels for Valerie.
ISBN 1-931513-59-7 $12.95

IN EVERY PORT by Karin Kallmaker. 224 pp. Jessica has a woman in every port. Will meeting Cat change all that?   ISBN 1-931513-36-8 $12.95

TOUCHWOOD by Karin Kallmaker. 240 pp. Rayann loves Louisa. Louisa loves Rayann. Can the decades between their ages keep them apart?   ISBN 1-931513-37-6 $12.95

WATERMARK by Karin Kallmaker. 248 pp. Teresa wants a future with a woman whose heart has been frozen by loss. Sequel to *Touchwood*.   ISBN 1-931513-38-4 $12.95

EMBRACE IN MOTION by Karin Kallmaker. 240 pp. Has Sarah found lust or love?
ISBN 1-931513-39-2 $12.95

ONE DEGREE OF SEPARATION by Karin Kallmaker. 232 pp. Sizzling small town romance between Marian, the town librarian, and the new girl from the big city.
ISBN 1-931513-30-9 $12.95

CRY HAVOC A Detective Franco Mystery by Baxter Clare. 240 pp. A dead hustler with a headless rooster in his lap sends Lt. L.A. Franco headfirst against Mother Love.
ISBN 1-931513931-7 $12.95

DISTANT THUNDER by Peggy J. Herring. 294 pp. Bankrobbing drifter Cordy awakens strange new feelings in Leo in this romantic tale set in the Old West.
ISBN 1-931513-28-7 $12.95

COP OUT by Claire McNab. 216 pp. 4th Detective Inspector Carol Ashton Mystery.
ISBN 1-931513-29-5 $12.95

BLOOD LINK by Claire McNab. 159 pp. 15th Detective Inspector Carol Ashton Mystery. Is Carol unwittingly playing into a deadly plan?   ISBN 1-931513-27-9 $12.95

TALK OF THE TOWN by Saxon Bennett. 239 pp. With enough beer, barbecue and B.S., anything is possible!   ISBN 1-931513-18-X $12.95

MAYBE NEXT TIME by Karin Kallmaker. 256 pp. Sabrina has everything she ever wanted—except Jorie.   ISBN 1-931513-26-0 $12.95

WHEN GOOD GIRLS GO BAD: A Motor City Thriller by Therese Szymanski. 230 pp.
Brett, Randi, and Allie join forces to stop a serial killer.   ISBN 1-931513-11-2 $12.95

A DAY TOO LONG: A Helen Black Mystery by Pat Welch. 328 pp. This time Helen's fate
is in her own hands.   ISBN 1-931513-22-8 $12.95

THE RED LINE OF YARMALD by Diana Rivers. 256 pp. The Hadra's only hope lies in a
magical red line . . . climactic sequel to *Clouds of War.*   ISBN 1-931513-23-6 $12.95

OUTSIDE THE FLOCK by Jackie Calhoun. 224 pp. Jo embraces her new love and life.
                                                               ISBN 1-931513-13-9 $12.95

LEGACY OF LOVE by Marianne K. Martin. 224 pp. Read the whole Sage Bristo story.
                                                               ISBN 1-931513-15-5 $12.95

STREET RULES: A Detective Franco Mystery by Baxter Clare. 304 pp. Gritty, fast-paced
mystery with compelling Detective L.A. Franco.   ISBN 1-931513-14-7 $12.95

RECOGNITION FACTOR: 4th Denise Cleever Thriller by Claire McNab. 176 pp.
Denise Cleever tracks a notorious terrorist to America.   ISBN 1-931513-24-4 $12.95

NORA AND LIZ by Nancy Garden. 296 pp. Lesbian romance by the author of *Annie on My
Mind.*   ISBN 1931513-20-1 $12.95

MIDAS TOUCH by Frankie J. Jones. 208 pp. Sandra had everything but love.
                                                               ISBN 1-931513-21-X $12.95

BEYOND ALL REASON by Peggy J. Herring. 240 pp. A romance hotter than Texas.
                                                               ISBN 1-9513-25-2 $12.95

ACCIDENTAL MURDER: 14th Detective Inspector Carol Ashton Mystery by Claire
McNab. 208 pp. Carol Ashton tracks an elusive killer.   ISBN 1-931513-16-3 $12.95

SEEDS OF FIRE: Tunnel of Light Trilogy, Book 2 by Karin Kallmaker writing as Laura
Adams. 274 pp. In Autumn's dreams no one is who they seem.   ISBN 1-931513-19-8 $12.95

DRIFTING AT THE BOTTOM OF THE WORLD by Auden Bailey. 288 pp. Beautifully
written first novel set in Antarctica.   ISBN 1-931513-17-1 $12.95

CLOUDS OF WAR by Diana Rivers. 288 pp. Women unite to defend Zelindar!
                                                               ISBN 1-931513-12-0 $12.95

DEATHS OF JOCASTA: 2nd Micky Knight Mystery by J.M. Redmann. 408 pp. Sexy and
intriguing Lambda Literary Award–nominated mystery.   ISBN 1-931513-10-4 $12.95

LOVE IN THE BALANCE by Marianne K. Martin. 256 pp. The classic lesbian love story,
back in print!   ISBN 1-931513-08-2 $12.95

THE COMFORT OF STRANGERS by Peggy J. Herring. 272 pp. Lela's work was her passion . . . until now.   ISBN 1-931513-09-0 $12.95

WHEN EVIL CHANGES FACE: A Motor City Thriller by Therese Szymanski. 240 pp.
Brett Higgins is back in another heart-pounding thriller.   ISBN 0-9677753-3-7 $11.95

CHICKEN by Paula Martinac. 208 pp. Lynn finds that the only thing harder than being in a
lesbian relationship is ending one.   ISBN 1-931513-07-4 $11.95

TAMARACK CREEK by Jackie Calhoun. 208 pp. An intriguing story of love and danger.
                                                               ISBN 1-931513-06-6 $11.95